The Girl Puzzle

Kate Braithwaite

"Grounded in historical research, brought to life by a novelist's imagination, here is Nellie Bly in all her fascinating complexity: outspoken, courageous, kind, clever, sometimes headstrong, other times self-doubting. In *The Girl Puzzle*, Kate Braithwaite has created a character who is not easily forgotten."
   Matthew Goodman, bestselling author of *Eighty* Days: Nellie Bly and Elizabeth Bisland's History-Making Race Around the World

"Everything a historical novel should be - illuminating, intriguing and intelligent. Kate Braithwaite has woven a fascinating and atmospheric story from what is known about the pioneering feminist journalist Nellie Bly (née Elizabeth Cochrane). Braithwaite skillfully blends Bly's early and later career to give a new insight into a remarkable and complex woman."
   Olga Wojtas, author of Miss Blaine's Prefect and the Golden Samovar

www.darkstroke.com

Copyright © 2019 by Kate Braithwaite
Cover Images:
Adobe Stock: © Sergey Kamshylin
Shutterstock: © Everett Historical
Library of Congress:
(1890 - H.L. Meyers) (Public Domain)
Library of Congress:
(1887 - The Sun/Chronicling America)(Public Domain)
Cover Design: Soqoqo
Editor: Christine McPherson
All rights reserved.

No part of this book may be used or reproduced in any manner whatsoever without written permission of the author or Crooked Cat Books except for brief quotations used for promotion or in reviews. This is a work of fiction. Names, characters, and incidents are used fictitiously.

Second Dark Edition, darkstroke. 2019

Discover us online:
www.darkstroke.com

Find us on instagram:
www.instagram.com/darkstrokebooks

Include **#darkstroke** in a photo of yourself holding his book on Instagram and **something nice will happen.**

To my own talented girl,
Maddie Braithwaite.

About the Author

Kate Braithwaite grew up in Edinburgh but now lives with her family in the Brandywine Valley in Pennsylvania. Her daughter doesn't think Kate should describe herself as a history nerd, but that's exactly what she is. Always on the hunt for lesser known stories from the past, Kate's books have strong female characters, rich settings and dark secrets. Her books have been nominated for several awards and she enjoys connecting with readers on twitter @KMBraithwaite, and @The GirlPuzzle1, and at **www.kate-braithwaite.com**

Find Kate on BookBub at: www.bookbub.com/authors/kate-braithwaite

The Girl Puzzle is her third novel.

Acknowledgements

I first came across Nellie Bly on Maria Popova's excellent blog, Brain Pickings. I bought a copy of *Ten Days in a Madhouse* right away and was instantly hooked on Nellie's story - not just in the asylum, but in the weeks, months and years that followed. This novel owes a great deal to historians Brooke Kroeger and Matthew Goodman who have done amazing work in uncovering Nellie Bly's history, and don't seem to mind answering odd questions from curious novelists. I'm also in debt to Stacy Horn for her book, *Damnation Island*, and Judith Berdy of the Roosevelt Island Historical Society. If you ever have a chance to go on one of her tours, I can highly recommend it! I'd also like to thank the Kennett Square and Chester County Public Library staff for their assistance in sourcing Nellie's articles. Huge thanks go to my family – my mum, Jean Taylor and husband, Chris - and to reading and writing buddies Jen Blab, Zoë Fairtlough and Kat Smith. Thank you to Laurence and Steph at darkstroke/ Crooked Cat for their support, guidance and this wonderful book cover. Thanks also to my editor Christine McPherson. For two Scots women producing a novel in American English, I think we have done okay! And of course, thanks most of all are due to Nellie Bly, whose life and work were so ground-breaking, yet whose story is often exaggerated or embellished. I hope this one is closer to the truth.

The Girl Puzzle

"What shall we do with our girls?"

"Take some girls that have the ability, procure for them situations, start them on their way, and by so doing accomplish more than by years of talking."

Orphan Girl
The Girl Puzzle, January 25th, 1885,
The Pittsburg Dispatch

May 20th, 1921

A middle-aged lady walks out of the Leake & Watts Orphan House in Yonkers, New York, holding hands with a small child. This child, a girl, is eight years old, but she's thin and small, most likely as a result of her recent illness. The lady whose hand she holds is smartly dressed in a long navy velvet coat with a fur collar. She wears a particularly fine cloche hat, trimmed with gold filigree.

The child's eyes widen a fraction as she takes in the lady's shiny, black Model T Ford and her tall driver. She holds her breath as he removes his cap and opens the door for them to climb inside. The engine is running, loud to her unaccustomed ears. They speed down the winding driveway, through tall iron gates, and out into the world.

"There, Dorothy," says the lady, smiling broadly and rubbing the child's long fingers. "What do you think of it? I am kidnapping you today."

She has always had a captivating smile.

"That's all right with me," says Dorothy. "I'd go anywhere with you."

Beatrice

December 1919

She was always Miss Bly to me, even though I knew she'd been married and that Bly wasn't her real name anyway. Her *real* name was Elizabeth Cochrane; but growing up, she told me, everyone called her Pink. I'd been working for her for several weeks by then, and had proved myself as a typist and secretary. I kept her diary on track, reminded her of promises made, and ensured she replied to as many letters as humanly possible. I even walked her dog – an enormous German Shepherd she'd called Brisbane, in honor of her friend and employer Arthur Brisbane, although what that gentleman thought about it, I didn't like to consider.

She told me to take the dog to Greeley Park, where he liked to scare off shoppers and snuffle around the statue of Horace Greeley. Miss Bly had no time for *The New York Tribune*, the newspaper Greely had founded. I sensed there was a story there – there was always a story with Miss Bly – but I never quite got up the courage to ask.

She didn't eat regular meals, so I started bringing some extra cold cuts and fruit to work with me. I suppose it was an odd set-up. She had a suite of rooms in the McAlpin Hotel on Thirty-Fourth Street. Pauline, Mary and I worked in the main living area, and there were two other rooms. One was Miss Bly's bedroom, and the other a small sitting room with a cot where the children she helped could sleep.

When the other two left, I'd stay back a little, share some food, and then she'd talk. I wasn't like Pauline and Mary, with men to go home to and dinner to cook. I didn't rush to leave when five o'clock came, and I didn't want to. I'd never met anyone remotely like Miss Bly.

Everyone had called her Pink, she said, and everyone meant her older brothers, Albert and Charles, her younger sister, Kate, and her baby brother, Harry, who was born when she was five years old. She told me how she loved to play mother when he was young. Given all the children she was so busy finding new families for, it looked like she still did.

She was born in 1864 – the last full year of the war – in Cochran's Mills, Pennsylvania. Only a small town, she said, but named after her father, Michael Cochran, a successful lawyer, judge, and businessman. That made her fifty-five, more than thirty years older than me. I asked her about her name, noting that she now spelled Cochran with an 'e' on the end. She rolled her eyes and gave a rueful smile. Just a family thing, she said.

The judge had been married and widowed before he met Miss Bly's mother, Mary Jane. Miss Bly grew up around a clutch of half-siblings – ten in all – from her father's first marriage. Some were still at home when Miss Bly was born, but others were grown and had their own children, the same age as she was.

"What do you think of it? Pink? As a name?" she asked. "You've heard my brother Harry call me Pink by now, haven't you?"

"Yes, Miss Bly," I said. "It seems like a nice kind of family name; a pet name. I did wonder why Pink, but didn't like to ask."

"It was the judge. Or my mother. I don't know which, but I can't ask him and I *won't* ask her."

There was no doubting that "won't". She couldn't speak of her mother without grimacing. The correspondence between their lawyers flew in and out of our office like hot sparks.

"She dressed me in pink calico and white stockings," she said. "And I loved it. I loved pink so much they made it my nickname, although I won't wear a hint of it now."

"Not ever?"

She shook her head. Miss Bly has a soft face, her features still pretty, but her eyes are tired and only really sparkle when her temper's unleashed: usually when she doesn't like where they've placed her articles in *The New York Evening Journal*.

"It's a ridiculous name," she said. "Although I clung to it, with the memories of my father, through all the rottenness that followed."

"Rottenness?"

"Oh, ignore me. A sad story for another day." She smiled, but not with her eyes.

It was late, and I took that as my cue to stand up and gather my coat and purse.

"I was Pink until Pittsburgh and Q.O.," she said. "My best and oldest friend. He gave me my first job as a reporter. He and George – our editor – even gave me my name, Nellie Bly. A name that still means something in this town, at least to some."

"I'd love to know your full story, Miss Bly," I said. I was gushing, I'll admit it. "You must have had the most amazing life."

"Ha. You are a sweet girl. My life? I suppose there have been some highlights."

"Goodnight, Miss Bly," I said, turning back at the door, sorry to go. She was staring into space. I don't think she even heard me.

"The adventures of Nellie Bly," I heard her say. "Or of Elizabeth Cochrane. Or both."

***

The next day, she handed me some extra typing.

"Don't show it to the other two," she said. "Let's keep this just between ourselves."

I was desperate to open the folder and see what it contained. And yes, I enjoyed being singled out and set apart from Pauline and Mary. They could talk about anything for hours those two, although they hushed up fast enough when Miss Bly swept back in and started rifling through folders or demanding to see the letter backlog.

I set up my things on the desk and positioned her big leather

Webster's Dictionary in front of the folder so neither of them could see what I was working on from the other side of the room. I had a letter she also wanted typing just beside it. I could cover things up in seconds. It surprised me to see that she had given me a story, and I read several pages before realizing that it was *her* story but written as if it belonged to someone else. She was a puzzle, Miss Bly, with all her columns and crusades. Perhaps she was handing me the key. I made steady progress initially, but after the phone call all work went out the window.

Pauline answered. Her face dropped as she listened.

"Miss!"

Miss Bly had only come in moments earlier and was in the room next door, tidying her hair. "What on earth is it, Pauline?" she called out. "Come here and speak properly. Don't just screech out my name."

"There's a woman in the lobby asking for you. She says she's Love of Mike's mother!"

Miss Bly only raised her eyebrows. "Beatrice. Go down and talk to this woman. If she is credible, bring her up. If not, get rid of her. And Pauline? Do try to calm down."

I took the elevator down to the lobby, wondering what kind of woman I would find when I got there. "Love of Mike", as the newspapers had dubbed the baby, had been found abandoned at Grand Central Station a week earlier. The note pinned to his chest was printed in the *Journal* and several other city papers. It read:

For the love of Mike, take this kid. He is too much for the family. Give him to Nellie Bly of The New York Journal. *He is seven months old and as healthy as they make them.*

The baby had been taken to Bellevue Hospital, and Miss Bly had rushed over as soon as she heard about him. She'd spent hours there, finding the baby quite captivating, and although she could not remove him from the hospital, she had vowed to find him a wonderful home. She had used her column to tell his story to the world, and the publicity had produced quick and unexpected results. A married couple – the Wentzes – came forward and identified the baby as their own child, Arthur, who had been kidnapped months previously. Miss Bly trumpeted this happy ending in another edition of the newspaper. It was the kind of story that she was well known for. Her column was growing in popularity. She'd been given a raise, Pauline said.

But now someone else wanted the child.

The lobby was quiet, and I saw only one woman anxious enough to be the person I was looking for. She sat hunched in a lounge chair, fiddling with the clasp of a large bag and chewing on her lip. Her face was puffy, and her shoes were scuffed and worn. I wondered if she was hoping to wheedle some money from Miss Bly. She certainly looked in need of help, and not a day older than me. Conscious of my crisp new shirt, purchased with my last paycheck, I raised a smile that I hoped was warm and friendly.

"You wanted to meet with Miss Nellie Bly?"

"Yes. Can I see her? It's really most urgent."

"You told the receptionist that you wish to speak to her about the baby left in Grand Central Station."

"My Harry, yes, that's right." The woman clasped and unclasped her hands. "What will she think of me? I just wanted a better life for my boy!"

She was on the verge of tears. I pulled a handkerchief from my sleeve and handed it to her. "There now," I said. "Miss Bly is the kindest woman I know. But how can you prove to her that your son Harry is Love of Mike? Another family has already come forward to claim him."

"I know!" She leaned forward. "That's why I've come. That family will do no better for the boy than I can. I thought Miss Bly found homes for orphans in the country with well-to-do families. That's what I've read in *The Journal*. But the Wentzes are no better than I am. Harry's father is dead, and there's only me and his brother to care for him, but he should be with us. It was all a mistake!"

"You have another son?"

"Yes. He's over there."

She pointed at a small boy, not more than three, lying on the carpet behind her chair, pushing a tiny toy train back and forth.

He'd been so quiet I'd no idea he was there.

"Come here, Tommy," she said.

The boy came at once and leaned against his mother's knee. He looked at me with soft brown eyes. "Is Harry here?" he said.

I was lost for words for a moment or two. I'd gone with Miss Bly to witness Love of Mike go home from Bellevue with Mr. and Mrs. Wentz. There was no missing the resemblance between the baby and this young boy. Brown eyes, snub of a nose, deep chin dimple, even the same cow's lick of hair above a wide forehead.

"You had better come upstairs and see Miss Bly," I said. "My name is Beatrice Alexander. I'm her assistant. And you are?"

"Mrs. Lena Lisa."

"Come this way."

***

Miss Bly, thankfully, was not the kind of woman to be easily daunted. She looked over Mrs. Lisa and Tommy, and knew at once what had to be done.

"We will go to see Ernest Coulter at the Society for the Prevention of Cruelty to Children. He is not a favorite of mine, but if anyone will know how to fix this, he's the fellow."

She got to her feet and put on her hat and coat before swinging young Tommy up into her arms. "There now, little man," she said, patting his woolen cap. "What I'm really wondering is whether you have ever ridden in a taxi-cab anywhere?"

The boy shook his head.

"Then today is your lucky day."

She marched to the door with Mrs. Lisa following in her wake, her expression a mixture of hopefulness and wonder. Miss Bly's enthusiasm and energy had that effect on people. It was catching. Mrs. Lisa gave a grin that made her look even younger than I'd supposed, and then she scurried off to keep up with Miss Bly.

Pauline and Mary wanted to gossip, so naturally we had a cup of tea and speculated about Mrs. Lisa and whether the Wentzes would have to give up the baby. None of us understood why Miss Bly wanted to involve herself in such matters.

It was hours before she got back and told us what had happened.

While we waited, I worked on her story.

Dear Q.O. --- *I am off for New York. Look out for me.*
                                                                    BLY

Elizabeth
I
September 1887

North of Ninety-Third Street, the Western Boulevard narrowed and turned dusty, and a layer of grime attached itself to Elizabeth's skirts. The walk from the streetcar made her uncomfortable. There were too many dark alleys and shadowy doorways. The click of her boot heels on the hard ground bothered her. She missed the racket of the main city streets and the comfortable pressure of many-storied buildings.

This far north on Manhattan Island, the skyline ebbed low and became fragmented, with many empty lots. Dogs and goats wandered in gaps between houses, and sporadic street lighting made the distance between the Ninth Avenue station and her boarding house on West Ninety-Sixth Street seem longer than it really was. Only a block or two south there were brightly-lit restaurants and bars. Streetlights lined Central Park but that was further behind her with every step. After dark, this broken forest of cheap boarding houses was a silent world apart.

She saw the man up ahead, still some distance away, sitting on the steps of a house only three or four doors from her destination. Elizabeth slowed and weighed her options. She could barrel past, ignoring the dryness in her throat and the heat rising in her gloved hands. She could cross the street and circle back down further on. He might not even notice her passing by. She tucked her portfolio under one arm and opened the swinging purse under her coat to find her door key. Crossing the street now would be ridiculous. The night air was cold and clammy on her cheeks.

He got to his feet.

She sucked in a breath, hating the anxiety burning in her chest. The noise of her boots drummed in her ears. Elizabeth was twenty-three years old, independent and proud of it. She straightened her spine and kept walking. He was four houses away, three, two, now one. As she drew level, he stood up and blocked her path.

"What's a pretty thing like you doing out alone at this hour?"

The horrible predictability of it made her temper surge.

The face, the accent, even the intent might change, but this wasn't the first time she had been accosted at night.

"I am just on my way home, sir," she said. "Please let me pass."

"In a moment, in a moment." He threw out his arms, filling any path forward she might have taken, and releasing a volley of unwelcome odors – stale, dirty clothes and whiskey-breath. His face and expression were hard to see. He had a scarf wound high around his neck and chin, and a cap pulled low to his eyebrows. Let him only be a harmless drunk. Let one of the doors to the nearby homes swing open. Let someone else appear on the street.

"My landlady has been expecting me this half hour," Elizabeth said, avoiding his eye. "I'm afraid I must be going."

She stepped to his left, one hand raised to carve a path past him, but he grabbed her wrist.

"Not so fast."

"Take your hands off me right now!"

Up close, they glared at each other. He was young, and his gaze was predatory.

"That's not a nice way to talk, not ladylike, is it?" He twisted her round and shoved her against a metal railing, pressing his body against her back. There were no lights in the basement kitchen just yards below. "I think your landlady will have to wait a while longer. We need to get to know each other better. Perhaps find somewhere a little more private."

"No!"

Elizabeth lifted one foot and stamped her heel back into his foot as hard as she could. His grip on her hand slackened and she twisted round, swung a hand across his face, and gouged his skin with her key.

"Bitch!"

He stumbled but then lunged, knocking the folder from her arms and pushing her towards the steps of the house. He moved to pin her again, but she squirmed out from under him. His hands clutched her long coat. She spun, and heard the cloth rip as she tore herself away and ran for safety.

A light glowed behind thick curtains at the window beside her front door. Elizabeth banged on the glass and fumbled to fit her key into the lock. Before she could turn it, the door swung open and she crashed over the doorstep.

"What in heaven's name?"

As Elizabeth pushed past, Mrs. Tanner poked her head out into the street.

"Is he there?" said Elizabeth.

"Who? Were you followed?"

"Grabbed. Nearly assaulted." She got to her feet and put her hands to her cheeks. "My portfolio. I dropped it. Everything is in it."

"I'll send Ned to look. Come. You are shaking."

The hiss of gaslights in Mrs. Tanner's cramped parlor soothed her. While her landlady bustled off to find the boy, Elizabeth bent to catch her breath. Her pulse slowed. She'd been close to disaster. If Ned could not gather her folder of news clippings, she might be even closer. A sob formed in her throat as her difficulties bore up on her. She had been in New York for months, barely subsisting on money she earned from articles sent back home to *The Pittsburg Dispatch*. No New York editor would look at her. And now this.

She sank into an armchair and her hands fell on her torn coat. One pocket ripped half off, the rest intact, but then her fingers found torn ribbon. Her purse was gone.

One hundred dollars – all her savings – gone with it.

She was penniless.

Mrs. Tanner backed into the room bearing a tray, and presented Elizabeth with a steaming cup of tea, a nip of whiskey, and her portfolio, muddied but safe. She was as buttoned-up and proper as her high-necked dress, stiff back, and thin lips suggested, but the presence of hard liquor on her tray betrayed some sympathy for Elizabeth. Perhaps she expected to find a weeping, emotional young girl shedding tears in her armchair. Instead, she was confronted by a pale but determined young woman, jabbing a needle and thread into her coat.

"I must ask you to lend me my car fare tomorrow morning, Mrs. Tanner," Elizabeth said. "It is not my habit to ask, but my situation demands it."

The landlady opened her mouth to refuse. She never gave handouts. And yet the words did not come.

"I will repay you, be assured," Elizabeth said. "By this time tomorrow night, you will have the full amount. Will you assist me, Mrs. Tanner, in this one thing?"

Not quite knowing why, the landlady nodded.

II

Elizabeth slept badly. She dreamed she abandoned her mother on a station platform in Mexico. She left Mary Jane crying and alone as the train steamed out. The anxiety of it woke her, and only the shadows of her small room coming into focus brought her relief. They had returned from their Mexican adventure unscathed and, above all, together. That they were not together now was her real failure. The plan, when she dashed off her note to Q.O. – her colleague at *The Pittsburg Dispatch* – had been to find a job in New York and have Mary Jane join her within a matter of weeks. Already four months had passed.

But dwelling on a problem didn't fix it. Only action did. Elizabeth splashed cold water on her face, pinned her long brown hair into a tidy chignon, and tweaked her curling bangs into place. Lastly, she forced a wide smile at herself in the looking glass. An air of confidence was essential, however assumed. She must look and be at her best. Today she must succeed. She had to.

Elizabeth had surveyed her limited options overnight, and this morning her conclusion was the same: her best chance lay with Colonel Cockerill at *The World*. In her four months in New York Elizabeth had learned that it was damned near impossible for a woman journalist to gain employment on Newspaper Row – she had even written an article about it.

"Journalists," Q.O. had said, "need a pretext. Find your way in, lie your way in if you need to. But once you are in, find the truth and report it."

Unable to gain admission to a single editor's office on her own behalf as a lady writer seeking work, Elizabeth had come up with a pretext. She invented a letter from an aspiring female journalist, asking how hard it was for women to find work in the great newspapers of New York. On the strength of that, she'd arranged to interview the Gods of Gotham for an article presenting their views about women journalists. It had been revealing, galling, depressing even. But the article had been well received, and today she intended to put what she had learned to good use.

She had met with six editors in total: Charles A. Dana at *The Sun;* Dr. Hepworth of *The Herald;* Miller of *The Times;* Colonel John A. Cockerill of *The World;* Foster Coates of *The Mail and Express;* and Robert G. Morris of *The Telegram.*

Morris was the most infuriating. A tall, spare-framed man in his fifties, he had little interest in her questions. Women were fit for some purposes, he supposed – like reporting on the clothes worn by other women at a reception, or any and all details to do with a wedding. They were useless for anything physical, however.

"If there was an emergency just as we were ready for the last edition, I could not send a woman sliding down the bannister and have her return up three flights of stairs four steps at a time," he said.

Elizabeth had challenged him to a race, offered to race any man he had in the office at that very moment. Morris was not impressed.

Foster Coates at *The Mail and Express* at least had some charm about him, even if the message was ultimately the same. Women were "invaluable", but only at reporting all the same society or fashion events that Morris had outlined. At least Coates had the honesty to admit that there was a prejudice against women in the industry. Others, particularly Miller at *The Times*, had pointed out that they had more male applicants – only Coates had admitted the unvarnished truth. But that didn't mean he would be any more open to employing Elizabeth today than he had been a month ago. *The Mail and Express* was well staffed, perhaps even over-staffed. She had seen it as soon as she walked through the building – too many men lounging around with little or no urgency. She did not need that kind of workplace, and it clearly did not need her.

In his comfortable office at *The Herald*, Dr. Hepworth had blamed the modern taste for sensationalism for his reluctance to employ more women. With so much newspaper space devoted to crime and scandal, he said, he needed men, not women, as his reporters. A woman sent to a courtroom would be ushered out just as the most important news was taking place.

Elizabeth kept her tongue between her teeth but very nearly loosened it when he claimed that women in the workplace made life difficult for the poor men who would have to rein themselves in and speak and behave more guardedly than they would in a male-only area. Only her need to note down his words exactly prevented an unseemly explosion. No, no amount of money would induce her to work for either Dr. Hepworth or Robert Morris. If Dr. Hepworth had seen only the half of the things that Elizabeth had seen in her short life, he would not be so quick to patronize.

That left Dana at *The Sun* and Cockerill at *The World*. She had liked Charles Dana the most of all these powerful men. His office was everything she had imagined a New York editor's to be. Every wall was lined by well-filled bookshelves. A tidy desk, soft carpets, and comfortable office chairs gave the room a cozy yet studious appearance. Mr. Dana sat at his desk twirling a pair of gold-rimmed spectacles. He looked to be in his late fifties, judging by the silvering of his hair and beard. She had been nervous, but his thoughtful, intelligent responses had put her at ease. He said he had no prejudice against women as journalists, but just as her hopes began to climb, they were quickly dashed.

"Accuracy," Dana said, "is the greatest gift of a journalist. It is difficult for most people when they are told that two and two make four, not to write that they make five, or three, or anything except the exact truth. Women are generally worse than men in this regard. They find it impossible not to exaggerate."

It was beyond infuriating.

Still, she persisted, turning the conversation to her work at *The Pittsburg Dispatch*. She described her travels in Mexico – with no hint of exaggeration – and Dana had appeared interested, even impressed. Yet his final handshake had been just that: final.

"In the end," he told her, "men are always preferable, because they have been educated to the business." A fatherly twinkle in his eye softened the blow in the moment, but the message rankled. There was no job for her at Charles Dana's *Sun*.

No, Colonel John Cockerill at *The World* was her only hope, and for several reasons. The man was a maverick, even by New York standards. In St Louis, a few years back, he had shot and killed another man – a lawyer, who had taken exception to some article in Cockerill's paper, *The St Louis Post-Dispatch*. There had been a trial, and Cockerill had been found guilty only of committing a justifiable homicide in self-defense, despite claims by the dead man's friend that he had been unarmed when the altercation took place. Whatever the truth of it, Cockerill had moved north to run *The World* for Joseph Pulitzer. And while he seemed no more enthused at the idea of women journalists than his colleagues were, Elizabeth recognized something in him – call it bravery; call it passion; call it guts. She did not know what it was, except that it was there.

She didn't forget that it was Cockerill who'd had the nerve to suggest she found herself a man and set up a family rather than pursue a career in journalism. But when she'd ignored that nonsense and pressed right on with her questions, she'd gained a glimmer of respect in return, she thought. Just a glimmer. With everything on the line, that glimmer was another reason to target *The World* this morning. Colonel Cockerill was a risk-taker. Perhaps he would gamble on her.

There was also plain honest ambition. Joseph Pulitzer's paper was the fastest growing and most daring. Why aim low? *The World* was the paper she wanted to write for. She just had to get herself into Cockerill's office again. She had to.

***

Elizabeth breakfasted with Mrs. Tanner and assured the old lady that she was none the worse for her run-in the night before, although her stomach rebelled at the thought of food. It was all she could do to sip at a cup of tea. With her pride in her boots, she took the handout she needed for the streetcar. The train was faster but more expensive, and she didn't want to test the boundaries of Mrs. Tanner's generosity.

It was chilly outside. The sky, grey and oppressive, threatened rain. She held the lapels of her long coat tight against her neck and bent her head into the wind as she set out. The street outside was much changed from last night. Shutters were up on shops on the corner. People bustled past. Horses pulled carts and carriages. Doors stood open and curtains were pulled wide. Children jumped on the steps of their homes or into piles of leaves blown down from trees overnight. She passed a bakery, but the smell of fresh bread, normally so heartening, had her picking up her feet as a lump of bile rose in her throat.

Elizabeth waited for the streetcar on Columbus Avenue, gripping her portfolio bag with both hands, like any other young, working woman. Under her coat she wore a pleated full-length navy skirt and a matching tight-sleeved bodice with a high collar. It flattered her figure but was purposefully plain. She pinned it with a simple brooch, and there was no fashionable puff at the shoulders. A silk flower-trimmed hat was her one extravagance, bought during her trip to Mexico and a reminder that a free American girl could go anywhere and do anything she put her mind to do. She still believed it, but what if this was her last morning? Tomorrow she might be heading to Penn Station and a train back to Pittsburgh as a failure.

She grew hot and was sure her face must be turning pink. Elizabeth studied the people waiting with her on the street. Most stood much as she did, hands gripping bags or thrust in pockets, heads bent low, feet tapping a beat to keep warm, everyone lost in his or her own thoughts and concerns. Who knew what turmoil and worries they were experiencing? Perhaps someone else here was struggling as much as she was. Perhaps even more. Elizabeth swallowed her panic and raised her chin as horses pulled the streetcar to a stop.

She was too anxious to sit but the trolley lurched repeatedly, and she stumbled. She banged her shoulder against a tall man bundled up in a long wool coat with the lapels turned up. His glower at being knocked quickly turned to a smile as she apologized. Good. A pleasant look from a handsome man was welcome. Elizabeth needed to charm her way into Colonel Cockerill's office, and here was yet another reason for making a beeline for the offices of *The World* out of all the choices before her. The day editor had taken a shine to her on her previous visit. He'd made that more than clear. If a little flirting was what it took to get her up to the fourth floor this morning, then Elizabeth Cochrane was up for the game.

The line ended at City Hall, an area that was busy whatever the hour. In Pittsburgh the streets grew quiet mid-morning but that was never the case in New York. The newspapers on Park Row produced several issues throughout the day and employed hundreds of people – largely men, unfortunately – and attracted thousands more. They came seeking jobs, selling wares, or using City Park as a convenient meeting point with space to walk and talk, to buy peanuts or a milkshake, to spread some gossip, or pick a pocket or two. Horse-drawn carriages and trolley cars vied for space and made any road crossing a hazardous adventure. Newspaper Row was at work every hour of the day, and the area boasted saloons and restaurants ready to supply the hard-working employees of an industry on the rise. The stink of horse manure and cooking fat was enough to turn stomachs on a warm New York day.

Elizabeth marched past *The Sun* building on the corner of Nassau Street. She didn't look at the door of *The Tribune* or cast her eye up at the statue of Ben Franklin. She glanced at *The New York Times*, only to lift her chin and pull in her stomach. A horse, hitched to a milk wagon, stamped its hooves and whinnied as carriages rumbled past. And behind her, on its iron elevated tracks, a train pulled in from over the new bridge to Brooklyn with a roar and a squeal of brakes. She blocked it all out and marched into the offices of *The World*.

The first-floor area had a range of functions, from selling papers to recruiting and dispatching delivery boys and taking enquiries. Elizabeth skirted past the boy guarding the elevator and skipped up two flights of stairs past the composing rooms. The rattle of the basement presses reverberated through the floor, a familiar beat on the soles of her boots. The City Room took up the entire third floor. A maze of desks squatted under a thin cloud of cigar smoke, but the room was quieter than she had hoped and there was no sign of the day editor. Two or three men scribbled at their desks while a few others had gathered by the window, smoking.

"Yes?" This was a boy, no more than twelve years old, lounging at a large double desk that was shared by the day and night editors.

"I'm here to see Colonel Cockerill." Elizabeth raised her eyebrows and then nodded at the quiet room. "But I imagine his editorial meeting is in progress. If you would kindly find me a chair, I will wait."

"A chair?"

"Do you expect a lady to stand around for an hour, hopping from foot to foot?"

"I don't expect no lady in here at all!"

"Well, that is honesty, at least," she laughed. "But you may find your viewpoint is shortly to undergo an alteration." The boy looked puzzled but still made no move. "A chair?" she said.

He looked around the office as if for instruction, but the men at the window showed no interest and the others were too occupied to care for her existence. With a shrug the boy vacated the seat he had been rocking on and moved around the other side of the desk.

"Do you imagine the meeting will go on much longer?" she asked.

"Maybe an hour?" he replied. "They've not been up there long. Although the boss isn't here. So they might be down sooner."

The boss was J.P. Pulitzer. Elizabeth crushed a sigh of disappointment. She had held a vague idea that if she failed to convince Cockerill, she might somehow be able to inveigle her way into Pulitzer's office and talk him into giving her a chance. But now that he wasn't even on the premises, her eggs really were all in one basket.

The hour crawled by. More reporters came and went. Compositors ran up, asked questions, and ran downstairs again. The elevator rumbled up and down the building and the presses vibrated down below. Few of the men paid her any attention but her continued presence proved to be a source of concern for the boy.

"Here," he said, "I hope I won't get into no trouble for letting you sit here like this."

"Why would you? I'm not bothering anyone, am I?"

"No. But—"

"But nothing. What is the name of the man whose desk this is? The day editor?"

"Philips."

"Mr. Philips will be happy to see me." She flashed him a merry smile. "You will see."

"I don't know," came the grumbling reply. "I don't think he holds with women in here much."

She ignored that. She ignored the sly looks, the raised eyebrows, and odd elbowing of one man to another as they moved in and out of the office and spotted her sitting calmly at the desk.

"Is someone helping you?"

A young man, smartly dressed in a neat-fitting suit, stopped at the foot of the stairs to the next floor and called out to her. He had an air about him that didn't sit with the normal rumpled look of a newspaper reporter. His hair was neatly parted at the center, his moustache artistically tweaked at the ends, and a pair of small round glasses gave him an intelligent look. She stood up.

"I am waiting to see Colonel Cockerill," she said. "I thought to ask Mr. Philips to let the Colonel know I was here, but I believe the editorial meeting is still in progress. You are not a member of that group?"

"Lucky not to be!" the man declared, crossing over and putting out his hand in greeting. "Walt McDougall."

"The illustrator?" Elizabeth smiled broadly. "I am a great

admirer of yours."

"How very kind of you to say so. But why are you waiting here? The Colonel's office is right up here, near mine. If I might be allowed to show you the way? I'm sure his meeting will be over shortly."

Elizabeth got to her feet and straightened out her skirts. "You are very kind, Mr. McDougall," she said.

At the bottom of the stairs, she cast a quick glance back over her shoulder. The boy at the desk had leaned so far back in his chair that he looked at imminent risk of toppling backwards. His eyebrows knocked at his hairline in his surprise at this turn of events.

She planned to surprise him a lot more in the future.

For now, she just winked.

The floor upstairs presented a very different picture. Here were the offices of the management of *The World*: a brown paneled warren of walls and doors half filled with frosted glass. Scruffy, unfussy, warm, smoky, and airless, these were the lairs of the business manager and his minions, of the owner, of the managing editor, of the features editor, the sports editor and so on. Also, it turned out, of *The World's* chief illustrator and cartoonist, who insisted she called him Walt. He ushered her into his office after casually patting a young clerk at the desk outside Cockerill's office and asking him to "Tell the old man I'd like a word when he's free."

Elizabeth thought her heart might pound out of her chest with shock at this good fortune, but Walt was grinning and holding open his office door to usher her in. She nodded and walked past him into a light and frankly charming space, but even as she exclaimed at the drawings pinned to every surface, she was glad to note that he had left the office door wide open.

"You are the girl that came here a month or so ago, aren't you? The one who wrote the piece about women journalists?"

"Yes."

"I thought so. We don't often have females in this building. And you did make something of an impression on the Colonel. Your article did well, too. It was syndicated to *The*

Journalist?" She nodded. "You are tougher than I am, you know."

"I am?"

He gestured her toward a chair near the window and settled himself behind his desk. "I didn't make it past the lobby. I lost my nerve."

"Whatever do you mean?"

"That I was like you. That not so long ago I was desperate for a job at *The World*. I'm not mistaken, am I? You're here to talk the Colonel into employing you as a reporter."

"I won't leave until he takes me on."

Walt nodded. "Good for you. You have grit. Show him that."

"I intend to. Thank you. But what about you? What do you mean you didn't make it past the lobby?"

"Just what I said. I had drawn a cartoon – for *Puck* magazine originally – but they didn't want it. I was downcast. My tender, artistic feelings hurt, I suppose. It was my last hope, my last roll of the die." Elizabeth nodded; she knew how that felt. "So, I dropped it off with the elevator boy. I couldn't watch Cockerill – or whoever – look at it and shake their head over it. I was sure that, if it even made it that far, it would still wind up in a wastepaper basket."

"But it didn't."

"It did not. It was something like that one." Walt pointed at an old copy of a front page tacked on the wall near the door. Called *The Royal Feast of Belshazzar Blaine and the Money Kings,* it was one of the most celebrated of the many influential cartoons that lampooned Republican politician James G. Blaine a couple of years earlier. It filled the top half of the newspaper, screaming its message and impossible to ignore.

"It's wonderful."

"What was wonderful was that the drawing was just the right size. It sat across all the normal five columns of the paper. Cockerill and Pulitzer put my drawing on page one the very next morning. I was summoned back and brought up here. They gave me an office and a salary. I was 26 years old."

"So, you are telling me that miracles can happen?"

"I'm saying these are men who are prepared to take chances and try new things."

"Yes!" Elizabeth moved to the edge of her seat and clasped her hands together. "That's what I am hoping and praying for. There is a place for a female reporter, I'm sure of it. I am as a good as a man in most places and can do better than a man in others. I just need a chance to show them that, but I can't simply leave my portfolio. I won't stand out from the crowd in the way that you could."

"You'll convince him with your self-belief. And your smile. You are blessed with a very charming smile, you know. Even my wife will not mind me saying so."

"I like the sound of your wife," Elizabeth said.

"You can meet her! As soon as we are colleagues."

She blushed. "*If* we become colleagues."

"Not if. When." He broke off, stepped to the door, and poked his head out. "Listen. That's the editorial meeting over. Let's give Cockerill a few moments and then see if he'll give you a chance. I hope you're ready."

Elizabeth nodded and pursed her lips as she ran through the proposal she was about to make in her mind. McDougall seemed to realize she needed to gather her thoughts, and he busied himself at his drawing desk. A few moments later and the clerk appeared at the door.

"Sorry. He's too busy today. He says to write him a letter."

"No." She jumped to her feet. "Tell him that I have an opportunity for him that he will not want to miss. Unless he prefers that I take it to Mr. Dana at *The Sun*?"

The clerk hesitated. Another figure appeared at the door.

"Mr. Philips!" She saw the day editor's eyes widen and knew that he remembered her, too. "I was just telling this young man here that I have a most important idea to put before Colonel Cockerill. He doesn't know me, so I suppose he may be forgiven for his reluctance. But won't you tell him that the Colonel will be most unhappy if he finds I've taken myself off to one of your competitors?" She smiled as brightly as she knew how.

Philips was a pale man with thinning hair, and a moustache and beard that merely served to hide a weak chin. He might be charmed by her, but he was a career man with a position to protect and likely reluctant to put his reputation on the line for someone he barely knew. Even less for a woman. "I promise," she said. "The Colonel will thank you."

Philips looked at McDougall. She raised her eyebrows expectantly and stood as tall as she could.

"Tell the old fellow that McDougall and I think she might have something interesting for him," he said, tapping the clerk on the shoulder. "I'll bring her along in a moment."

As the clerk departed, Philips turned and put out his hand. "Since I am about to introduce you to the boss, perhaps you might introduce yourself to me first. I recognize you from an earlier visit, I believe, but I don't have your name."

Elizabeth placed her hand in his, resisting an intense desire to throw her arms about the man.

"My name," she said, "is Nellie Bly."

Beatrice

December 1919

I noticed him in the hotel lobby, the moment I walked through the door. He was standing by the elevator with his back to me, but he was tall with broad shoulders, and smooth dark hair cropped neatly at his collar. I always looked to see who might be hanging around downstairs hoping to catch a word with Miss Bly. She publicized her address widely in *The Journal* and the hotel staff had long since given up complaining about all her visitors, many of whom were far from charming to look at.

This man was smartly dressed, tapping his fedora against his leg while he waited. He was most likely a guest returning to his room for something. I had Brisbane with me, and he snuffled at a couple of chairs before letting me drag him into the elevator just as the doors opened.

"What floor?" The man had chocolate brown eyes and I liked his voice. He didn't sound like a New Yorker. I thought perhaps he came from somewhere farther north. Boston, if I had to guess. "I've never ridden in an elevator with a dog before," he said.

I looked at the button he had already pressed. "Same floor as you. Brisbane lives here but he's not mine. He belongs to my employer."

"Is that your job? To walk the dog?" he asked, bending to fondle the dog's black ears. I liked that he was confident. You can tell a lot about a person through the way they handle animals.

"Oh no." Did I blush? I know I did. "I'm a secretary." I smiled at him. "And I love what I do, but it is nice to have a reason to step out of doors every once in a while. I'm always happy to take him for a walk."

The doors of the elevator opened, and the man stepped back to let me leave first. I wanted to carry on the conversation, ask him some question, but how could I? I walked down the hallway, conscious of him walking behind me, aware of the inches I'd raised my hemline by just the other day, and glad I was wearing a new pair of shoes with a generous heel. I wondered if he'd say anything else, perhaps when he passed me. The last thing I expected was for him to head to the very same place.

"You work *here*?" he said, as I stopped at the door. "For Nellie Bly?"

He was frowning. Why was he frowning? "Yes," I said. "I do. Do you have business with Miss Bly?"

"Oh yes."

His change in tone and demeanor did not please me. "Then I hope you have an appointment. Miss Bly is extremely busy and—"

"I have an appointment all right," he said, following me inside. "My name is Ernest Coulter. Miss Bly is expecting me."

They were stiff and unsure of each other, that much was evident. Miss Bly ushered him into the small second bedroom that she used as a sitting room, having insisted the hotel remove the bed and install a pair of wingback chairs and a small table. When it wasn't in use as a playroom and bedroom for orphans, she used it for meetings, leaving the door wide open as she always did. Pauline, Mary, and I had long since stopped pretending not to listen. If there was a perk of working for Miss Bly we could all agree on, it was that there was always something dramatic going on. Whenever she had a visitor, we all found tasks to do that were quiet – filing, proofreading, recording letters received and replies sent out. Any typing could wait.

"To what do I owe the honor, Mr. Coulter? I must say I was surprised to hear you wanted to see me again so soon."

He made a choking noise and I imagined him fingering his

collar in discomfort. "Indeed, I had not thought so either. Although, I must say again that your assistance with Mrs. Wentz was most helpful."

"The boy had to be restored to his mother. But that did not mean overlooking the suffering of the Wentzes. So you were glad, after all, that I accompanied you?"

Miss Bly had entertained us all with the story of how Ernest Coulter had tried – and failed – to send her packing when the time came to remove little Love of Mike from the arms of the Wentzes and reunite him with Mrs. Lisa.

Again, he made an uncomfortable noise before replying. "I have some reservations about reporters Miss Bly – based on experience, I may say. I'll admit I was unsure of your motives."

"You thought I was along for the ride simply so I could report on the woman's misery and disappointment?"

She sounded indignant, but we exchanged a grin in the outer room. She was like a cat toying with a mouse. Enjoying herself.

"I wouldn't put it quite like that…"

"How would you put it then?"

"The handling of families in such situations is something the Society believes is best left to trained individuals." He cleared his throat. "However, in this instance, I have already acknowledged that you were most helpful with Mrs. Wentz. I did read your account of the events in last night's *Journal* with interest."

Pauline put her mouth over her hand to stifle a giggle. He was a brave man this Ernest Coulter. I was certain Miss Bly's presence had been a comfort to Mrs. Wentz, but she had also made sure that the write-up of the story in *The Journal* cast herself in a flattering light. The paper had described how Mrs. Wentz had wept and thrown her arms around Miss Bly, who had comforted her and called her a "dear woman" who had "simply made an honest mistake out of pure mother-love".

"Love of Mike's story has captured the city's imagination," said Miss Bly.

"Indeed, and that is what brings me to you today. I have a

request to make."

"I'm listening."

Ernest Coulter's request concerned a six-year-old girl named Dorothy Harris, who had recently come under the care of the Society and been admitted to Willard Parker Hospital with a severe case of diphtheria.

"She first came to our attention in June," Coulter said. "Her mother was arrested for stealing a doll from Riker and Hergemane's drugstore in Times Square. When she told the police she had a young child at home in her apartment in the care of a maid, one of my officers was sent to the address. The girl had not eaten, and the alleged maid was nowhere to be seen. The mother, Grace, was also in possession of cocaine."

Mary shook her head and got up and walked over to do some filing. I think her brother may have had a drug problem. This story seemed to touch a nerve.

"A doll? For the child, I assume. There is good in everyone, if you wish to see it, you know," said Miss Bly.

I imagined Coulter nodded. At any rate, he carried on with Dorothy's history.

"After some to-ing and fro-ing, the girl was lodged with a decent woman who agreed to board her until Grace Harris, the mother, attended court on the shoplifting charge. But Grace Harris has disappeared. She hasn't paid the woman for Dorothy's board, and when the girl fell sick the woman washed her hands of her. The child may die. We need to find the mother, and at the very least ascertain if the child is Catholic or Protestant. If she does survive this illness, we will need that information before we can place her."

"How can I help?"

"Publicity. Tell your readers Dorothy's story. Help us find Grace Harris."

"I will need to see the girl."

"I thought you might say that."

"Then you might look more happy about it, Mr. Coulter! Come. I see no need to delay. No child deserves to be abandoned. And none will be, if I've any say in it."

With that, she marched into the office and set about

gathering her coat and purse. Mr. Coulter followed her out, looking slightly wary although not displeased. Brisbane, who had been lying by my desk, sat up, and Mr. Coulter, seeing him, crossed the room and fondled his ears.

"You have got what you came for then, Mr. Coulter?" I said.

He looked at me and smiled wryly. "I may have got more than I bargained for."

Miss Bly was back in the room and tucking her arm in his before I could respond. She whisked him out of the room without a backward glance. Not that there was anything out of the ordinary about that. She was always happiest with a mission to execute. At times like that I could see the girl in her story, full of drive and energy, confident, daring. I thought of all the intervening years and all she had gone through with her husband, her mother, and the war. Despite it all, she was the same at heart. A woman who made a difference. Someone who needed to be needed.

In the moment, I was glad for her and for this poor child, Dorothy. And I did also find myself imagining tucking my arm into Ernest Coulter's as she had.

I thought it might be very pleasing indeed.

Elizabeth
III
September 1887

Cockerill remembered her. That was a start.

"I don't have much time, Miss Bly," he said, but he gestured toward a chair, so she tucked her skirts and sat down. "You did a good job with your piece on women journalists. No. Don't smile. That smile will do you no favors in this business. I'll be honest. You'd be a distraction in any newsroom. Plain and simple. Far too pretty."

"I don't plan to be much in the newsroom, Mr. Cockerill. And believe me, when I am, I'll be writing and working hard, just as hard, if not harder, than any man."

"Well, you don't lack confidence." Cockerill leaned back in his chair. His office was plain. It had none of the bookish warmth of Charles Dana's lair, or the creative disorder of McDougall's workspace. There were papers, yes, and a few reference books on a corner bookshelf, an old revolving globe, a heavy agate paperweight, and a magnifying glass, but it was the window that drew the eye. Cockerill must spend hours looking out of that window, she thought, watching the scurrying crowd below or staring at the tall square pillars of the Brooklyn Bridge.

"I can find you new stories," she said. "I can bring a perspective on life that others can't. Women read newspapers just as much as men do. And our lives are about more than wedding dresses and society fundraisers. For most of us, anyway."

"There are places where a woman simply cannot go."

"Perhaps. But then aren't there equally places where only a woman can go?"

"Name one."

"The women's workhouse."

He looked unimpressed.

"Anyway, women are no longer only in the home," she said. "In Pittsburgh I interviewed a woman who ran her own opera company. Every aspect of it. There must be hundreds of women like that in New York."

"Feature work. Not news."

"There could be exposés. Explosive revelations and discoveries work well in *The World*. I'll take a factory job and report from the inside. I'll talk to prostitutes. They'll far more likely talk to me than to a man. The city is full of scandalous behavior – charlatan doctors, and girls treated like slave labor. Women are getting involved in every sphere of life, even politics. I'll report on issues like that." She looked him right in the eye. "I'm not afraid of anything."

"Apparently not."

"But first, I want to offer you a major story. Let me travel to Europe and then return by steerage." She had his attention fully now. "I'll travel with immigrants heading to New York. I'll tell their stories first-hand. I'll describe conditions on board as accurately as if you saw it through your own eyes. I'll detail every indignity and discomfort from departure to arrival on the city's streets. I'll tell the stories of the people I meet – men, women, and children. Everyone in the city will be talking about it."

"An assignment of this nature requires an investment up-front. We don't even know you."

"*The Pittsburg Dispatch* sent me to Mexico last year. I filed six months' worth of reports from any number of locations and on a wide range of topics. I have them all here."

She patted the leather satchel on her knee and this time, finally, someone held out their hand for her portfolio.

The Colonel took his time. Elizabeth watched him skim over her series on factory girls and take a closer look at her reports from Mexico. The urge to talk him through it was almost overpowering, but she held her tongue. He picked out one clipping and held it up as he read her own words out to her.

"*For the first time I saw women plowing while their lords and masters sat on a fence smoking. I never longed for anything so much as I did to shove those lazy fellows off.* You don't pull your punches, Miss Bly. Are you what we might call a man-hater?"

"Not at all," she said, straightening in her chair and smiling. "I don't like to see unfairness though. And I don't think all men are better than all women, just by virtue of their being men."

"I suppose we can agree on that, at least," Cockerill said. He shuffled her papers back into the folder but kept it on his desk.

Cockerill got to his feet and stood staring out of the window. With his back to her, he spoke: "I will consider it," he said. "Our owner, Mr. Pulitzer, is out of town for a few days, and such an irregular expenditure as you suggest needs his seal of approval." He turned and contemplated her. "I am prepared to discuss you with him. You have something about you…"

She smiled – how could she not? – but he shook his head.

"Lord knows, that smile of yours is as likely to get you into trouble as out of it, young lady." He put out his hand for her to shake. "Come back at this same time a week from today and we will see what work we might have for you."

His handshake was firm and his expression serious, but not unkind. She got to her feet, and with her heart in mouth said, "There is just one more thing…"

Elizabeth shared her good news with McDougall and Philips and was delighted to see something very like respect appear in their eyes when she showed them a money order for twenty-five dollars written in Cockerill's lazy scrawl. McDougall even invited her to be the guest of himself and his wife for lunch at Delmonico's at Twenty-Sixth Street and Fifth Avenue in just a few days' time.

Downstairs at the cashier's desk, she gave her smile full rein. The young clerk's obvious surprise at the money order she handed him only made her happier. It had been awkward, admitting to Cockerill that she could not afford to wait in New York, not even for a week, but as she told him of the theft of her purse the night before she made sure to turn the story in her favor. She was penniless, true, but she had fought off an attacker. Cockerill's eyebrows had risen when she described how she ground her heel into her assailant's foot and then swiped at him with her key. The event, in fact, had been turned from an unmitigated disaster into a positive advantage.

As she folded the bank notes into her pocket, Elizabeth wished the clerk a wonderful day. She stepped back out into Park Row and stood for a moment breathing in the city, the rumble of carriages, the shouts and the hustle. A tall black man in a suit, carrying a stack of books tied in string, almost knocked her over but she waved away his apologies with another unbridled smile of delight.

She was in.

IV

The week passed quickly. Elizabeth dashed off an enthusiastic letter to her mother. As soon as she completed her first assignment for *The World,* she'd find suitable lodgings for them both and send the fare to bring her to New York. Mrs. Tanner was repaid, but Elizabeth promised herself that she wouldn't be living so far north of anywhere worth being for many more weeks. She explored the city with a new sense of confidence and belonging, drawing up a list of ideas certain to have Colonel Cockerill slapping his desk in appreciation and make her the toast of the fourth floor. And she dined at Delmonico's with the McDougalls, trying not to stare open-mouthed at the plethora of mirrors and glittering chandeliers, or the sight of a fountain in the center of a dining room.

Walt's wife, Annabel, proved to be both friendly and fashionable. Elizabeth couldn't wait to be able to overhaul her own wardrobe. Macy's on Fourteenth Street, she thought. Or Arnold and Constable on East Nineteenth between Broadway and Fifth Avenue. Probably both.

***

Back at *The World* at the appointed time, she strolled up to the elevator boy and announced her meeting with the Colonel. No running up the stairs this time. Cockerill's clerk stood up when she presented herself at his desk, causing her lips to twitch just a little. She suppressed a desire to giggle, and nodded as he held the office door for her. Cockerill wasn't alone. The other man was smaller, slighter across the shoulders and a little stooped, although she knew he was no more than forty years old. He had a thick, dark head of hair and an equally dense moustache and beard. His eyes were deep-set, and she straightened her spine as he looked her up and down.

"It's an honor to meet you, Mr. Pulitzer." Elizabeth squared up to him and stuck out a hand. He took it and shook her hand firmly, but deferred to Cockerill who asked her to take a seat.

"This transatlantic crossing idea of yours," Cockerill said. "It just won't work."

Elizabeth tightened her grip on her purse. "Why not?"

"Too much investment in someone we know nothing about."

"You still have my clippings." She nodded at the folder on the desk. "I was sent to Mexico. I fulfilled my role there, and more. I can do the same for *The World*. I can do it better."

"How better?" asked Pulitzer.

"I'll be one of them, on board all day, every day. I can talk to anyone. People talk to me. I'll show you who these people really are. Why they come. What they go through to get here. I'll suffer every deprivation alongside the families making the journey. I'll learn what their dreams are. Find out their fears. Discover what they leave behind and what they hope to gain."

"Our readers already know these things."

"Only as a set of facts. Not through the stories of real people. And not told by someone with critical eyes and a determination to report the details."

"Still. The answer is no."

Cockerill folded his arms, watching her reaction closely. If this was some kind of test, she wasn't about to fail it by looking disappointed.

"A shame," she said. "But I have other ideas. I—"

The two men exchanged a glance. Pulitzer nodded.

"Before you launch yourself into those, Miss Bly," said Cockerill, "perhaps you will listen to an idea of our own. You've heard of Blackwell's Island?"

She nodded. Blackwell's Island, a long sliver of land in the East River, was home to a range of public buildings that no man or woman ever had any ambition to inhabit: the smallpox hospital; the penitentiary; the poorhouse; and the insane asylum. Everyone had heard of Blackwell's Island.

"There have been several scandals reported recently," said

Pulitzer, leaning forward in his chair. "Allegation of abuses in the treatment of lunatics. Are you familiar with this issue?"

"I am." Elizabeth had spent the last few months in New York doing nothing but looking for work and reading the city's newspapers. "I read last month about the ill treatment of inmates in the Ward's Island Asylum. A report was commissioned. Our asylums are over-crowded, under-funded, and under-staffed. I believe the food is poor and the care is inadequate."

"Good," said Cockerill. "We want you going in there with your eyes open."

"In there?"

"Into the Blackwell's Island Insane Asylum for Women."

How to react? Elizabeth had faced difficult questions before. At fourteen, she had sat before a range of lawyers and been relentlessly grilled on the evidence she wanted to give the court. She wasn't about to get flustered by Cockerill and Pulitzer.

"You want the inside story from the lunatic asylum?"

"We do."

"Then I will need to be committed as a lunatic." It wasn't a question, and she didn't look to them for confirmation. "What are my options?"

She saw Cockerill throw Pulitzer a grin and knew he was pleased with her response.

"You can use your friends and contacts," he said. "Have a breakdown of some sort at a friend's house. Let them call medical help. But you need two doctors' signatures before a committal to the lunatic asylum can be made."

Elizabeth's list of friends in New York was short to the point of non-existent, although she'd never admit it. She imagined recruiting the McDougalls to help her, but the whole idea of involving others in an enterprise so unlikely to succeed was not attractive.

"Or?" she asked.

"Find a way to be arrested. Appear at the Police Court. Convince the authorities that you are insane. They will likely send you to Bellevue Hospital, and from there to the Island.

You'll need to be a fine actress. And use a false name."

"We thought you might use a pseudonym that we agree in advance – in order to keep track of you. There are many dangers involved." Pulitzer's eyes narrowed as he spoke. Perhaps he was waiting for her to back out.

"I can see that," Elizabeth said carefully. "My linen is initialed N.B. for Nellie Bly. Shall I be Nellie Brown? I must be a poor and plain girl."

Cockerill snorted. "Ha! And that's the place you will find most difficulty. Plain you decidedly are not!"

"Why thank you, Colonel." She allowed a demure smile to peep out. "But I have already smiled far less than normal, based on your advice on my previous visit. I'm a fast learner, as I hope you will soon see. I won't go into this unprepared. And I can trust you to get me out again, can't I?"

"Young lady, if you can work your way into the asylum, as you believe you can, we will leave you there only for long enough to see – to really see – what goes on. And then we will pull you out."

"And offer me a permanent position with *The World*?"

"You have my word on it," said Pulitzer.

***

She wasted no time after the meeting. Dwelling on the prospect in front of her was never going to make it any easier. Experience had taught her that it was always better to just *do* a thing, rather than spend hours in pointless angst and hand-wringing. The memory of her mother weeping night after night, trying to hide the fingermarks on her neck but doing nothing to save herself, always propelled Elizabeth into action.

Mrs. Tanner looked curious that evening, when she told her she was going out of town the very next day.

"I have an assignment," she said. "A difficult one. But if I am successful, then… well, we will see what happens then." She smiled widely. "I'm writing to my mother. Mrs. Mary Jane Cochrane. She may arrive while I am away, and will stay in my room. Here, let me pay you in advance."

The color of her money was all that was needed to quiet the old lady. Elizabeth escaped upstairs with Mrs. Tanner's copy of *The New York City Register*, and dashed off a letter with instructions to her mother before settling down with the directory and examining the list of asylums and homes she might use as her springboard to insanity.

Four columns were devoted to establishments aiming to rescue and relieve the struggling masses. She discounted many in the list at once: the Colored Home and Hospital on First and Sixty-Fifth Street, the National Home for Disabled Volunteers on Broadway, and many others were not what she sought. Others merited more consideration. The Home for the Friendless, she ruled out because it sounded too sympathetic. Two homes for "young women" were too much of a risk. They were no good to her if they were trying to save girls in their teens or women in trouble. Many establishments claimed religious affiliations. The last thing she wanted was someone trying to save her soul when her only goal and purpose was to be committed. At length she settled on the Temporary Home for Women at 84 Second Avenue. It was an unremarkable location with an unremarkable listing. The word "temporary" leaped out at Elizabeth. She intended to be there for as short a time as humanly possible.

That thought led her to consider how best to present herself. She abandoned the directory and sat down at her dressing table to peer in the mirror. Could she appear mad? What did mad people really look like? What did they say? She opened her eyes wide and tilted her head. She let her jaw drop down and set her tongue between her teeth. She pulled her nostrils back. No. That was too much. She worried she looked too well-fed and too healthy. The shiny hair she prided herself upon was, for the first time, rather a nuisance.

Elizabeth shivered. The room was colder than she had realized. She abandoned the mirror and knelt to turn on the small gas fire in her grate. It took several matches to get it lit, and even then she had to crouch on the floor with her hands held in front of it for many minutes before her fingers grew warm. As the light whoosh of gas burning filled the silence, she looked at the worn carpet returning to thread beneath her feet. She studied her narrow bed with its thin layer of old blankets. She considered the curls of wallpaper peeling from the walls by the window and mold stains rising at the bottom of her curtains.

Against the grim prospect of failing, all her doubts fell away. To return here unsuccessful was not an option. She wouldn't even be able to afford to live in this miserable house if her plan failed. She'd be forced back to Pittsburgh, back to leaning on her mother, when her whole aim was to offer support. It would mean back to living with Albert and Harry in a tiny house with no space for thinking or writing, or breathing even. No dinners at Delmonico's. No fine clothes and pretty shoes. Nothing. It was unacceptable. She reached for her notebook and looked at the first page where she had written:

Energy rightly applied and directed will accomplish anything.

All the unpleasantness of these disappointing four months would be nothing compared to the difficult days ahead, supposing she did manage to get herself committed to the asylum. But she never turned back from a challenge.

Elizabeth rifled through her wardrobe. She found a long navy-blue skirt with a sagging hem and a worn seat. A black tight-waisted jacket with a dark stain down the front worked well too. It was a little fashionable – it had been one of her favorite pieces – but hopefully the mark was obvious and helped create an impression of carelessness and self-neglect that might be fitting for a struggling girl. No proud or sane girl would wear the jacket and skirt together, she was certain. Satisfied that she had a costume prepared, she hung and folded her better clothes with great care and then shrugged on a thick flannel nightgown that went all the way to her ankles.

In bed, she resolved to prepare her mind by staying awake for as long as possible and reading the most unnerving stories in her small book collection. Edgar Allan Poe was the obvious choice. *The Tell-Tale Heart* – a murder story written by a madman trying to convince his unseen audience that he's sane

– was all the more vivid, given the challenge before her. Sounds taunted her as she read: the closing of a door downstairs; the creak of the bedframe in the room next door; a man whistling on the street below.

Elizabeth's hand went to her heart as the murderer described his victim's startling eye and his heart beating a tattoo, driving him on to murder and dismember. She had to force herself from the grip of the story itself and to focus on the aspects of madness she might display in the morning when her adventure began. She would speak slowly sometimes and too fast at others. She would be vague. She would hear noises no one else could. She would stare people out of countenance. She would laugh inappropriately, and mutter and weep if she could.

The women at the Temporary Home for Women were in for an interesting day and night tomorrow.

Beatrice

January 1920

I was barely familiar with Nellie Bly's history before I started working for her. I'd got the job through word of mouth. Pauline's sister worked with a girl who was walking out with my brother, and she'd mentioned my name. Although I'd never heard of Miss Bly, my Nan knew exactly who she was – or who she had been, at any rate. She'd told me about the asylum and the trip round the world, and as I'd got to know Miss Bly I'd read through her clippings folder. Elizabeth's version was different, though. Some details jumped right off the page at me. That line about her mother, for one.

I was typing a new section of Miss Bly's story when the telephone rang. I saw Mary put her hand over her mouth as she listened. Something was wrong.

"It's little Harry," she said. "That was Mrs. Lisa on the telephone from Bellevue. She sounded terrible upset. He's very sick."

"Get my hat." Miss Bly was on her feet in a moment. "Beatrice. Put your coat on."

Miss Bly was quiet as we left the hotel. Harry Lisa was so young, still not a year old. She had last seen him at the hospital with his widowed mother, Lena, just before Christmas. Two days after he was returned to his mother, Harry had fallen sick with bronchitis. Miss Bly had answered Mrs. Lisa's call for help at once, just as she did again now. She'd helped with his admission to Bellevue, but hearing nothing further, we had assumed all was well.

In the cab to Bellevue Hospital, she shared her worries. "He has spent far too much time in this damned institution already.

If that fool at Grand Central Station had brought him to me instead of taking him to Bellevue, he might be healthy now." She stuck her head out of the Checker Taxi cab and groaned at the traffic in front of us on Lexington Avenue. "And then that nonsense with the Wentzes." Her gloved fists were clenched in frustration. "If he has been in the pit of sickness that is Bellevue all through the holidays, then I dread to think what diseases might be plaguing him now."

"Let's hope it's not pneumonia," I said.

She surprised me by taking my hand and giving it a squeeze.

"We'll soon find out."

The taxicab turned onto First Avenue and then through the arch in the red brick gatehouse of Bellevue. We were out of the vehicle in no time, and I trailed in Miss Bly's wake as she marched into the ward and waved off any nurse who wanted to know her business. While the hospital was generally clean and tidy, the sheer number of patients, packed in beds barely feet apart, was unnerving. All the city's indigent, poor, incapable, and incapacitated souls were here. We passed a row of Italian women shouting, in their own language, at a nurse who scurried past them, looking harassed and tired. "The doctor is coming!" she called back at them. "Any *momento*."

When we found Mrs. Lisa, it was clear that Harry was every bit as unwell as we feared. He lay asleep in his cot but looked weak and listless. I heard each individual rasping breath of air he took.

"He has this rash too now," said Mrs. Lisa. She was even paler than I remembered. She had a nasty sore on her lip, and I saw her fingernails were bitten down and bleeding as she pulled the bed clothes down just a little so Miss Bly could see the poor baby's back. "I called you as soon as I saw it."

"You did perfectly right." Miss Bly took a moment to look around. "This is no place for a young boy in such condition. Lord knows, I admire the work done at Bellevue, but there are better hospitals in this city and we must find the means to pay for one."

Mrs. Lisa's eyes brightened for the first time since we had

arrived, and the tension in her body eased a fraction now that Miss Bly was there to lean on. Tears of gratitude shone in her eyes, but Miss Bly was not attending. Instead, her brows knotted suddenly and her gaze narrowed on something across the ward, by the doors. Her head tilted on one side. I turned to see what was distracting her.

It was Tommy, Mrs. Lisa's older son. I recognized him at once and began to smile, but then I saw, as Miss Bly had, that he was holding hands with a man who looked – and there was no doubting what our eyes were telling us – exactly like both boys. The same eyes, the same wide mouth and rounded cheeks. The boys' father was dead.

Except he wasn't.

"Daddy!" Tommy dragged him toward us as he recognized Miss Bly. "Look who is here to visit Harry and Mama. Quickly, come say hello."

Miss Bly knelt and opened her arms to the boy, who dashed at her and threw his arms around her neck. His father, meanwhile, stood before her, red-faced and awkward, glancing at his wife, who clutched Harry's cot with one hand and covered her mouth with the other.

I don't suppose any of us breathed until Miss Bly stood up.

"Mr. Lisa?"

He nodded miserably as his wife rushed in. "Oh, please forgive us, Miss Bly. We thought you might despise us for trying to give away our boy. We thought everyone would have sympathy for me if I were a widow."

Now her husband found his tongue. "I'm ashamed of it, Miss Bly. And have regretted it from the moment we started the lie. We only wanted a better life for Harry. We are not smart, educated people. But we do love our children."

They hung on her reaction like two poor puppies begging for a bone. There is no other way to describe them. I knew what her answer would be.

It began with one of her famous smiles.

A half hour or so later, we walked back out of Bellevue. The Lisas were forgiven. Plans to have Harry transferred to the

Willard Parker Hospital were in place. The fresh air was welcome and the front of the hospital was unusually peaceful. I watched her look up at the January clouds hanging low over the vast hospital complex.

"Will you write about what has happened today in *The Journal*, Miss Bly?"

It was her habit to keep her readers up-to-date on all news concerning her foundling activities, but I wasn't sure she'd want to reveal that the couple had duped everyone, especially Nellie Bly.

"What?" She turned to me and blinked. *The Journal* and even the Lisas were not on her mind after all. "Will I? I don't know yet. I'm sorry, Beatrice, I was miles away. I was thinking about this place and the first time I ever came here. Over thirty years ago. Not to this building, though – a different one, a pavilion; it's gone now. It stood over there." Her shoulders shifted and she shook her head.

"But enough of that," she said. "I have an appointment with Coulter to discuss little Dorothy and I don't have time to go back to the hotel first." There was only one taxi-cab in sight. She looked at my feet and pulled a face. "Well, you can't walk back in those shoes, and I don't have time to drop you off. You will have to come with me to the Society. Just make sure you don't distract Mr. Coulter from the task at hand!"

She was in the cab before I could lift my jaw from the ground.

"Oh, for goodness sake get in, Beatrice," she said. "I may be an old woman, but I was young once, you know. Pretty girls turn heads. Always have, always will." I climbed into the taxi beside her, hardly knowing where to look or what to say. "And he is a handsome fellow, don't even think of denying it." She patted my hand. "But I won't say another word on the subject, unless you want me to."

She gave the cabbie our direction and then leaned back in her seat, letting out a peal of laughter. "Oh, my dear girl, your face is a picture."

Ernest Coulter's office on East Twenty-Third Street was located in an imposing eight-story building, erected by the Society decades previously to house their administrative offices and offer shelter for the numerous children in their care. We saw at once that they were in the midst of some upheaval. Boxes lined the hallways. Noisy footsteps and banging from above suggested a large number of children in a state of some excitement. Several staff rushed past us without asking us who we were or what our business was. Perhaps they just looked at Miss Bly and saw that she knew what she was about. She led me through a warren of hallways until finally she rapped on a door and swept inside.

Mr. Coulter was at his desk. He had his jacket off, his sleeves rolled up, and was leaning back in his chair with his feet up, reading a letter.

"Miss Bly! Miss…"

"Alexander," said Miss Bly, smiling broadly. "I fear we are a little early. Do you need a few moments? We could wait outside."

Wait outside? Early? She had told me we were late and marched straight in. But if her intention was to catch him off guard, she did not succeed. He shrugged on his jacket and ran one hand through his hair.

"Not at all. Please sit down." He indicated a table and four chairs next to a tall bookcase crammed with folders and books. "I was just reading over a report I received about Dorothy this morning. But first, are you warm enough? May I offer you some refreshment? We are in the process of moving our facility up to One Hundred and Fifth Street – more space needed, you know – but I think I could manage to order us some tea."

Miss Bly indicated that a cup of tea was acceptable, and he disappeared into the hallway.

"Tea," she said, winking at me. "I've never been offered tea before."

"Miss Bly!" Blood rushed to my face. Mr. Coulter was back in the room before I could say more. I grabbed my purse and dug in it for a handkerchief until my face cooled down. In the meantime, they made small talk about the relocation of the Society to new premises opposite Central Park.

"It will be wonderful for the children," said Miss Bly.

"It will," he said. "Although it creates some transportation challenges. Mr. August Heckschler's generosity knows no bounds, thankfully, and we will have additional cars to transport our staff to the courtrooms."

Tea arrived, and I sipped quietly as Miss Bly and Mr. Coulter got down to business. Miss Bly's article about Dorothy had caught the public imagination, and several lines of enquiry were developing. The Society had managed to contact Dorothy's father, but the man had claimed she was his step-child, not his daughter at all. In the short time he'd been married to her mother, he'd only met the girl once, when she was three years old.

"He is a vaudeville actor and harmonica player," Mr. Coulter said. "My investigator believed him when he said the child was not his. He said that Grace Harris appeared to love the child but was never capable of looking after her. She was a nervous wreck and a drug addict. She had the child boarded out but visited her regularly. He has no idea about where Grace Harris is now, and doesn't know what her religion is."

"Perhaps this woman will know." Miss Bly dug into her purse, pulled out a letter, and passed it to Mr. Coulter. She had shown it to me the day it arrived. Helen Love-Beauregard of New Haven, Connecticut, claimed that she had been the woman who had boarded Dorothy for Grace Harris until they moved to New York almost exactly one year ago. She did not paint a pretty picture of the mother. Mrs. Love-Beauregard described Grace Harris as a drug addict and "inmate of a house of ill-fame". I watched Ernest Coulter's eyebrows rise as he read the details.

"Do you see how she describes the mother?" asked Miss Bly. She took the letter back and found the line she was looking for. She is a woman of "good birth but bad environment". The world is not fair, Mr. Coulter, and that's a fact. Sometimes I think we are all but one step away from chaos or disaster. The choices that bring us three here –

educated, well fed, clean living, and kind – were not all our own doing. Luck plays too mighty a part in the way people's lives play out. Who knows how different life might have been for Grace Harris? A wealthy young man seduced her. She is to be pitied, not reviled. And even if the woman is at fault for her sins and errors, the daughter has none. If the mother is beyond redemption, the child is not."

"I agree," said Mr. Coulter, spreading his hands on the table. His fingers were long, his nails clipped and clean. "This woman may have some knowledge of the child's faith. I will write to her and then take the letter to Judge Levy so he can add it to Dorothy's case file."

"Already done," said Miss Bly. "I'm waiting to hear from Mrs. Love-Beauregard and Judge Levy is already familiar with everything here." She tapped the letter and appeared not to notice Mr. Coulter's obvious surprise.

"You have already seen Judge Levy in this matter?"

"I have."

She raised her eyebrows as if daring him to challenge her.

"Why?" He kept his voice calm, but his jaw stiffened and his eyes narrowed.

"I have several excellent families interested in adopting Dorothy."

He leaned back in the chair and crossed his arms. "Oh, you do, do you?"

"I do. The article bore much fruit, as you so cleverly thought."

He wasn't interested in her flattery. "So, tell me about them. Who are they? Where do they live?"

"I have told Judge Levy the particulars. No one else needs to know."

"Shouldn't the Society know? She is under our care."

"Legally, yes, but I have promised these potential parents anonymity."

"And the Society is supposed to simply take your word that they are fit for the task. You? With no training or background or experience?"

"Yes," was all she answered.

He wasn't satisfied. "You know that no one can adopt Dorothy unless we know her religion. That is the fruit that we need to pluck. Not prospective parents."

"But we could have that information at any moment. And the girl needs a home. Her health is much improved, isn't it?"

"It is."

"Then as soon as we have determined this ridiculous question of faith, she can be adopted. She is six years old. That is a tender time in a child's life."

"I'm aware of that."

"Are you?"

"I might just as easily ask the same of you!"

They'd become heated so very quickly. Coulter's suspicion of Miss Bly wasn't unnatural. She operated outside the framework of support for children that the Society had been at the heart of for nearly fifty years. He was proud of his work, and dedicated, that was abundantly clear. I just wished he could trust her like I did.

"Miss Bly was six years old when her own father died, Mr. Coulter," I said. "So I believe she understands Dorothy's position very well."

"Oh, you do, do you?" He turned his gaze on me and did not hide his scorn. "When you have seen what I have seen, then I will welcome you back here and be most interested in your opinion."

"That's enough, Mr. Coulter." Miss Bly pushed back her chair and stood up. "I believe your irritation is with me, not with Miss Alexander, and we'd be grateful if you would mind your manners. You may not like my methods, but do not think that I have not seen and understood the misery that affects children and women in this metropolis. Until *you* have seen what *I* have seen, Mr. Coulter, I find I do not care for your opinion on my activities regarding Dorothy Harris, not one bit. No. Don't get up. Miss Alexander and I are perfectly capable of finding our way out of here by ourselves. Good-day to you."

With that, she swept out of the room and I followed her without a backward glance. I had been a fool for admiring him. He was pompous. Arrogant. And so wedded to his rules and regulations that he had no heart to see that Miss Bly only had Dorothy's best interests at heart. I was afraid she'd be cross with me for saying what I'd said about her, but when we were out of the building and in a taxicab, the girl was all she was thinking about.

"We will go and see Dorothy at the hospital for ourselves in the morning, Beatrice, that's what we will do. Wait until you meet her. She truly is most charming. If anyone deserves a decent chance in life, it's Dorothy. We're going to make sure she gets it. You'll see!"

Elizabeth
V
September 1887

In the morning, Elizabeth slipped out the door without a word. No need to let Mrs. Tanner see her leave on her assignment with no more than the clothes she stood up in.

It was a lengthy walk, through Central Park and down Fifth Avenue, and her thoughts were busy with the task ahead. Her fingers rubbed at the few coins in her pocketbook. The sky was clear blue, but cold air bit at her cheeks.

She entered the park at the South Meadow and passed the reservoir and lake before turning along the Mall. It was too early for the daily parade of fine carriages of society elites, seeing and being seen, but there were nursemaids wheeling their charges, riders on horseback, and visitors to the city enjoying the open space.

She continued south, down Fifth Avenue to Madison Square Park, and then followed Broadway to Union Square. She had the route mapped out in her head, and crossed to Fourth Avenue, still heading south until she reached The Cooper Union. From there, Elizabeth turned left, into a tree-lined street that narrowed and darkened as a sweep of cloud hid the sun. She passed McSorley's Ale House, ignoring the calls of two men rolling barrels. Second Avenue was just ahead. In a matter of moments, she found the building she was looking for.

The Temporary Home for Women at 84 Second Avenue was every bit as miserable-looking as she had hoped: a tall, thin, red-brick tenement building crowned with a bottle green architrave, and grimy drapes hanging at the three dirty windows on every floor. A series of decorative green diamonds on cream panels between its attic windows suggested an architect's bright hopes when the building had been erected, but paint peeled at the door and wet leaves lay in soggy heaps in the front yard. At least the doorbell worked.

"Well?" A scraggly, sharp-faced girl with frizzy blonde hair looked Elizabeth up and down, her hands balled into fists at her hips. She looked thirteen at most.

"Is the matron in?" Elizabeth's voice cracked. She needed no acting skills to appear nervous.

"She is, but she's busy," said the girl. "You can wait in the back." She flattened herself against the fully open door and pointed Elizabeth down the dim hallway. "There. In that one. It's not that difficult!"

Elizabeth found herself in the back parlor. It was a gloomy excuse for a room, papered in dark brown stripes, with no lamps yet lit, and only the weak light from one window to bring any brightness. She saw a forlorn old organ, a plain wardrobe, several unmatched dining chairs, and three odd armchairs – each as uncomfortable and badly sprung as the next, she discovered, as she tried out each one in turn. There was no mirror, but Elizabeth took off her sailor's hat, picked at the short veil, and retied her hair more loosely. She hoped she looked tired and anxious. She *was* tired and anxious.

An age passed before the door opened. A slender woman with tidy hair pulled back from her face and wearing a dark, plain dress came in and stood before her with her hands clasped in front of her.

"Well?" she said.

"Are you the matron?"

"Her assistant. She's busy. What can I do for you?"

"I need somewhere to stay. Only for a few days. Can you accommodate me?"

"Not in a single room, if that's what you are looking for. But if you will share, I can do that much for you. We are very busy."

"I'm happy to share. How much do you charge?" Elizabeth stood up, clutching her pocketbook.

"Thirty cents a night. To be paid each morning before noon. I can take that now. Name?"

"Nellie Brown."

They had no sooner exchanged the coins than a knock came at the door and the woman disappeared. Elizabeth was unsure what to do next. She took a seat again, but the noises of the house – the clip of heels up and down stairs, the tread of feet on the ceiling above, and the rattle from the kitchen below – kept startling her. At last a loud bell clanged somewhere below and a steady trample of feet began, suggesting that dinner was served. Elizabeth didn't know whether to join them or not.

Deciding to wait, she pulled a small notebook from her pocketbook and made some nonsensical jottings that might help confirm her case of insanity should anyone look at it in the days ahead. She was still writing when the assistant matron stuck her head back round the door.

"Don't you want to eat?" she asked.

"I do. But may I know your name first?"

The request produced a frown. "Mrs. Stanard."

Elizabeth knew the woman's eyes were on her as she bent to write the name in her notebook. Good. She planned to be as odd as possible. Jumping to her feet, Elizabeth gave Mrs. Stanard a broad and over-friendly smile. She rushed to the door and abruptly stopped smiling before following Mrs. Stanard down to the basement.

The dining area was an uninspiring sight. There were upwards of ten small rough wooden tables with nothing on them but knives and forks, and no table linen. Thick smells of stewing meat filled the air, and the hum of the women talking was broken only by the clatter of the kitchen and the arrival of trays of steaming food. Mrs. Stanard found a space for Elizabeth and disappeared. Her fellow diners nodded briefly but were not inclined to talk. A few moments later, the blonde girl from the door appeared, again, fists on hips.

"Boiled mutton, boiled beef, beans, potatoes, coffee or tea?" she said.

"Beef, potatoes, coffee, and bread."

"Bread goes in." The girl pointed at Elizabeth's neighbor's

place where a bread roll had sunk in the gravy of her meat. It might have been mutton. Or beef. Or something else entirely. At least the meal was not long in coming. As there was no conversation to be had in her small group, Elizabeth took the opportunity to observe her fellow boarders.

In her job for *The Pittsburg Dispatch*, she could have made a story of these women into an article in a heartbeat. They were worn creatures, plainly dressed and badly groomed. She felt a rush of sympathy, listening to a woman at the table next to her respond to the blonde serving girl in heavily accented English. German, Elizabeth thought. No doubt many of them were immigrants, newly arrived and struggling to find work and a home. It occurred to her that pretending some foreign origin, using the Spanish she'd picked up in Mexico, might help her charade succeed.

At the end of the meal Elizabeth followed a group of women upstairs and into the front parlor. The doors had been opened between this and the back room she had waited in earlier. Now, as this front area filled, Elizabeth sidled towards the back parlor, hoping to find a vantage point from which to observe these women and find a way to execute her mission. The front room was similarly furnished with a muddle of dining and armchairs. Really the only difference between the two was in the light afforded by the front window, shining on a formal oval table covered in brown velvet and topped with a curling dried-up fern display. She sat in the armchair in the back and composed her face into as lifeless a pose as she knew how, keeping her lips closed but letting her jaw sag, and moving her eyes as little as possible.

It made for a dull and anxious afternoon. One woman had her son Georgie with her – an obnoxious, snotty creature of six or seven years who made it his business to squirm around the floor between the dining chairs, disturbing their occupants and talking back whenever his vapid mother summoned up the energy to try and remonstrate with him. Elizabeth's fingers twitched with a desire to tweak him by his ear, and for a moment she thought of doing it. That would make a stir. But before she could make up her mind, the assistant matron was back in the room. She saw Elizabeth sitting apart and seemed concerned.

"What's wrong with you? Are you troubled?"

"No. Why?"

"Your face looks very troubled."

"Perhaps I am. I am very sad. Everything is very sad these days, don't you think?"

"Why, not at all," said Mrs. Stanard. "We all have our worries and troubles, of course, who does not? But we can't let them weigh us down. You are looking for work, I suppose. You won't find it by sitting here. What are you looking for?"

"I hardly know. It's all so sad."

"Well, what about being a nurse? I'm sure children like you. You have a gentle face. Wouldn't you like a pretty white cap and apron?"

This jollying-along was unexpected and Elizabeth struggled not to giggle.

"But I have never worked," she managed to whisper.

"Well, you will learn. Every lady here works. They have to." The matron waved her arm at the five or six women in the other room. Two were knitting. One slept in an armchair with her mouth hanging open. Georgie's mother was reading a book and ignoring him drumming his feet on the table leg.

"They all look crazy to me. They are horrible. I'm too afraid to go in. And so I stay here."

The matron pulled a chair up and sat next to her. "They are good, honest women," she said. "We do not keep crazy people here."

"But how can you tell?" Elizabeth leaned toward Mrs. Stanard and widened her eyes as much as she could. "There are so many crazy people these days. So many murderers. The police never catch them. A woman could murder her husband and run to a place like this to hide herself."

Mrs. Stanard stiffened. "I'll come back to see you later," she said, scraping back her chair and taking a step away from Elizabeth.

She did not come back.

As dusk fell, Elizabeth ate another meal in the basement

and joined the women trooping back upstairs. Now that all the working women had returned, the seats were quickly taken. With her purse nearly empty, Elizabeth knew she had this one night to achieve her objective. Where to start?

Her eye was drawn to two women seated near the window in deep conversation. They were both in their late twenties and gave an appearance of good sense and good manners. When a chair beside them became vacant, Elizabeth hurried over.

"May I join you?" she asked in a low, uncertain voice. "I'm terribly lonely."

"Of course," said one. "I'm Ruth. Ruth Caine. And this is Lizzie King. Lizzie was just telling me about her sister's wedding plans."

"My name is Nellie Brown."

"Well now, I have a little niece named Nellie," said Lizzie. She spoke with a soft southern drawl and smiled, but when Elizabeth did not reply, Lizzie grew a little pink at the cheeks. She glanced at Elizabeth's hat, which she still wore, along with her gloves, even though every other woman had removed theirs before dinner.

"Nancy wants pink roses everywhere," Lizzie said, turning back to Ruth Caine. "My mother wrote me all about it. It will be a fine affair."

"Don't you think the women here all look a little crazy?" said Elizabeth, leaning toward Lizzie and enjoying the way the older woman pulled away.

"Not at all," said Ruth.

"I wish you weren't leaving tomorrow, Ruth," said Lizzie.

"Where are you going? Must you leave so soon?" Elizabeth knew she was unsettling the women, although both tried not to show it.

"I am," said Ruth. "I must go home. I have been working here for some months, but my eyesight has altered for the worse."

"I wish you could find a physician to treat you. Do you need new eyeglasses?" asked Lizzie.

"I can't afford New York prices. I must go home to my parents and do some other work until I can pay for treatment.

By then, my position here will be filled so I must start all over again. At least I will see my little girl again."

"What position are you leaving?" asked Elizabeth.

"I work at the William Wood Company as a proofreader. But my headaches..." She sniffed and tried to smile a little at Elizabeth. "Enough about me. Do you have work?"

She shook her head. "Don't you think it's very sad?"

"What is sad?" Ruth asked. "Working?"

"Yes. So many women working. Your poor daughter managing without her mother. When I think of your poor eyes, I could weep."

"There, there, now." Ruth was consoling, but Lizzie took the chance to excuse herself, claiming tiredness and a desire to retire for the night.

"Tell me," said Ruth, "how old are you?"

"Nineteen."

"And where is your family?"

"I don't know."

Their conversation faltered. Elizabeth stared vacantly at the floor, but in her mind, she was busy. She needed to act and act soon.

When the scrawny serving girl appeared to bid all the women to their beds, she sprang into action.

"No!" she declared. "No, I won't. I'm afraid to! I won't go upstairs with these strangers. And you can't make me do it!"

This brought a crowd about her, with Ruth at the center, pleading with her to just go upstairs and rest.

"How can I rest? How can any of us? We could be murdered in our beds. Smothered or strangled."

"What nonsense is this?" Mrs. Stanard appeared in the doorway. "Ladies, to your rooms, please. I will deal with Miss Brown." Several women were reluctant to leave, and made their objections to Elizabeth known. She should be put out at once, said one, while another declared as she left the room that "the crazy creature" had better not be sharing a room with her.

"Come now," said Mrs. Stanard. "We run an orderly house here and I cannot have this kind of disruption."

"I will sleep here," Elizabeth announced. "Just leave me

here. Get me a pistol! I will be safe with a pistol in my hands."

"No." Mrs. Stanard's temper rose with the color on her cheeks. "This room is locked, and all women sleep in their assigned rooms. No exceptions!"

"Then I'll sleep on the stairs!" Elizabeth twisted past her and out of the door. She sat down firmly on the stairs and pulled her knees to her chest. "I won't move. I'm afraid of them. Are there no guns in this house? Why can't I have a pistol? I can't go upstairs with those crazy women."

"Them crazy?" snorted the serving girl, leaning over her, as if ready to throw a punch. "There's only one crazy bird in this house and I'm looking at her."

"Enough, Emily," said Mrs. Stanard. "Miss Brown, you will take yourself upstairs or I will call the police and tell them you are drunk. I'll have you thrown in a cell."

The police! The police were just what Elizabeth hoped for, but she needed them to be called because she was crazy, not drunk. Seeing no other choice, she got to her feet. "Very well then. I'll go. But I shall not sleep a wink."

"That's up to you," said Mrs. Stanard. "All I care about is that you are quiet. Now follow me. And no more funny business."

Elizabeth followed her up two flights of stairs, considering her next move. Women stared out from each doorway. She was an event, that was certain – as exotic as a lion in Central Park Zoo.

"You've got to be kidding me." As Mrs. Stanard paused at a door to show Elizabeth inside, a thick-set woman with greasy brown hair moved to fill the doorway. "I'm not sharing with a lunatic," she said. "Take her elsewhere. I won't be stabbed in my bed."

"Don't be ridiculous, Sarah Feathers," said Mrs. Stanard.

"You can't call her ridiculous," called out a woman behind her, bringing the rest of the women on the floor from their rooms.

"That's right, you can't. Where's the senior matron? Someone should fetch her."

"Someone should fetch the police!"

"Ladies!"

Elizabeth saw Mrs. Stanard was floundering. She opened her eyes wide and began twitching her nose up and down while clenching and unclenching her fists. Sarah Feathers saw it at once.

"I won't have this madwoman in here with me for all the money of the Vanderbilts, and you can't make me!" she shouted, slamming the door in Mrs. Stanard's face. Elizabeth stopped twitching and attempted to look as innocent as possible, but as soon as Mrs. Stanard turned her back she started again.

"I'll share with her," said Ruth Caine. "Sarah can take my bed in with Lizzie and I'll share this room with Miss Brown."

Mrs. Stanard sagged with relief. Ruth told the other women to go to their beds, and once Sarah had pushed past Elizabeth with her bags and her clothes, she and Ruth were left alone in the bedroom.

It made her little room at Mrs. Tanner's boarding house look luxurious. There was no fireplace, no mantel to set a photograph on, and no dressing table to set out one's brushes and combs. There were only two narrow beds, two high-back wooden chairs, and a table with two cracked jugs and bowls, beneath a speckled old mirror. The walls were bare, and a dirty brown rug filled the gap between their beds.

Ruth wanted to help Elizabeth take off her hat and unpin her hair but was refused. When she realized that Elizabeth had no luggage with her at all, Ruth urged her to take one of her own nightgowns. Again, Elizabeth said no.

"You must rest," Ruth said. "And in the morning, we will find you some assistance."

"No one will help me."

Perched on the side of her bed, Elizabeth let her shoulders curl and her chin sink.

"Where are your family?"

"I don't remember."

"Are they here in the city?"

"I don't remember. I promise you. No one will help me. No one."

"Of course they will! This city is full of good kind people. Why don't you take your boots off, dear? We should sleep soon."

"I'm afraid to sleep." Elizabeth tried to stand but Ruth clasped her hands and sat next to her.

"We must try soon. Perhaps we can talk until you fall asleep. Won't you take my nightdress and lie down?"

"I won't be found murdered in another woman's nightdress!"

"Hush, hush. These walls are like paper."

As if proving her right, there was a knock at the door. "Quiet in there, for pity's sake!"

"See," said Ruth in a whisper. "The door is locked. We are completely safe." She looked directly into Elizabeth's eyes. "I am going to put on my nightgown and lie down now. There is nothing for you to fear tonight." She stroked her hair and Elizabeth found a tear sliding down her cheek.

The kindness of the other woman was genuine. This performance was wearisome. Tiredness washed over her. For a moment, she thought of how wonderful it would be to wake up tomorrow morning on her own bed on West Ninety-Sixth Street, but the faces of Cockerill and Pulitzer rose up in her mind, demanding results.

"You must lie down," said Elizabeth. "I'll watch over you and make sure you are safe. I won't let them touch you."

Ruth shook her head but bent and unlaced her boots. "Can you truly remember nothing of your parents? Are they alive?"

"My mother is dead. My father, too. I had a grandfather, but he is also gone now."

"I'm so sorry. Was this long ago, do you remember?"

"My mother died when I was born. My father, Juan Marina, used to take me sailing at the Hacienda. But he died and I was alone."

"Marina? Didn't Mrs. Stanard say your name was Brown?"

"Did she? Why does my head hurt so?"

"It does? Perhaps we should turn the light off." Ruth lay down on her bed. "I only want you to be comfortable. Don't you wish to rest?"

But Elizabeth could not lie down for fear of falling asleep and missing any opportunity to further her cause. No. She was determined to stay awake all night, and did so although the hours crawled by. She tried to amuse herself recounting the events of her life but snagged too often on unpleasant memories. She turned her mind instead to daydreams of a rosy future at *The World*, of new fashionable clothes and expensive dinners at Delmonico's.

At one point Ruth was woken by cries from the room next door.

"What is it? What is it?" Elizabeth pulled her knees to her chest and rocked on the bed until Ruth promised to investigate. She was gone for a few minutes and came back quite irritated.

"That silly woman dreamed that you attacked her, of all things," she declared. "I have never heard of anything so ridiculous. But I do wish you could get some rest. We could all do with it."

"I don't think I'll ever sleep again."

Ruth lay down again on her bed and suggested Elizabeth do the same. "Where are you from, Nellie? Where did you grow up?"

"I don't remember."

Ruth sighed. "I wish I could help you. Let's sleep."

***

By morning, Elizabeth had a plan. She was silent through breakfast, and when they returned to their room she again sat rocking on the bed.

"How can I help you?" asked Ruth. "You must have friends. Or family. Everyone does."

"I have no friends, but I did have trunks! Oh, where are my trunks?"

Elizabeth's voice rose and she began looking under the beds as Ruth tried to calm her.

"I'm sure we can find them. I will help you. I won't go to Boston until they are located. I promise."

Elizabeth grabbed Ruth's hands. "No. You must go home to

your family. Your little girl. Think of her. Don't let her think you have forgotten her. I only need my trunks. I need them. Someone must fetch them. I won't move until I have them. Do you hear me?"

"Let me go and I will fetch Mrs. Stanard."

Elizabeth saw how anxious she had made the poor woman, but had no time to ponder the rights or wrongs of it all. When Mrs. Stanard appeared, she dug her heels and refused to move until they located her trunks. At last, the surly serving girl whispered loudly in Mrs. Stanard's ear that she should call a policeman. Elizabeth could have kissed her.

Two policemen arrived and were shown upstairs to her room. Elizabeth ignored them, sticking to her rocking and twitching and muttering about her missing trunks. She heard the men and Mrs. Stanard decide to tell her they were taking her to a lost property office to help her find her missing possessions. The matron was determined that Nellie Brown leave quietly, ideally by the basement back door.

Elizabeth said goodbye to Ruth Caine, pulled down the veil on her sailor's hat to hide her eyes, and went along without any fuss. Mrs. Stanard accompanied them, and Elizabeth was glad of it. She was sure that the matron was determined to get this strange Nellie Brown girl off her hands for good.

But she knew a moment's worry when she realized the police station they took her to was one she had visited only ten days earlier for an article she had written for *The Pittsburg Dispatch*. Worse, the very captain she had spoken to at length that day turned out to be the man on duty. Elizabeth shrank behind Mrs. Stanard and kept her eyes on the ground, praying that he did not recognize her.

He did not.

When asked to confirm her name was Nellie Brown, she didn't look up and answered only that she supposed so. Mrs. Stanard stepped forward and took it upon herself to fully acquaint the police captain with all of Elizabeth's deranged behaviors, and the captain barely looked at her. After a few moments, she was told to wait in a chair while her situation was discussed.

"Come along then, Miss Brown," said one of the policemen, a burly Irishman named Brockert, a few minutes later. "We have another place to go and look for your trunks and will find them very soon, I'm sure of it."

"Do you really think we will find my trunks?"

"Oh, most certainly," he replied. "We'll take you to Essex Street. They put all the lost bags there."

The streets were busy and the voices she heard were mostly foreign – German, Jewish, Russian voices – calling children to behave, cutting business deals, going and to and from factories and sweatshops, selling food, furniture, shawls and blankets; everything from pots and pans to livestock could be bought on these crowded streets. The oddness of their party caught the eye of a group of children who followed them, asking questions about who they were and what Elizabeth had done. They only disappeared when the Essex Market Police Station and Courthouse came into view. It was a squat stone building, and scores of people waited to go inside. The line was so long it wrapped around the corner into Ludlow Street.

"This many people have lost their trunks?" Elizabeth asked wide-eyed.

"Yes. That's why they're here," said Brockert.

"Are they from here?" she said. "They all look so strange."

"Foreigners. Just landed. They've lost their trunks and come here to find them."

"And must I wait with them? I don't like the look of them."

"No. You don't need to wait," he said. He gripped her elbow, steered her past the line and into the courthouse.

VI

The courtroom was busy although conversation was muted. The judge was in session and had a kindly aspect about him that surprised Elizabeth. She thought of her own father, who had died when she was just a girl. She watched the judge read papers and smile kindly at a German couple struggling to speak to him in English. The wife did the talking, speaking painfully slowly while her husband, a little older, frowned, whispered in her ear, and gesticulated in obvious frustration.

There were people of all ages, colors, and countries here. Two dark-skinned women huddled opposite Elizabeth. They wore identical shawls of red and orange, and each had a long, thick plait of black hair. Their features were the same, only their skin revealed their different ages. The younger stroked her mother's hands, talking quietly. Next to them, a young man in an ill-fitting suit cracked his knuckles and tapped his feet. To Elizabeth's left, a fat old woman with beady dark eyes and a plain black dress rolled her eyes at her balding husband. He sat slumped and defeated, as if he wished himself anywhere but here.

She tried to guess their stories, and imagined herself on her way across the Atlantic to report on immigration as she had proposed, rather than trying to prove to the authorities that she was insane.

Her spirits foundered. This task was impossible. As a young American girl, she was already attracting too much attention. There were a couple of reporters in the building – men, of course – lounging around on benches waiting for some drama to arrive, and their eyes were on her from the moment she entered the room. While Brockert and Mrs. Stanard presented their story to the judge's clerk, one of the reporters, a thin man with slick hair and a nervous smile, slid along the bench beside her.

"What's your story?" he said. "Maybe I can help you."

She kept her eyes on the floor, swallowing a desire to tell him just exactly what she thought of his offer of help.

"What's your name at least?" he asked. "It can't hurt to tell me that."

"Here you! Scram!" Brockert waved the man away and called Elizabeth up to speak to the clerk.

"Full name?"

"Nellie Brown." She made sure to give a Spanish edge to her accent. "I have lost my trunks and need to find them."

The clerk was a small, round man who looked as warm as a boiled ham in his thick wool suit. He noted her reply and then moved to another question on the form in front of him. "When did you come to New York?"

"I did not come to New York."

That made him put down his pen at least. "But you are in New York now," he said.

"No. I am not. I did not come to New York."

"Where is this girl from?" He spoke sharply to Mrs. Stanard. "Is she from the West? She is not from round here."

Mrs. Stanard shrugged, as ready as any woman was to wash her hands of another.

"She sounds Southern to me," said the young man who had been cracking his knuckles.

The clerk returned to Elizabeth and sighed. "So, you are telling me you have no idea where you are or how you got here? Take a seat. Judge Duffy will want to examine you himself."

Mrs. Stanard looked on the verge of complaining, but the round little clerk waved her away and scraped back his chair. He crossed the room and conferred with the judge who stared over at Elizabeth.

"Come here, girl, and lift your veil," called Judge Duffy.

She walked over, holding herself stiffly, imagining she walked a tightrope.

"Now lift that veil so I may see your face. Even the Queen of England must do as she is asked in my courtroom, you know."

Elizabeth complied and the judge leaned forward and studied her.

"What is wrong, young lady?"

"Nothing. But this man," she gestured toward Brockert, "promised to help me find my missing trunks."

"And what are you to do with this young girl?" the judge asked Mrs. Stanard.

"I know nothing of her! Nothing except that she arrived at the home yesterday, asking for a room for the night."

"The home? What home?"

"A temporary home for working women. At 84 Second Avenue."

Elizabeth was aware of the reporters moving across the room in order to hear this exchange with Judge Duffy.

Mrs. Stanard explained to the judge about Elizabeth's arrival at the home and the disturbance she had caused overnight. "She asked for a pistol. The other women were terrified. She said her name was Brown, but she told the girl who shared a room with her that her name was Marino. She did not sleep a wink last night."

"Does she have any money?"

"I paid for everything," said Elizabeth. "Although the food was some of the worst I have tried."

She heard Brockert mutter behind her. "She's not so crazy on the food question, then."

"Well, my dear," said Judge Duffy. "Your English is impeccable. But I wonder, where are your family, where are you from?"

"I only know I need my trunks, sir. Won't you help me find them? I have nice clothes in my trunk. Nicer than this hat. It's not even mine." She opened her eyes wide. "When I have my trunks, I can go home on the railroad. Perhaps I can go home to Cuba. Is my home in Cuba, do you think? Do they always speak Spanish there?"

Judge Duffy shook his head. "You are a puzzle to me, young lady. And I do not like to see you so confused."

He turned to his clerk and spoke as if no one were there.

"She reminds me of my sister, my poor dead sister. I'm sure someone must be looking for her. It is really most unfortunate. You," he pointed at a reporter squatting on a nearby bench with his elbows on his knees and leaning forward to catch every exchange. "Can't you locate the family of this poor girl? Isn't that what your lot are good for."

The last thing Elizabeth wanted was a reporter on her case.

"I don't like that man and his questions," she said shrilly. "There are too many impudent young men in this courtroom, and they are staring at me. I don't want to stay here. Not for a minute longer." As if to underline her agitation, she rolled her thin veil back down.

"She's a crazy lunatic," said Brockert. "Send her to the Island."

"Oh, surely not," said Mrs. Stanard. "She's so young. And clearly a lady. I cannot think of her in such a place."

Elizabeth ground her teeth. She wanted to shake Mrs. Stanard. Thankfully, the matron's compassion quickly proved to have its limits.

"Could she return with you then, Mrs. Stanard?" asked the judge. "Perhaps someone will claim her soon. I'm sure this young man from *The Sun* will report on her case in his newspaper."

"Oh, my goodness, no. No, I'm afraid that's impossible. The household was in chaos. She may seem quiet now, but she wasn't last night, I can assure you."

"Hmm." Judge Duffy took a moment to stare at Elizabeth and then spoke to his clerk. "There is some foul play here, I suspect. Perhaps drugs, hopefully not something worse. She needs somewhere safe to stay while we see if her memory returns. Make out the papers and have her taken to Bellevue."

He looked at Brockert. "Take her and the matron to wait in the back room."

The moment they were away from the judge, the matron began to grumble about the time and her need to return to the post. After a while the judge appeared briefly and questioned Elizabeth again about her home and the idea that she was of Cuban origin. There was no doubt he was more inclined to send an immigrant girl to the Island than he had been earlier when she provoked memories of his dead sister. Elizabeth let her feigned accent grow stronger with every word she spoke.

The reporter she so dreaded made an attempt to come in and ask her more questions, but Elizabeth raised a fuss at his intrusion and paced the room in an agitated manner until the ambulance and doctor from Bellevue Hospital arrived.

Judge Duffy brought him in to examine her. "Here is the poor girl who has been drugged," he said. "Look in her eyes. I believe her pupils are enlarged."

"You are right," said Mrs. Stanard. "I noticed it particularly. They have been that way since her arrival yesterday."

"It may be belladonna," said the doctor, talking over Elizabeth's head as if she were not present, even as he took her pulse and listened to her heartbeat. He shone a light in her eyes and Elizabeth forced herself not to blink.

"Yes. Highly likely belladonna," he said.

"Well, I want you to take good care of her, as others cannot or will not," said the judge. He frowned at Mrs. Stanard.

"I'll go anywhere but back to that home with its crazy women and its terrible food!" said Elizabeth.

That was enough for the other woman to take umbrage. "I wish to be excused, your honor," she said stiffly. "I'm needed elsewhere."

"Yes, yes, woman. Off you go."

Elizabeth didn't give Mrs. Stanard a backward glance. Her attention was on the doctor, who was as young as she was. Belladonna indeed. She really did have a chance of succeeding here. He asked her to stick out her tongue.

"I'm not sick and I don't want to," she said.

"You must. You are sick and I am a doctor. You must do as I say."

"I am not sick and am only here to ask for my trunks."

The doctor sighed. He folded his hands and looked at her with his eyebrows raised. Confident a moment ago, she suddenly quailed. She was completely alone in the hands of these three men – judge, doctor, policeman. A knot formed in her stomach and she stuck out her tongue.

When the doctor concluded his examination, he made several notes in his notebook. He nodded at the judge, who clasped Elizabeth's hands in his own. "This man will be kind to you, I am sure of it. The staff at Bellevue will do all they can for you. We will not give up hope of those trunks. But at least you will be safe while we look for them, my dear."

Elizabeth tugged at her veil to hide her emotions. With Bellevue in sight, the Island was in sight. Her head throbbed and her eyes burned through lack of sleep, but her spirits soared. Brockert led her back out through the busy courtroom and past a clamor of people surrounding the black and red Bellevue ambulance.

Outside, the driver stepped away from his horse and grabbed at her, pinning her arms.

"What is this? Take your hands off me!" She turned to look for Brockert, but his back was to her as he tried to break up the crowd. The driver pushed her against the side of his vehicle and pressed himself into her.

"Shall we take a little detour on the way?" he whispered. "No one should be in a rush to get where you are going."

She twisted, trying to free herself.

"I will ride in the back with the patient," said the young doctor. The driver's grip on her relaxed.

"Just helping her in," he said.

Elizabeth shrank away from him and tried to move toward the doctor, but the pock-faced driver wrapped one arm around her again, lifted her, and shoved her inside the ambulance. She landed on her knees and scrambled up, scowling at the doctor who climbed in behind her.

"Did you see that? Did you hear him?" she said.

But he did not meet her eye. "Lie down," he said.

Inside the ambulance were two flat roll beds, each with a thin yellow blanket. She did as she was told, while the doctor perched himself on the end of the other, near the door at the back.

She closed her eyes as the driver hollered and shouted at the swarm of onlookers to get out of their way. Every jolt of the carriage shook her. The sides of the ambulance rattled as people banged it as it rolled along.

One thought consumed her. There was no way back now.

She had put her safety in the hands of two men at *The World* – she, who prided herself on not depending on anyone for anything. She barely knew whether to laugh or cry. Elizabeth glanced at the doctor, a stranger, only a foot away from her, staring out into the streets. He was all that stood between her and an assault. She turned her head the other way and chose to hope for the best.

Beatrice

January - February 1920

Working for Miss Bly was an education in itself – far more instructive than anything I had learned in school or from my family. She was a force of nature and we never knew what might happen on any given day. At the end of January, Arthur Brisbane sent her to witness and report on the execution of Gordon Fawcett Hamby at Sing Sing. Hamby had shot and killed two bank clerks and a policeman during a robbery in Brooklyn just over a year earlier. Miss Bly had some correspondence with the murderer leading up to his death, and although he admitted his guilt and wrote that he was ready to get "it over as quickly as possible", she was haunted by what she witnessed.

"The commandment says – 'Thou shalt not kill'," she said to me. "If that applies to Hamby, then why not to all of us? None of us should kill. And that is what I saw. Legal killing, yes. But still wrong."

I had never thought of it in such a way, but in the ensuing weeks I typed up column after column in support of the Boylan-Pellet bill which would abolish capital punishment, and found myself coming around to her way of thinking. At the same time, she wrote about the evils of gambling, about the problem of homelessness, about criminal justice, and fairness for first offenders. She battled with her family over finances. She had inherited a business from her husband, but had left everything in her mother and brother's hands while she worked overseas during the Great War.

I didn't agree with everything she did. She took up the case of one young man who had been imprisoned for theft, helping him find a job on his release and insisting that he had served his time and reformed. Yet when he came to thank her in person, and I was taking Brisbane out for a walk, she told me to be sure and take my purse with me.

"This young man here has light fingers," she said to me, with him standing right by, hearing every word. I don't think she even knew what she had said, but I saw the poor man blush to the roots of his hair.

She wasn't consistent either. She wrote regular articles slating anyone who gave up their child, even calling for a law whereby any mother who abandoned her child lost all claim on it. Yet she had forgiven the Lisas. She had nothing but good words for them, despite their deception. And she wrote letter upon letter trying to track down Dorothy Harris's mother. I hardly thought she did all that only to tell the woman she could never care for her own child again.

On the subject of women working, she was particularly puzzling. She was the strongest, most independent woman I knew. She had changed the newspaper industry forever when she was twenty-three years old. She wrote frequently and passionately about women's rights, equality, and fair pay. This was where she had begun. Miss Bly didn't keep all her work, but her first published article, *The Girl Puzzle,* published with her original pseudonym, "Orphan Girl", was in her clipping file in her little sitting room, and I had read it several times. In it she had called for greater employment opportunities for women. She said women could be more than teachers, or clerks, or factory girls, or cooks, chambermaids, and washerwomen. There were too many girls at home, and they needed their chance. Girls were just as smart as boys and a great deal quicker to learn.

I agreed with her. Whenever I read her words, I felt their truth like a physical lump in my chest. Even then, aged only twenty, she had wanted action, not talk. People shouldn't debate and discuss making change, she had insisted; people should make change happen.

Now, although her head-on approach was the same, some of her ideas were different. She wrote this in one column: *No home can be a home where the wife and mother works outside. No marriage life can be ideal or true or worthwhile where the wife and mother "goes to business". No children can be cared for and brought up as they should where "mother works downtown".*

That did not sit too well with Pauline, who had two boys at home in the care of her mother while she travelled "downtown" every day to type letters for Miss Bly. Pauline groused around our room for days afterward, muttering that she was about to quit. When she asked me what I thought I'd do when I had children, I laughed off the question. But I did wonder about my future. I looked at Miss Bly who, for all her charm, all her cleverness, and all her energy, was widowed, estranged from her own mother and, despite all her generosity and charitable instincts, far from comfortably off. She worked because she needed the money. And the attention, yes, and the drama; all that was true. But we three, who saw her correspondence, who saw her face when the letters came from her mother's lawyers, who saw the love and the longing in her eyes when she looked at the children she found homes for: we all felt sorry for her in our own ways. I don't think any of us wanted to change places with her. I know I didn't.

But my heart broke with hers when we heard about Harry Lisa.

The little boy never left the hospital.

Miss Bly had arranged for him to be moved from Bellevue, but by that time it was already too late. Bronchitis, whooping cough, measles, chicken pox, and pneumonia, they said. It was all too much for him.

Miss Bly was distraught. We all were.

As the days passed, she grew only more tearful and more angry. The system had failed him, she said. If he had been brought to her in the first place, none of this would have happened. Keeping children in institutions for too long was dangerous. Institutions. She knew something about them, she said. None of it good.

As a consequence, she turned her energies toward Dorothy Harris, who was also at the Willard Parker Hospital. Dorothy, she declared, must not suffer the same fate as Harry Lisa.

And truly, Dorothy was an engaging child. She was blonde, with a charming smile and a musical laugh. It was impossible to meet her and not be interested in her fate. Ernest Coulter wrote a chillingly formal letter to Miss Bly, reiterating his argument that although Dorothy was cured of diphtheria, any decision about her future remained in limbo while her religion remained unknown.

Miss Bly responded by hiring a lawyer.

He negotiated with the courts and the Society to obtain the agreement of all parties that Dorothy could be released from hospital and into the care of the Catholic Church, at least until the question of her faith could be resolved. Dorothy left Willard Parker, and we visited her in Campbell Cottages where she was sent to convalesce.

Dorothy Harris was fast becoming Miss Bly's most important cause. She wasn't about to let Ernest Coulter, or his Society, get in her way.

Elizabeth
VII
September 1887

As the ambulance rolled its way to Bellevue, Elizabeth closed her eyes and tried not to panic. The coarse driver had opened her eyes to her own vulnerability. Women were always at a disadvantage, but now she had no money, no reputation or family to support her; only her wits and the clothes she stood up in. She had allowed herself to do something she had sworn never to do: be reliant on men – policemen, judges, doctors, and two newspaper men – for her own honor and safety. She had been to Mexico, yes, but in her own name, with her own mother at her side, with papers in her pocket and money in her purse. This was a different proposition altogether.

She opened her eyes just a fraction and looked at the young doctor riding with her. He was staring out of the back of the wagon, lost in thought, tapping his fingers against his lips. He had a long, full moustache – grown, she guessed, to make him look mature. She had some sympathy for that, having found more than once that age was often a barrier to her ambitions, although never so challenging as the inconvenient – yet inescapable – fact of being female.

The ambulance arrived at Bellevue. Thankfully, the doctor pre-empted their driver's interest in manhandling Elizabeth out of the ambulance and led her up the hospital steps himself. He took her to a small office where the familiar questions as to who she was and where she came from were asked. She responded as vaguely as ever. Paperwork was completed, confirming her admission to the Insane Pavilion. An orderly arrived and pinched her so hard by the arm that she cried out and refused to go with anyone but the young doctor. For the first time, panic started to rise. Although the doctor agreed to walk her to the Pavilion, she knew he intended to leave her there.

They followed the path between manicured lawns and tidy flower beds that led to the Insane Pavilion. Bellevue was superficially ordered and maintained. Yet behind every stone wall there were wards overflowing with suffering humanity. It was a cold September day, but it wasn't the chill in the air that made her shiver and her arms prickle like goose flesh.

From the outside, the Pavilion had an almost homely air about it, with net curtains at the glass double doors and stained glass glinting red and blue in the odd ray of sunshine breaking through the clouds. A nurse in a black dress and a white apron and cap looked over Elizabeth's papers and ushered her inside. The door was closed behind her and a large black key turned in the lock.

A bitter smell of lye lingered in the air. She stood in a wide hallway with floorboards scrubbed bare. Three downcast-looking women sat on plain wooden benches, under a couple of faded seascapes, hung askew.

"Dining room and nurses' sitting room." The nurse pointed at the first two doors in the hallway. Elizabeth counted six others, but no comment was passed on these and she assumed they must be the patients' rooms. At the end of the hallway she saw a cast iron door hung with a hefty padlock.

"The men are on the other side," said the nurse, following her gaze. "We only keep women here. Take a seat and make yourself comfortable. I'm Nurse Ball. I will come if you need anything."

With that, she stepped into the nurses' sitting room and pushed the door until it was nearly closed. Elizabeth was left to contemplate her fellow inmates. One burly woman sat asleep with her chin sunk low on her ample chest. On the bench beside her, a disheveled young woman chewed her nails. Her skin was blotchy, and Elizabeth could see scabs and cuts on the back of her hands. The last of the three sat further away, quite upright, with her feet together and her hands clasped on her lap. She glanced at Elizabeth but only briefly, turning her head to gaze into space. It almost seemed unfair to disturb her, but Elizabeth was keenly aware that a more thorough doctor than she had encountered so far might easily rule her sane and send her packing. She needed to get to work.

"May I sit with you?" she asked, presenting herself in front of the woman.

"If you wish to."

"Thank you. My name is Nellie Brown. I hope you don't mind me joining you. I'm not quite sure what I am supposed to do."

"There is little to do, I'm afraid," said the woman. Her voice was soft and pleasant. "Although the nurse will give you sewing to do, if you ask her."

"Ha! Don't tell anyone, but sewing is not my strong suit." Elizabeth smiled again and saw the other woman relax. "Won't you introduce yourself?"

"Of course! How silly of me. You must think me very odd, but I have been a little unwell and have barely spoken a word to a soul since I came here. My name is Anne Neville."

"Anne is one of my favorite names! I'm so glad already that I have found you here. I am quite in the dark about what is going to happen to us."

"To be honest, I am not sure myself. I only came to Bellevue because I had been ill, and my nephew could not afford my care. I was brought to this building yesterday."

"You saw a doctor, though?"

"Yes. So many doctors and so many questions. I'm not sure I answered well. They said I was confused."

Elizabeth looked at Anne. Her eyes were clear, her voice calm, and her words measured. She was tidily dressed, unlike the slattern on the other side of the room. She seemed every bit as sane as Elizabeth.

"You don't sound confused to me."

"Thank you. That's very kind. I am not confused, just deeply tired and a little anxious."

"You know where we are, though, don't you? That only insane people are sent to this place?"

"Yes, but I am not insane. It doesn't seem like you are either. How did you come to be here?"

"I have lost my trunks and become separated from my family. I'm hoping they will find me."

"Oh, I am sure they will. A girl like you must have a family that is missing you terribly."

"I certainly hope so. But I am here now, and so hungry I could weep!"

Anne smiled and looked younger instantly. "The food, I have to tell you, may not be to your liking. Look, here is Mary now. She serves us meals."

The women lapsed into silence as the maid of work bustled in to prepare their midday meal. A new nurse arrived just before the women went to eat. She was young and cross-looking, with thin hair tucked behind her ears and a down-turned sullen mouth. She conferred with Nurse Ball and stared down the hallway at Elizabeth.

"Nellie Brown," she called. "Take off your hat."

"I will not. I am waiting for the boat and I need to be ready."

"Boat?" The nurse walked over to Elizabeth and poked her in the shoulder. "You are not going on any boat. This is an asylum for lunatics. And you need to do as you are told."

"I didn't want to come here. I'm not sick and I'm not insane. I can't stay here."

The nurse snorted. "That's what you all say! Let me tell you something. It will be a long time until you set foot out of this building if you can't do as you are told. Take your hat off or I will take it off for you. Give me trouble and I only have to ring the bell to bring men in here to do it for me."

Elizabeth was aware of the eyes of the three other patients on her. "I am not afraid of you," she said. "I am cold, and I wish to keep my hat on."

The nurse's face darkened. She stepped back and her voice rose. "I will give you a moment to consider and if you won't take it off, I will not be gentle with you."

"Do you think I don't recognize a bully when I see one?" Elizabeth stood up and the nurse took a step backward. "Touch my hat and I will take your cap from your head. See if I don't."

They stood staring for a few moments. The nurse chewed her lip. Elizabeth raised her eyebrows and waited.

"To the dining room, ladies!" The maid, Mary, bustled past carrying a tray. The nurse turned on her heel and retreated to her sitting room. Anne Neville rushed to Elizabeth and grabbed her by the arm.

"Oh, won't you take off your hat and gloves and come and eat with me?" she said. "Nurse Scott is a bully, you are right, but she will bring the men in and I am afraid they will hurt you."

Elizabeth hesitated.

"Please," said Anne. "Come. You are hungry. You said so yourself."

"That is true," Elizabeth admitted. She took off her hat and gave Anne a shy smile. "I do need to eat. And after all, how bad can it be?"

In fact, it was worse than she expected: prison fare, served on a tin plate, and cold as stone. She tried to eat but the lump of beef was tough, cold, and tasteless. She chewed but could not swallow it. In the end, Mary brought her a glass of milk and a soda cracker instead. Elizabeth looked at her fellow inmates, so quiet and uncomplaining. The older lady, Mrs. Fox, was preoccupied by some unknown misery. Elizabeth tried to draw her out, but she was unwilling to talk and simply muttered that her case was hopeless. With that attitude, Elizabeth thought, it certainly was.

The young girl, whose name was Maggie, appeared simple of mind; dim-witted more than mad. In Cochran's Mills or even Pittsburgh, they would call her a half-wit, but she was the kind of girl that might help in a laundry or as a kitchen maid if someone kindly and patient were prepared to take her on. Why place a girl like that in an asylum?

The afternoon passed slowly. The doors to the bedrooms stood open, but the women were told to remain on the benches in the hallway where they could be supervised. Nurse Scott went from bedroom to bedroom, opening windows and allowing in sweeping draughts of cold September air. Despite Anne's quiet counsel, Elizabeth grew agitated.

"Why make us cold unnecessarily?" she grumbled. Her fingers grew numb and her toes ached in her boots, but her complaints elicited no sympathy. Nurse Scott reluctantly produced an old gray shawl, moth-eaten and musty. Elizabeth settled into it and slept in her chair.

At some point, a doctor appeared. Already her sense of time was bleeding away. He asked her the same questions as everyone else. Who was she? Why was she in New York? He felt her pulse and examined her tongue.

And then he asked her if she was a woman of the town.

"I do not understand you," she said, although she did, very well.

He tilted his head on one side. She saw an insulting, speculative look in his eyes. "I mean have you allowed men to provide for you and keep you?" he said.

She wanted to slap his face. Her eyes flitted over to Anne, who shook her head and put a finger to her lips.

"I don't know what you are talking about," Elizabeth said, and turned away.

A little later, two more patients were admitted. A wide-faced, blonde German woman named Louise Schanz was brought in and left there by a teenage boy, presumably her son. She spoke little English and was tearful when the boy left, but she was soon occupied with sewing. She kept herself to herself. The next arrival was a young woman of about twenty-five. She was thin and ill-looking and said she was recovering from a fever. It had frayed her nerves, she said.

After another poor meal, they were all six ushered to their beds. Elizabeth got undressed and pulled on a long flannel nightgown. She handed her own clothes to Nurse Ball and watched the nurse remove the whole bundle. Another layer stripped away.

The windows were finally closed and the bars pulled to check they were firm. Elizabeth's bed was narrow and hard and lined with oilcloth that chilled her through the thin sheet stretched over it. She settled down under a blanket, determined to sleep and gather her resources for the days to come. The sick girl wept in the room next door. Voices from the hallway came and went. The night nurses arrived at some point during the evening, and she heard her door unlocked. They stood over her for a moment and then left. Later she heard them talking in the hallway. A reporter was looking for Nellie Brown. She was a hopeless case, the man was told, but when one of the nurses agreed to his request to search her clothing, Elizabeth was on her feet in indignation. She knocked and called but all she heard was laughter and the voices floating away down the hall.

She had barely settled down again when the nurses were back. One unlocked the door and poked her head in. "A doctor is here. He wishes to speak with you."

Elizabeth hastened to sit up and wrap her single blanket around her as modestly as possible. The idea of a man – a doctor, yes, but still a man – entering her room and speaking to her in such a state of undress made her gasp. If it were the same doctor as from the afternoon, she'd call for a nurse. She'd scream her throat raw if she had to.

It was not the same man. This one was younger, with soft brown hair and a dimple in his chin – handsome, she thought, as he turned up the oil light and sat down beside her on the bed. Another man followed, but he remained in the shadows, just by the doorway, with his arms folded. The young doctor was full of smiles and friendly overtures, but he made no mention of his companion by the door.

"How do you feel tonight, Nellie," he began. He spoke as if they knew each other, as if he had been visiting her every night for weeks.

"I am fine, thank you."

"But you are sick, you know. You've been very sick."

"I am?" Elizabeth glanced at the other man by the door. He was staring at her in a way that made her insides quail.

"When did you leave Cuba?" asked the doctor.

"Do you know Cuba?"

"Of course. I remember you there. Don't say you have

forgotten me?" He edged nearer on the bed and put an arm around her.

All her muscles tensed. "I've no memory of being in Cuba. Although I remember my grandfather. And my father also."

"In Cuba. On the hacienda? I met them there with you many times." His hand slid up and down her arm.

"I don't recall it." Elizabeth stood up and wrapped her arms around herself. "But tomorrow I will be leaving here to find my trunks. My address is inside. When I find my family, I will tell them very carefully of all the good care I received here." She looked at the doctor and then at the door, still slightly ajar. The other man moved his hand and placed it on the handle. "Shall we call for the nurse?" she asked.

The two men looked at each other. She thought that the silent man flattened his lips and tilted his head just a fraction toward the door. The doctor slapped his legs and got to his feet.

"It has been our pleasure, as always, Miss Brown. I'd love to stay longer, but I have many patients to visit tonight. Sleep well."

He reached out and ran his fingers down the side of her face.

Then they were gone.

Elizabeth lay down on the bed and wept.

***

Tilly Mayard was the name of the girl who was recovering from fever. She attached herself firmly to Elizabeth and Anne at breakfast. Tilly struggled to eat and Elizabeth, looking down at the bowl of chicken broth in front of her, slick with grease and only a few scrapings of meat, understood her difficulty. But Tilly was terribly pale and thin. The bones of her wrists stuck out like rivets and her dress hung loose at her neck and shoulders, suggesting recent dramatic weight loss. She seemed at ease when sitting with them, however, and although she said little, she was happy to hear Anne talk about her job as a chambermaid at the Buckingham Hotel, where she had worked until she fell ill.

It was bitterly cold again in the hallway. Elizabeth asked the nurses to turn on the radiators, but was informed that the heat was never switched on until October. If they could survive the chill, the nurses said, so could she.

At least she'd had her own clothes returned to her. When the young doctor who had frightened her during the night arrived back and called her into the nurses' sitting room for a consultation, she was composed and ready for anything he might say.

"Name?" he asked, with none of the previous evening's familiarity.

"Nellie Moreno."

"Moreno? Your name is Brown."

Elizabeth shrugged.

"And what is wrong with you?"

"Nothing." She looked at a space to the left of his head, intending to make no eye contact. "I did not want to come here but people brought me anyway. I need to go home. Won't you let me out?"

"I could take you out," he said, lowering his voice. Her eyes snapped to his. "But if I do, will you stay with me? I'm afraid you will run away from me the moment we are on the street."

She longed to slap his handsome face. In different circumstances, she would do it, too. Instead, she forced a smile and a coy comment. "I can't promise I will not."

Nurse Scott poked her head round the door before he could respond. "Are you finished with the patient, Doctor?"

Elizabeth was allowed to return to the hallway and her bench with Anne and Tilly.

"I'm immensely glad you are both here," she said, squeezing their hands.

The hours ticked past. Reporters arrived and asked to interview Nellie Brown. The young doctor gave permission, but she refused to answer questions beyond admitting to her name and that she believed she was from Cuba. Each time, she feared being recognized. Each time someone approached

Elizabeth, Tilly became agitated on her behalf. Why were they so interested in her? Who did they suspect she was? Was this how missing persons were found? Did she think her family would come for her soon? Tilly's hands flapped nervously and her face turned pink and then pale again. From the reporters' questioning, Tilly realized that this wasn't a convalescence ward but a place for the insane. She rushed to the doctor and begged for an examination to prove her sanity. "Test me, why won't you test me?" she asked.

"We have all we need on that score," was his only reply.

Anne soothed her.

Elizabeth made light of it.

The hours ticked past.

After dusk, the visitors stopped and the women were sent to bed. Elizabeth's mind turned to the doctor's visit of the previous evening and she slept fitfully, but the door didn't open and she was not disturbed.

VIII
September 26th, 1887, a Monday

In the morning, the women learned that they were to be taken to the Island at 1.30pm.

When the time came for their departure, a crowd of medical students watched the women leave the pavilion and climb into an ambulance. Anne went first, with Tilly close behind her, then sad Mrs. Fox and the quiet German woman. The Maggie girl had been spirited elsewhere. Elizabeth left the pavilion last, taking in the curious gazes of the crowd and moving too slowly for the waiting attendant's liking. He wrapped his arms around her and half-lifted, half-dragged her to the vehicle. She shook him off and clambered inside, but he followed her in and sat down, far too close. Dirt clung to the rings of skin at his neck, and the lines in his fingers. He leaned his body into hers as he pulled the door closed and turned the lock. The smell of him – of alcohol, sweat, and urine - filled every inch of air in the ambulance. They travelled in silence and darkness, with the windows covered.

At the wharf she heard a disturbance. People milled around the ambulance, ignoring the driver's shout and the horse's whinny. The attendant climbed down but locked the door behind him. Some cursing, pushing, and shoving followed. The ambulance rocked. Tilly started to shake. Elizabeth put an arm around her. The German woman hugged herself and rocked back and forth. Anne looked like she might cry. Bells rang as the police arrived. Eventually, the ambulance rolled forward.

Elizabeth was the last to leave the ambulance and board the boat. She looked across the East River toward Blackwell's Island. It was no distance really. Grey water swirled under the plank and the breeze caught her skirts. The same attendant hustled her into a cabin smelling of wet wood and brine. The floor was a black, watery mess. A bunk in one corner was piled with soiled blankets. Elizabeth smelled vomit and her gorge rose. A young girl was brought in and made to lie on the bunk. She looked too sick to care where she was. Lastly, an old wrinkled woman, bundled in shawls, lumbered in carrying a basket with chunks of bread and a slab of meat. Two female orderlies blocked the doorway. Both were wide-hipped with hefty arms crossed under their chests. One spat tobacco juice on the floor and glared when Anne gasped in surprise.

Elizabeth, Tilly, and Anne kept their eyes on the floor and held hands. The boat docked but they were told not to move. Only the sick girl and the old woman were escorted off. At the boat's second stop, the women were removed and shuffled into another ambulance to take them to the asylum. A nurse accompanied them, dressed in brown and white stripes, a cap, and a large white apron. She had a green cord tied at her waist, with a large bunch of keys attached. She was young, and not unkind-looking, but she sat beside Anne and didn't say a word to any of them.

"Do you know where we are?" Elizabeth asked Tilly, as they walked up the steps of Blackwell's Island Insane Asylum. It was an imposing stone building, with two wings spreading out from a central octagonal tower four stories high. It squatted, grey and brooding, stoic and remote, even while the city burst its seams just across the water.

"Yes. The insane asylum. I know it."

"But you are not crazy?"

"Not a bit. Yet here I am, and how will I ever escape? Will any doctor even give me a chance to prove my sanity?"

Elizabeth bowed her head and followed Tilly inside, feeling a wash of unexpected guilt. She entered confident that her stay was to be temporary. But Tilly and Anne? For them, this was a prison sentence. Maybe worse.

As at Bellevue, the inside of the asylum was austere and sparsely furnished. They passed a wide sweeping staircase to their right, and were led through a pair of columns to a waiting area with an old grandfather clock, one wicker chair, and a dried-up rubber plant wilting on a wicker stool. From there the silent nurse led them down a long, uncarpeted hallway to a room she called Hall 6.

Elizabeth braced herself.

She was in the madhouse.

IX

The arrival of five new patients caused a stir. There were perhaps forty women in Hall 6, dressed uniformly in ugly blue and white calico checks. Most were seated close together on wooden benches set out at intervals around the walls of the large room. It was bright, at least. Light shone down from barred windows, reflecting off white walls whose only decoration were three small lithographs – one of the composer Fritz Emmett, and two others of negro minstrels. While the patients crowded the benches, two nurses in uniforms sat at a central table covered in a clean white cloth. At one end of the room stood a square grand piano, not a fine-looking instrument but serviceable, and at the other end were doors leading to what Elizabeth thought might be a doctor's office or perhaps an examination room.

A couple of the patients sprang up at the sight of the newcomers. Two crossed the room and stood in front of Mrs. Fox with their arms folded, demanding to know her name. A nurse called out at them and got to her feet with obvious reluctance. While she shushed those two women, a third crept up behind Elizabeth and whispered in her ear.

"Who sent you here?"

"The doctors." Elizabeth turned to see what kind of person was addressing her. The woman was tall and bony, her nostrils raised in a permanent sneer.

"And what did they send you here for?"

"Because they say I am insane."

"Insane?" The woman's lips curled. She grabbed Elizabeth's chin and pinched it between her forefinger and thumb, hard enough to make Elizabeth wince. "It cannot be seen in your face."

"What's your name?" asked Elizabeth. "How long have you

been here?"

"Never you mind."

"Nancy! Get back to your bench this instant!"

"Of course, Nurse Grupe. At once, Nurse Grupe." Nancy melted away and Nurse Grupe, the same nurse that had been in the wagon from the boat, now ordered the new women to follow her into the offices at the end of the hall. She told them to sit and opened another door and stood at the doorway talking, presumably to a doctor. Elizabeth could only hear the nurse's words, but the change in her tone was remarkable.

"Why thank you," she said. "I do like to go down to the boat and enjoy a little fresh air." There was a pause and something further was said, clearly to the nurse's liking. "Do you think so? Then I'll make sure I always do."

She turned and looked back at the women. Her eyes found Tilly's. "You. You can go first."

Elizabeth and Anne nodded encouragingly. Tilly was older than Elizabeth, but seemed so young and fragile. Although Nurse Grupe followed Tilly into the doctor's office, she left the door open so the women remaining could easily follow what was happening inside.

"She sounds very calm," Anne whispered to Elizabeth as they listened to Tilly explain her illness, but she spoke too soon.

"Give me a chance!" Tilly suddenly cried out. "Why won't you give me a chance? I don't belong here. I should be at home with my family, don't you see? Test me. Ask me anything."

There was a pause.

"Why won't you give me justice!" shouted Tilly, as Nurse Grupe manhandled her out of the office. She thrust Tilly into a seat in the corner and glared at the other women. Her eyes fell on Mrs. Schanz.

"You. Come now."

As the nurse and the German woman disappeared into the office, Elizabeth rushed to comfort Tilly. The girl's helplessness was real. Elizabeth had her own case as direct evidence that sane women were being locked up by these ignorant men. She stroked Tilly's thin hair, and made a vow to help the girl as soon as she was able.

A tinkle of laughter from the doctor's office distracted her.

"What's happening?" she asked Anne, who sat nearer the door.

"The doctor is teasing the nurse to speak German," she whispered. "Her name is Grupe – perhaps her parents are German? Anyway, she says she can't speak a word and so poor Mrs. Schanz can't make herself understood." Her hands went to her cheeks. "How can they be so unfair?"

Soon it was Mrs. Fox's turn, and then Anne's. Elizabeth had been nervous initially, but now it was clear that this inspection was cursory, she grew curious to see what kind of man this doctor was. He made a far from favorable impression.

"Name?" He didn't look up. She judged he was aged somewhere between thirty and forty. He had a round face that might almost have been handsome, but his nose was upturned and rather ugly, to her mind at least.

"Nellie Brown," she said. She sat awkwardly in her chair, holding one hand to her head as if it pained her.

"And where is your home, Nellie Brown?"

"In Cuba."

He paused in noting her answers and looked up at Nurse Grupe.

"Ah! Is this the girl that was in *The Sun* on Sunday?"

Elizabeth kept her eyes firmly on the deep red carpet. This was excellent news. If her committal had been reported, then Cockerill at *The World* must know of her success already. She spent a glorious moment or two imagining Cockerill and Pulitzer's reaction to her achievement, but the doctor's questions pulled her back to the present.

"What color are her eyes, Nurse Grupe?"

"Grey, Dr. Kinear," the nurse said, without even pretending to look. Elizabeth's eyes were brown. Or hazel. Not grey by anyone's estimation. She bit her tongue and said nothing.

"What is your age?" he asked her.

"I turned nineteen last May." That wasn't true, although her birthday was in May. In truth, she was twenty-three, but Mary

Jane had brought her up to believe that her age was no one's business but her own.

The doctor was barely attending her anyway. "When do you get your next day pass?" he asked the nurse.

She tittered, and Elizabeth's temper rose. "Next Saturday," the nurse replied with a blush.

"Measure her, please."

Elizabeth submitted to standing under a wooden measure with the nurse's breath on her cheek as she tried to read the results.

"What height?" the doctor asked.

"I can't tell."

Elizabeth forced herself to look straight ahead. It was impossible to know if Nurse Grupe was actually illiterate, or if she simply wanted the doctor to come to her aid. Certainly, when he did and took the woman's hands to point out Nellie Brown's height as five feet five inches, the air was thick with flirtation.

Elizabeth marveled at this whole new experience. It was almost like being invisible. As an insane woman she was no longer even seen by this pair of dalliers. She longed to stamp her foot and tell them what she thought of them, but now she was on the scales and again Nurse Grupe required Dr. Kinear's help to record that she weighed 112 pounds.

They talked so familiarly, even referring to each other by their Christian names that Elizabeth decided to remind them she was there. "I am not sick, and I do not want to stay here," she declared. Her voice was controlled, and normal. Nothing hysterical, no Spanish accent, no hesitation. "No one has the right to shut me up in this manner."

But Dr. Kinear and the nurse simply ignored her. The doctor made some more notes and then dispatched her back to the others.

Worse followed. On their return to the hall, they were quizzed by Nurse Grupe's colleagues: Nurse Grady, a flame-haired, freckled Irishwoman; and a younger, skinny girl called Nurse McCarten. Their clothing was pawed at, their shoes inspected, and their dresses commented upon. Near the piano, six patients competed for space on a bench intended for no more than five. Elbows poked and fingers pinched. One woman started crying. Nurse Grady confronted them, screaming at the women to sit still, while Nurse McCarten tried to distract another group nearby by calling on one of the new women to play a tune. Elizabeth obliged, but winced to find the instrument so jarringly out of tune. Her disgust was not missed by the young nurse.

"Not good enough for you, is it?" she hissed in Elizabeth's ear. "I'll send a note that we need another one for the fine ladies we have staying with us nowadays, shall I?" The nurse had a long face and deep-set eyes, with the hint of a squint. She snapped shut the lid on the piano, missing Elizabeth's fingertips by a hairbreadth.

Elizabeth looked for Anne or Tilly, hoping to find space for her to sit with them while she took in Hall 6 and its occupants, but before she could join them, the double doors to the hall were flung open and someone called for the women to gather in the hallway. She threaded her way to Anne Neville in the crowd of women pressing their way out. It was uncomfortable to be so suddenly in the midst of a crush.

"I'm so hungry," whispered Anne.

"I'm so cold!" said Elizabeth, eyeing the open windows. "How do they stand it?"

All around them, the women were shivering and complaining. Some jigged on the spot. Others wept. Many stood still with their heads bowed and shoulders slumped. Several talked to themselves. A few sang quietly. One woman set up a loud rendition of *Home Sweet Home* but was quickly silenced by a slap in the face from Nurse Grady. An older woman with long grey hair, matted at her head and falling in tangled curls down her back, tugged at Elizabeth's sleeve. "Don't mind them, dear. They are all mad. Lost souls every one."

"And you?"

"I am as right as rain, dearie. Can't you tell?" She winked and broke into a barking laugh that set Elizabeth's nerves jangling.

"What are we waiting for?" she asked.

"Nobody knows," said the old woman. "But it is always so. In little while they will shove us through there." She pointed to the door at the end of the hallway. "If you are cold now, you will be even colder on the stairs." Again, the bark of laughter. "And after a little time shivering there, we will descend to the feast!"

"Descend to the feast?" She looked at the old woman, trying to see if there was any truth to be found in her or even any spark of sanity in her watery eyes, but a hand fell on the woman and Nurse Grady pulled her away.

As the woman had said, they were herded into a freezing stone stairwell and waited again before shuffling downstairs and into a narrow dining room filled with one long, narrow table. At the door, several women pushed forward and scrambled for the benches. Each place was set with bowls filled with pinkish-looking tea, a plate with a slice of bread and butter, and a small saucer holding five prunes. One large lady crushed Anne's foot as she barged past and scooped up several saucers. She tipped the prunes onto one and then poured them into her mouth, filling her cheeks like a hungry groundhog. Elizabeth stifled a hoot of laughter and climbed over the low bench.

"Benches like these? For women? It's ridiculous." She had barely sat down when the woman across from her shot out a hand and grabbed her bread, cramming it all in her mouth and glaring as she chewed it down.

"Nurse!" Elizabeth called to Nurse Grupe, the nearest woman in uniform. "My bread has been taken."

"And?"

"And I'd like something to eat, of course."

"Well, I'm sure the doctors will be pleased to know that you haven't lost your appetite with your memory." Nurse Grupe stalked off and returned moments later with a new slice of bread and butter which she slapped down onto Elizabeth's plate without another word.

The butter was rancid. The mouthful of tea she took to

cleanse that away tasted coppery and sour. She craved sugar. She craved sustenance but couldn't stomach another bite.

"You must eat something," said Anne. "Ask for bread without butter."

"You think I dare ask for anything more? No. I am not hungry."

"You may not think you are, but you must force yourself. Else you may be sick, and who knows but that being sick in such a place might not turn a sane woman crazy."

"I will try tomorrow, I swear it," said Elizabeth. Despite Anne's continued urging, she did not touch another thing.

Before long they were shepherded back up the stairs, through the hallway, and into Hall 6. Tilly found them and begged Elizabeth to play the piano again, so that she might sing. Her eyes were bright, and her cheeks flushed. Elizabeth could not say no. Tilly insisted on singing *Rock-a-bye Baby* and the room fell silent until a few other fragile voices joined in. Elizabeth found her mind wandering to her childhood, to her father's death, and to the man her mother married a few years later. She saw Tilly was singing with tears streaming down her face. As she played the last note, she found that she was crying, too.

After Tilly grew tired of singing, they went to sit near Anne and Mrs. Schanz, who had found a fellow German to talk to. Her relief at finding someone to share her troubles was evident and could not be dimmed, despite some rude interruptions from the nurses who seemed to dislike anyone enjoying themselves every bit as much as they objected to any woman creating a disturbance or scene. Elizabeth, occupied with observing the women before her and considering how she might learn their stories and use them in her reports, barely registered it when Nurse Grupe summoned the newcomers from the room.

The nurse led them into a large bathroom and locked the door behind them. For the first time since they had left Bellevue together, Elizabeth was selected to go first instead of last. In the center of the room stood a tin bath filled with water.

Beside it waited Nancy, the woman from the hall who had pinched Elizabeth's chin. She held a filthy towel.

"No," said Elizabeth, taking a step back and crossing her arms. "No. I am perfectly able to clean myself."

"Our patients do not wash themselves, Brown," snapped Nurse Grupe. "Take your clothes off."

"No!" Heat rushed to her cheeks.

"If we need to, we will strip you ourselves." Nurse Grupe sounded bored, but Elizabeth knew she meant every word. "Take your shoes off."

With a distressed glance at Tilly and Anne, she did as she was told. She rolled down her stockings and stuffed them in her boots. The floor was wet and cold. When her hands faltered on the buttons on her bodice, Nurse Grupe grabbed her. She called Nurse McCarten to help, and the two women stripped away Elizabeth's bodice, skirt, and corset, leaving her in nothing but her thin cotton chemise and drawers.

"No!" cried Elizabeth, clutching at the thin fabric.

"Enough!" Nurse McCarten yanked Elizabeth's hands and held them behind her back while Nurse Grupe took a pair of scissors, slit open the chemise, and ripped her drawers to her ankles. Elizabeth's body burned. She threw a sharp glance at Anne and Tilly who were staring at the floor, and then clambered into the bathtub where at least she could be covered.

The water was so cold she couldn't breathe.

She shrieked and tried to stand, but Nancy's hands were on her shoulders. She forced her down so hard that Elizabeth slipped, and she was submerged. Her hands scrabbled for the edges of the bath and she lifted herself back out, gasping for air. Wet cloth slapped her face. She couldn't see. She tore at the material at her face.

"Sit still, you stupid bitch!" shouted Nancy, her face enraged and her mouth only inches from Elizabeth's ear. The cloth lifted. Elizabeth had a moment to see and take a proper breath, but it was only for a moment, as Nancy's arms plunged in and she rubbed soap all over Elizabeth's body, face, and hair. She tasted soap in her mouth. It stung in her eyes and nostrils. Although her instinct was to fight, she realized the quickest way to end the misery was to sit still. Nancy shoved and rubbed, swirling the cold water around so that the flesh of her arms erupted in goose bumps and her teeth rattled in her head.

Suddenly one, two, three buckets of freezing water were tipped over Elizabeth's head in quick succession. She gasped and spluttered. Hands grabbed her under the armpits, and she was dragged from the water and deposited on the floor. Nancy threw a towel and nightgown at her. Elizabeth rushed to dry herself, pulling the gown over her head. It stuck to her damp skin and she winced, fearing her skin might tear. She was pushed to a bench in a corner while Anne, Mrs. Schanz, and then Mrs. Fox underwent the same treatment in the same tub of icy water.

Watching Tilly was the most distressing. She wailed at the cold and cried that she had been unwell. Nancy scrubbed at Tilly even more harshly than she had the others. When she came to rub soap in the girl's hair, she was cruel.

"What's wrong with your hair?" she said. "It's coming away in my hands. Disgusting." She made a great show of rinsing her hands in the bath water. "Have you got something wrong with you? Is it catching?" She grabbed the rag and rubbed viciously at Tilly's scalp.

Elizabeth couldn't stay silent. "What are you doing, letting that cruel woman treat Miss Mayard like this?" she shouted at Nurse Grupe. "You should know better."

When Tilly tried to push her away, Nancy slapped her. Nurse Grupe walked over then, Elizabeth thought to intercede, but no, she had no more sympathy for poor Tilly Mayard than a coach driver for a squirrel caught under his wheel. "Shut up now or I promise you'll get worse," she said.

While Tilly sobbed and tried to dry herself, Nurse McCarten called Elizabeth. Barefoot and shivering, she followed the nurse to a room with six beds, but no sooner had she lain down as directed than Nurse Grady appeared at the door.

"Nellie Brown," she said, "you've already spoken out of

turn to my nurses once. You won't do so again. And I won't have you in here causing trouble among my patients."

Elizabeth was ordered out and escorted instead to room 28. A tiny room, it contained nothing but an iron bed below a tiny barred window.

Nurse Grady thrust her in. Then she slammed the door and locked it.

Beatrice

Spring 1920

In April, Miss Bly was unwell. She kept to her room mostly, and we heard her coughing; wet, rattling chest-racking sounds that required doctor visits but didn't diminish her work-rate. She wrote a humorous piece about what she might do with a million dollars. I typed that one up for *The Journal* and sat at her bedside as she read it over for errors.

"Read this bit aloud," she said, jabbing at the paper. "I can't with this cough. Read that paragraph there."

I did as I was bidden, of course. "*I would become the greatest benefactor in the world,*" I read. "*I would become to suffering humanity what no human creature has ever been. I would immortalize my name with undying fame. The great names of history would pale behind the renown of mine.*"

"What do you think of my fine words, Beatrice?" she asked.

"I think you are honest. Ambitious. Aiming high."

"But vain, don't you think?"

I opened my mouth to object, but she waved me away. Her voice was thin, as if she spoke with insufficient air, skimming from the very top of her lungs to avoid getting trapped in the liquid that had pooled and slowed her almost to a stop.

"I have always been very vain, Beatrice, and it is not an attractive quality. Indeed, it has led me to make some choices that I wish I had not made."

"Choices?" I wondered what she might say next. There was her marriage – never spoken of. Her siding with the Austrians during the war – never referred to. The hostility towards her mother – surely not purely based on money troubles. Who knew what else she might mean?

"Things I can never put things right."

"What things?"

"People. People I left behind."

"Miss Bly, your brother Harry always says you more than cared for your family. That your marriage settlements were all made to ensure the family's prosperity and security. That you gave everyone jobs, helped educate your nieces and nephews. That you did all a sister could do and more."

"I don't mean my family." She rubbed at her forehead. "I mean the work. When I was young, I reported what I saw, but I never stayed. Never saw a thing through. I could have helped more. But always I moved on. I left people behind. I wanted to be famous. Rich. Well-dressed."

I thought of the story I was typing for her. About the madhouse and the other women there.

"No. You're wrong," I said. "You have always done wonderful things for other people," I said. "Money for the asylum, creating opportunities for women, challenging stereotypes. Exposing medical malpractice, conditions in factories, countless things!"

"I have been a jack of all trades, Beatrice. Master of none. A man I cared about once said that to me. He told me I was like a lighthouse shedding its light: useful in a crisis, but remote, and always moving on. I had flashes of brilliance, he said, but he wanted a constant beam. That was his way. He was constant and steady. I was not."

Was she speaking of her husband or of someone else? I didn't have the courage to ask. We sat in silence.

"I'm not going to let Dorothy down," she said after a while. Her voice was firm, but it cost her a coughing fit. I handed her some tissues and was thankful there was no blood. She saw me looking, of course.

"Don't worry." She seemed to shake off her dark mood. "I'll be better soon. I'm thinking of something grand to do to celebrate."

"Good!" I was relieved. "What kind of something?"

"An outing. Something for Dorothy, but also for other orphan children. An unforgettable day. It will take a lot of arranging. I need you to write to the Society for the Prevention of Cruelty to Children for me."

"To Mr. Coulter?"

"Yes, of course to Mr. Coulter. What? You are not still thinking of that little argument in his office, are you?" She shook her head. "Mr. Coulter does not approve of me. He dislikes my methods because he prefers his own. Rather like that man I used to know." She rubbed her forehead again. "But a grand day out for the city's orphans? Paid for by the generous families you and I will approach? Ernest Coulter will turn down nothing that does the children in his care some good. Write and we will hear from him within the week. You mark my words."

Elizabeth
X
September 27th, 1887, a Tuesday

At 5.30 the next morning, Nurse Grady marched into the room and dropped a pile of clothes on the floor. She pulled Elizabeth up into a sitting position and used her bed as a footstool to reach up and yank open the window. Wind whistled in and the temperature dropped instantly. Elizabeth felt the back of her head. Her hair was still damp from the bath the night before. She asked for her own clothes but was told that this was as good as she would get. The Irishwoman leaned against the door and crossed her arms, an ugly sneer curling her upper lip. Elizabeth understood the threat of violence if she did not comply. No words were needed.

She pulled on a rough cotton underskirt and tied it at her waist. Next came a flimsy calico dress. It wasn't even long enough to cover the underskirt. In other circumstances she might have laughed, but here, with the nurse daring her to make the wrong move, she stared down at the heavy and ill-fitting shoes she had been given and said nothing. When she was ready, Nurse Grady led her back to the bathroom. Now it was full of women from Hall 6, corralled in the room like cattle. Elizabeth sought out Anne.

"Did you manage to sleep?"

"Barely. You?"

"A little."

"I won't be using *those* towels, I can promise you," Anne whispered. "My underskirt will serve much better."

Elizabeth looked at the women ahead of them at the sinks, splashing cold water on their faces and using two shared towels to dry off. A large, broad-shouldered woman with matted brown hair was rubbing her face dry as Anne spoke. When she put the towel down, Elizabeth saw her face was red and splotchy with wet sores. They were painful just to look at.

"An excellent idea," Elizabeth said. "I'll do the same as you."

Large as the bathroom was, with so many women milling around, the air quickly grew warm and began to smell unpleasant.

"How often do we bathe here?" she asked a small woman who was standing next to her, chewing her fingernails and muttering that she was hungry.

"Once a week. Saturdays." The woman visibly shuddered. "It's the worst day there is."

After the previous evening and this morning's experience, Elizabeth could readily believe it. "And why are we waiting now? Why don't they send us to breakfast?"

"Combing," said the woman. "See. Here comes the bench."

Two young girls, kitchen orderlies, backed into the bathroom carrying a long bench, like the ones in the basement dining area. When they stopped to gawp at the shivering women, Nurse Grupe cuffed the back of their heads and sent them packing. Quickly Nurse Grupe and Nurse McCarten chose a patient to join them behind the bench and handed her a comb. The woman slapped the comb in her hand and grinned widely, like a child ready for a treat. Three other patients were called to sit down, and the combing began.

There was no gentleness. Every woman's hair was combed and tied into a single tight plait. The nurses and the patient raked their combs across the scalps of these women without consideration or concern. Even those women that most visibly steeled themselves to bear it, found themselves jerking, crying out, and trying to pull away. Nurse McCarten slapped a woman who moved too much, and then gripped the poor creature by the shoulder so tightly that all the blood left her fingertips. The agitation of the women being combed spread to the others watching. They winced and trembled in sympathy. Elizabeth saw several women clamp their hands over their ears or eyes. Others began muttering and shifting from one foot to another. She caught sight of Tilly Mayard shivering near the sinks, and slid through the melee until they were side by side.

"We will suffer it together," said Elizabeth. She saw how the nurses called the women over in groups of three, and made sure she and Tilly took their turn at the same time.

Elizabeth's hair – thick, matted, and tangled after the previous night's rough bathing – was a challenge Nurse McCarten attacked with enthusiasm. She grabbed Elizabeth's forehead and clamped her against her legs while she dragged the comb through her stubborn locks.

"Get your hands off me! I could do this myself!" cried Elizabeth as tears pricked her eyes.

"Be quiet!" hissed the nurse. Beside her, Tilly wept silently. They held each other's hand for support, until Nurse Grupe stabbed their fingers as hard as she could with the teeth of her comb.

"How did you sleep last night?" asked Elizabeth when their ordeal was over and they were waiting in the cold hall again, before being shuttled down to breakfast. Her scalp stung and her head ached.

"I almost froze," said Tilly. "It was so noisy. The nurses came in and out so many times." Her voice rose and her eyes brimmed with tears again, as Elizabeth searched for something calming to say.

"Tonight will be easier," she promised. "Especially as there will be no bath-time! My hair soaked my pillow and I was cold and damp all night long."

"How will we stand it?" whispered Tilly.

"We will stand it together."

After another unsatisfying meal, the women trooped back to Hall 6 and a morning of chores, scrubbing, and cleaning. Elizabeth stood in the doorway shaking her head.

"*This* is how the hall is kept clean? The *patients* do it?" Anger spiked in her gut as the nurses, wearing coats and thick stockings, gave orders to women dressed only in thin calico – some sick and some healthy, but all treated the same, without favor or discrimination – and set them to work. Elizabeth would have none of it.

"Did you make your bed?" asked Nurse Grupe.

"Did I?" answered Elizabeth. "If you mean did I fold that too-short blanket on the worst bed I have slept on in my days, then the answer is yes." She jutted out her chin and dared Nurse Grupe to contradict her.

"As if *you* would know," Nurse Grupe sniffed. "Aren't you the girl who can't remember where she came from or how she got here? Who knows what beds a girl like you has slept on?"

The inference set Elizabeth temper aflame.

"I want to see a doctor," she declared loudly. "I want proper clothing and to be warm. I did not arrive here sick, but that is what you will make me – make us all – in these cold rooms with no heat and that terrible food with no salt or flavor. Fetch a doctor now!"

"You will see a doctor when we are good and ready. And not a minute earlier. If you won't be useful, just get out of my way and sit down somewhere. Don't cross me again, Brown, or I'll have you sent to the Retreat. I've already had enough of you this morning."

Elizabeth opened her mouth to make a smart retort but thought better of it. She needed to remember her reason for being there. Standing out from the crowd, being any kind of agitator, brought attention she did not seek. But it was so hard to watch and not speak. So hard to tolerate conditions that could be changed so easily.

Walking away from Nurse Grupe, Elizabeth began approaching other patients with a view to gathering their stories. A young woman caught her eye, sitting alone on a bench near the sitting room and doctor's office. She crossed the room and sat down, not too close, so as not to startle her. The woman had blonde hair and pale skin. Her face was waxy looking and her mouth twitched, making a small, put-put noise.

"My name is Nellie," said Elizabeth. "I just arrived yesterday."

"I know that. I saw you," said the woman, another with a German accent. "You played the piano."

"I did. But I don't know if I will play it again today. Would you like me to?"

"I don't care." She hunched her shoulders and slid a fraction along the bench and away from Elizabeth.

Elizabeth slid toward her.

"No! Don't come any closer."

"I don't mean you any harm, I promise," she said.

"I know that, of course." The woman turned and stared at Elizabeth. Her eyes were stormy blue and unnerving – it was as though she saw Elizabeth but at the same time was looking far beyond her. "I am keeping the space for my parents, that's all."

"Did they leave you here?"

"No! Who would leave their daughter here?"

"No one. I'm sorry. Of course they wouldn't. That was a silly thing to say." Elizabeth fell silent and waited.

"My name is Louise Becker," the woman said. "My parents died on our way here."

"To America."

"Yes, to America. What a question. Oh!" She stopped and looked at Elizabeth again and then raised her eyebrows. "But you are the Cuban girl that can't remember. You may be more lucky than you know."

"I'm sorry about your family. My father died when I was young. I know how difficult loss can be."

"Thank you." Louise moved along the bench until their arms and legs were touching. "It was very dark on the boat. We all had a fever. They told me my parents died. I did not see them dead, but they didn't get off the boat. I waited and waited and cried and wailed, but they did not let me back on board to look at the bodies. There were too many, they said. Too many. They threw them into the sea."

Elizabeth tried to picture this woman landing in America and searching for her parents. She had visited Castle Gardens in The Battery twice. It didn't take much imagination to see how the distraught girl ended up on the Island. She must have been causing a scene. Being inconvenient. A problem. Grieving. Did that make her mad?

"But you said you were waiting for them. Do you still hold out hope?"

"Oh no. They are gone. I've come to terms with it. But sometimes they visit."

"Here? In the asylum?"

"Well, where else could they visit me?" She surprised Elizabeth by patting her hand almost in pity. "I do hope you get your memory back soon. Your family must miss you dreadfully."

"Hello, my dear." This new, cheerful voice came as a surprise. Elizabeth looked at the woman standing in front of her. She was short and round with pink cheeks and a wide brow half hidden by bangs cut on a slant. There was an odd air about her, but her smile was genuine. Elizabeth smiled back.

"Hello," she said. "I'm Nellie."

"I know, I know. We all know you already, what with the piano and the arguing."

"Arguing?"

"With Grupe and Grady and McCarten." She pulled up her eyebrows and rolled her eyes in excitement. "You have us all whispering!"

Elizabeth looked around the ward. There was no sign of women whispering. Some were sewing, others stared at the floor, some shifted and muttered or hummed – but to themselves, not to others.

"And you are?" she asked.

"Matty! They call me Matilda," she threw her head back in the general direction of the nurses' table. "But you must call me Matty, because we are going to be friends."

"Thank you. I'd be happy to call you Matty. Won't you sit with me?"

Matty turned even pinker with pleasure. She sat down as close as was possible to Elizabeth, her thighs slapping against hers. Matty's legs were short, unable to reach the floor. She was not young, but had an air of optimism that belied their surroundings. Was she mad, or just happy?

"The nurse threatened to send me to the Retreat," Elizabeth said. "I don't even know what she means."

Mattie shivered. "You don't want to go there," she said, screwing up her face. "Or the Lodge. Nasty in there. Very nasty. They're for the bad women. Very bad."

Mattie wouldn't explain, so Elizabeth changed the subject. "I was wondering how you came here, if you don't mind me inquiring?"

"Oh, it's a terrible story!" Matty put her hands to her face and rocked back and forward on the bench. "I have had money troubles. Terrible troubles." She dropped her hands and turned to face Elizabeth. She smiled, but her eyes were opened so wide and unblinking that it looked quite uncomfortable. Elizabeth's eyes widened to mirror Matty's.

"Lawyers! Never trust them." Her head quivered and her teeth clicked together. "All my money gone! Can you imagine? My house. Given to me by my parents but not mine, they said."

"I'm so sorry. That must have been so difficult for you."

Matty's head dropped. She rubbed her eyes with her sleeve.

"Forgive me for bringing up bad memories. Perhaps we could—"

She had been going to suggest they talk of other things, but Matty leaped up and ran to the nearest radiator where she stopped dead and began chattering.

"What is she doing?" Elizabeth asked Louise. The other woman followed where she pointed but her face betrayed no reaction to Matty's strange behavior.

"Talking," Louise said. "She does that."

"But no one is there."

"Perhaps that's why."

There seemed no answer to that, so Elizabeth turned her eyes around the room once more. She saw Anne and Tilly sitting together. Tilly was talking. Anne took her hands in hers and rubbed, as if to warm her, and Elizabeth glared again at the nurses. How could they walk around in coats and gloves while their charges shivered? It was a disgrace.

"Nellie Brown!" Nurse Grupe appeared at the sitting room door. "The doctor will see you now."

She was disappointed to find the same young doctor as the

day before, and resigned herself to another pointless and degrading interview. This time, Dr. Kinear wanted to listen to her heart and lungs.

"Do you really imagine that you will find the answers to my difficulties with your stethoscope?" she asked.

"Your doctor is concerned for your welfare," said a calm, male voice behind her. "Mental and physical."

She couldn't turn, but the man who had entered walked round behind her and sat in the chair in the corner. She saw that he was only a little older than her, perhaps in his late twenties. He had an open expression that she liked instinctively. She took in his wavy fair hair, neat sideburns, and trimmed moustache. He carried a file of papers that he opened and read, lifting his eyes to consider her from time to time. She had the uncomfortable sensation of being a spectacle, like a freak, a few years back, in Barnum's American Museum.

"Are you feeling well, Miss Brown?" the new man asked after Dr. Kinear had concluded his part of her examination.

"I am cold, Doctor," she said, and saw him frown a little. In truth, it was not so cold in this little office where the window was shut tight. "I am a little hungry."

"Did you not eat breakfast?" He looked at Kinear who referred to some notes.

"No issue recorded. She ate this morning," Kinear said.

"I read here that you are suffering from memory loss. Is that true?" The new doctor tilted his head on one side. She was suddenly anxious that he would see right through her.

"I've lost my trunks," she said slowly, opening her eyes wide and looking at him directly, trying to think of the German girl's expression and turn it to good use. "Can you help me, Senor?"

He shook his head and turned to Kinear. "Confirm previous assessments," he said.

She was no longer there for him, she realized, and she didn't like the way that made her feel.

"Make sure the nurses keep her quietly occupied and out of conflict with other patients." He turned back to his notes without even glancing at her. "Time is likely the best healer here."

"What's your name?" she asked, turning back as Dr. Kinear ushered her out. He still ignored her.

"Who is the other doctor?" she asked Nurse Grupe, tugging on her sleeve. The nurse looked down at her hand as if it were a fly in her soup. "Who is he?" she asked again. "I only want to know who is looking after us here."

Nurse Grupe let out a sigh. "That was Dr. Ingram. He is the Assistant Superintendent. He and Dr. Dent are the senior doctors on this ward. You will see Dr. Dent later, I am sure. Now, for pity's sake sit down somewhere and don't make any more trouble!"

Elizabeth made her way over to join Anne, while Tilly was called in to see the doctors.

"It's ridiculous that we sit here shivering while the doctor's office is perfectly snug and warm," she declared, keeping her voice low as Nurse McCarten stomped past.

"I hope it will stop poor Tilly from shivering," said Anne.

"Are you cold?"

"A little. This idleness makes me more so. I'm not accustomed to inactivity."

"You said you were a chambermaid."

"In a grand hotel, yes I was. I would have been at work for hours by now and be gasping for a cup of tea."

"Proper tea," said Elizabeth. "Just imagine it. Not the flavorless stew we had this morning."

"Proper tea. And a hot spice bun." Anne sighed and smiled a little.

"Or hot buttered toast. With salted butter. And a piece of fruit."

"Some hot chocolate."

"A slice of cake."

"Heaven."

***

"No rain today, ladies. We will take a walk."

Elizabeth wondered that something so simple as a stroll in the fresh air could seem so precious. Only five days had passed since she'd strutted into *The World's* office to meet Joseph Pulitzer. It was a lifetime ago. The women were herded into the hallway while shawls and hats were distributed. Not knowing what to expect, Elizabeth and Anne hung back a little and found that all the warmest shawls and better hats had been quickly snatched up. Many of these women might be mad in some way, but they still had their wits about them in others. The straw hat Elizabeth crammed on her head was a squashed and shapeless thing. Walt McDougall's fashionable wife sprang to mind. As soon as she had her liberty, Elizabeth promised herself a trip to Lord & Taylor to buy the finest hat she could afford. The shawl smelled musty and was damp to the touch. If anything, it made her even colder.

"We will be warm when we are moving," Anne told Tilly, who actually looked mad, Elizabeth thought, in her ill-fitting dress, ugly shawl, and too large hat.

"I don't want to go outside," Tilly whispered. "I'm afraid."

"Afraid of what?" asked Elizabeth. "The grounds are beautiful. It will be heavenly to breathe the fresh air and smell the grass."

Although she intended to find every ounce of pleasure in the walk, Elizabeth was soon disappointed. The three nurses lined up the women in pairs. Nurse Grady led the way, Nurse McCarten walked in the middle, and Nurse Grupe brought up the rear. Where Nurse Grady walked, the women were told to follow. They had to march at Nurse Grady's smart pace or face unnamed consequences on their return to Ward 6.

Elizabeth, separated from Anne, found herself with a tall Frenchwoman who initially was disinclined to talk. Elizabeth gazed across the East River, thinking of the future, but they were not the only hall taking a walk at that time and the sight of group after group of sad and demented women circling the manicured lawns around the asylum put all other thoughts out of her mind. There were so many women here. So many empty expressions and blank stares. So many woebegone creatures; tired, hunched, and hopeless. Not all were passive, though. Every so often, as the lines of women passed each other, hands darted out, seeking to pinch or shove.

The women in Hall 6 were generally tidy, but that was not true of all the women on the Island. Elizabeth's dress was clean, but women passing her on the walk wore dresses splattered with stains and collars rimmed with grime. She smelled less grass and more humanity, and her stomach turned. The other nurses showed themselves to be no better than Grady, Grupe, and McCarten from Hall 6. They called out as they passed, several asking where the Cuban girl who had been in all the newspapers might be, and Elizabeth found herself pushed out of line by McCarten to be exhibited and commented upon.

"The newspapers said she was pretty!" complained one nurse.

Elizabeth's walking companion snorted.

"The pig never admires the rose," she said.

"Thank you," said Elizabeth. "Although I do not feel like a rose in these clothes and this hat."

"I have seen more fashionable costumes, I'll admit," said the woman.

"You are French?"

"Yes. My name is Josephine Despreau."

Elizabeth took a moment to look at her. She had the tired, deflated look that so many of the women shared, but none of the agitation. She had strong features, olive skin, and thick dark hair lined with grey. "Forgive my saying so," she said, "but you do not seem to belong here."

"Thank you," said Josephine. She sighed deeply. "I do not belong here. And yet I see no way out."

"What happened to you?"

"I had not been in the country long – two weeks only, I think. I was staying in a boarding house and had found work as a seamstress. But there was a sickness at the place I sewed. I could not afford not to go. I had to continue to work, so I could pay my board and eat. I must have had a fever. I collapsed, they said. One morning at breakfast. My English was poorer then. The woman whose house I lodged in had no time or care for me. She called two officers. I was sick. They took me to a courtroom. How could I answer questions I could not understand? They brought me here."

"And your friends? Your family?'

"In France." Her head dropped and her lip trembled. "I have a husband. I sent him a letter when I arrived, with the address of the boarding house, but I promised to write again and now I cannot. I have been here for six months. Will he come from France and somehow find me here? Or does he think I am dead or have abandoned him because I do not write?"

"You must not lose hope!"

"I try not to. Look." Josephine inclined her head toward a nearby building with a low wagon waiting at the front. The doors were open, and it looked like another group of women were about to troop out. "That is what I fear more than anything. That is the Lodge."

Elizabeth watched as the women emerged. Each wore a thick leather belt through which was passed a rope. The women lined up in front of the wagon, and the end of the rope was tied to it. Two women, shrieking and wailing, were thrust into the vehicle and manacled to it by four nurses, each of whom made Nurse Grady look ladylike. Then the women on the rope began to walk, pulling the wagon behind them. Six nurses walked alongside, keeping the creatures moving with harsh words and slaps.

The women themselves were obviously devoid of all reason. They jerked, twisted, shouted, cursed and roared, biting each other and themselves, some hitting themselves with fists, others kicking and bucking, their eyes rolling like feral horses. Elizabeth shuddered to see them. She had vowed to uncover all she could about the asylum, but could she stomach The Lodge, even supposing she could act as mad as these women did? She prided herself on her courage, but the Lodge and these women might be a step too far, even for her.

***

The rest of the day followed the same pattern as the previous one, with the happy exception that the ice bath was not repeated. Elizabeth tried to focus her mind on the job that she had gone there to do, and longed for the notebook that she had been able to keep on her person until her clothes were taken from her the night before. The dinner hour arrived, heralded by the same long wait in the freezing hallway and stairwell. There was no need for it. The women were hungry, too closely confined together and too cold to be reasonable. Bickering and squabbling were inevitable. Again, several women charged into the dining room to grab more than their meager share.

Elizabeth looked at her portion. She saw a small bowl of soup, one cold boiled potato, a chunk of beef, and a butter-less slice of bread – all to be eaten with only a spoon. Watching her fellow patients attack the lumps of beef with their fingers and teeth made her want to weep. Hunger took over, though, and she was glad it did. Others, including Tilly, pushed their bowls away and left the food untouched.

Back upstairs, a couple of women played the piano and a third sang until Nurse Grady shouted that she was hopeless and told her to sit back down. Elizabeth watched the sky slowly drain of color through the asylum windows. She had chosen the bench nearest to the nurses' table so that she could observe more particularly how they treated the other patients. Any woman that asked a question, or tried to stand up and stretch her legs, or ease her back after an hour on a hard bench, was told to sit back down or she'd be "taken to the closet".

Threats were not enough to keep the nurses entertained, however.

Nurse Grady whispered something in Nurse Grupe's ear. Then she called to Matty, the old woman Elizabeth had talked with in the morning, and beckoned her over to their table.

"We want you to give Nurse McCarten a message," Grady said.

"I can do that," said Matty. "What do you want me to say?"

"Tell her she's a filthy whore," said Nurse Grupe, clamping a hand over her mouth and rocking back and forth.

"Tell her that her mother's a filthy whore," said Grady. She held her sides and rocked with laughter.

"I will not do it," said Matty, her cheeks flushed and her lips pursed. "It is not polite."

Elizabeth silently cheered the lost soul who was still so much better than the women employed to care for her. Then she saw Grady bend to Matty's ear again as if to whisper.

Instead, she spat in her ear.

Matty said nothing. Elizabeth wanted to slap someone.

The day looked set to crawl to an end. Only the appearance of a third doctor caused a reaction, particularly from the nurses who fell over themselves to greet him.

"Who is this?" Elizabeth whispered to the Frenchwoman, Josephine.

"Dent. He is the medical superintendent. He is normally here in the morning, but it was Dr. Ingram today. Ingram is a much better man. I hate this Dent."

There was certainly nothing to like about Dr. Dent on first glance. He was a tall man with dark hair, dark eyes, and a smart moustache. He should have been handsome – she almost thought that he was handsome – but the way that he looked first at the nurses and then at his patients, with an expression so cold, such a barely disguised disgust, destroyed any good impression. He circled the room, addressing some patients and stopping to consider others, but barely a woman there looked at him or answered his general how-are-you-todays.

"Can't we tell him how cold we are? Can't we at least ask him for the shawls we wore earlier?" whispered Elizabeth.

"You would not dare!" said Josephine. "Don't do it. He will only refuse, and the nurses will beat you."

Elizabeth had never refused a dare in her life. She would as soon refuse a hot meal or a new bonnet. But this was not her life. This was another world, where the rules she understood did not apply. Dr. Dent continued his way around the women and arrived at where she sat. Nurse Grady pointed Nellie Brown out and insisted she stand so that the doctor could look at her. It was like being stripped naked all over again. She did not know how much of this she could stand.

***

She couldn't sleep. Her mattress had a lump in the middle that she could neither lie directly on nor comfortably curl around. The night nurses were loud, opening and closing doors at regular intervals and walking up and down. Tilly had said sleeping in her shared room was impossible, but isolation seemed no better to Elizabeth. She heard so many noises: her own breath; the wind on the glass above her head; the creak of the oilskin under her sheet every time she moved an inch; the constant footsteps outside her door. And then the old woman started screaming.

Elizabeth had heard children crying. That could be harrowing, especially if they are hungry, or lost, or in pain. But it was a terrible thing to hear, an old person in distress. The cries of the elderly woman in the room next door hurt Elizabeth in ways she had not imagined. When children cried, it was because they had no other ways or means to express themselves. But that old woman's rights had been stripped from her. Elizabeth imagined her, chilled to the bone, underfed, neglected to the point where her mind was no longer her own. The woman had returned to childhood, to base instincts and to calling out in distress. Her voice was thin and shrill, but it was loud enough for her words to be discerned. She cried to God for help. She begged him to let her die so that she could be with him. The woman's distress only increased when the nurses try to argue her into silence. Elizabeth squeezed her eyes shut and balled her fists.

The woman's pain was unacceptable. Worse than that, it was unnecessary. She needed a warm blanket, a hot meal, and a kind word or two.

None of these things were on offer on Blackwell's Island.

Beatrice

Late Spring 1920

"I hoped I'd find you here."

Brisbane and I were loitering in Greeley Park. It was one of those hot spring days in New York where the air didn't move inside, even with every window flung wide open. Only the shade of a tree and a cold glass of lemonade would make a difference. I was settling for the shade.

"How is Brisbane?" he said.

"He is well. How are you?"

To say I was surprised to see Mr. Coulter would be an understatement, although I'd be lying if I said he wasn't on my mind.

"I received your letter."

"Yes! Miss Bly was certain you'd want to be involved." I smiled, but he was shaking his head. "You don't?"

Now he smiled. "Oh no, I do. Most certainly. The Society does, that is. Yes." He was flustered. I had never seen him so. I couldn't take my eyes from his. "But I didn't come to talk about that. I came to apologize."

"I—"

"No, let me speak. I was very rude to you in my office a few months ago. Perhaps it did not matter to you, but I have long regretted it. I'm embarrassed when I think of it. I was annoyed, but not with you. I was unprofessional."

He thrust his hand through his hair. Without thinking, I reached out and ran my hand down his arm. "Apology accepted!"

His shoulders relaxed and he grinned down at Brisbane. "Do you have a moment to sit? Or will Brisbane object?"

"He likes you," I said. "He'd be happy to sit for a while."

"Good," he said. "There's so much I want to talk to you about. Beginning with work, though, if you don't object."

"Of course not," I said.

"I've been thinking of this grand plan of Miss Bly's and I think it really could be a day to remember."

"That's what she is hoping for."

"Did she have anywhere in mind?"

"Not that she has mentioned. But I can see that you do."

He grinned again. "I do. Although to be honest, it will take a great deal of planning. We'd need to really put our heads together. Probably over dinner. Over several dinners."

He was confident again, now that the awkward apology part was over. I tried to look prim and reserved.

"I'm thinking of Coney Island," he continued. "The children will love it. We could take a hundred – several hundred – if we can find transportation, that is. It's not what it once was, but the children won't care. What do you think?"

"What do I think, or what will Miss Bly think?"

"You. What do you think?"

"I think it sounds marvelous. Although I've never been there myself."

"Never?"

I shook my head.

"Let me take you there this weekend!" His voice was bright with enthusiasm. "May I, Miss Alexander? We could call it reconnaissance."

"Only if you call me Beatrice," I said. "Then I'd love to."

***

Miss Bly embraced the idea of Coney Island, and threw herself into planning the event with the energy of a woman decades younger. She wasn't a lover of the telephone, but happily wrote letter upon letter, urging businesses to contribute to the event, calling upon the Mayor to support her, gaining promises of assistance from taxi companies, caterers, and more.

Whenever Ernest Coulter's name came up, as it inevitably

did, her eyes twinkled in my direction. Miss Bly made sure that every message or issue that required his attention was given to me to execute, never Mary or Pauline. She made such a big deal of it that very soon they were in the story, too, and all three teased me about Mr. Coulter, asking me questions until I'd grab Brisbane's leash and take him out in order to escape them. It was all good-natured, though. I was happy, and they were happy for me, I knew.

One day they got me to admit that he was taking me to dinner at Rector's in Times Square that evening, and Pauline launched into a long story about a dinner date with her boyfriend, now husband, where her mother had insisted her brother accompany her. Pauline's future husband had paid him to sit two tables away with his back to them, she said. That was when she'd known that he was "the one".

"I've never really held with the idea of 'the one'," said Miss Bly, looking up from a pile of letters that she'd been rifling through.

"No?" I said. Mary gave me a sharp look.

"No. Not when you consider the number of people in the world and the tiny fraction you ever get the chance to meet. Too much of life is made up of luck and circumstance as it is," she said. "Imagine if there's only one man for you. Even suppose you are lucky enough to meet him. What if the time isn't right? What if other people get in the way? What if you don't recognize that this man is 'the one' and let him go? What then? No." She shook her head and spoke quickly. "I'm very glad you are happy with your husband, Pauline, but I can't believe he was the only man for you in the world. Half the time we have no idea who is around the corner, or through the wall, for that matter."

None of us said anything. Miss Bly's face was stormy. I wasn't sure what had gone wrong but there was something upsetting her, anyone could see it.

"Besides," she continued. "It's all too easy to be attracted to a man, only to find out later that's he's not the person you thought he was at all."

I didn't ask any more questions after that. There was

something in her voice that stopped me, if Mary's glare at me hadn't already been quite enough. The atmosphere in the room changed completely. Miss Bly turned on her heel, went into her private room, and closed the door. She never closed the door normally. I wanted to ask Pauline and Mary a slew of questions but neither of them made eye contact with me, even when they went home for the night.

The next day, we all just went on as if nothing had happened. But I waited for the next installment of her story, even more eagerly than before.

Elizabeth
XI
September 28th, 1887, a Wednesday

In the morning, she felt dull. She didn't want to wash her face or stand in line for another poor meal that left her hungry. She didn't want to sit in Hall 6 and interrogate other patients. She'd seen enough of the place and its unkind doctors and mean-spirited nurses. She thought back to her meeting with Cockerill and Pulitzer. They promised to get her out, but didn't say after how long. She was naïve in that conversation, she realized now. Thank heavens for Anne and Tilly. And the French woman, Josephine.

When Nurse Grady ordered her from the room, she roused herself planning, if nothing else, to make sure that Tilly ate a proper meal.

In this, she was quickly disappointed. Tilly sat down heavily on the bench in front of her cup of tea, a bowl of oatmeal and molasses, and a slice of bread and butter, and didn't touch a thing. There were dark circles under her eyes and her skin looked almost grey.

"Won't you take a sip of tea?" Elizabeth urged, picking up her own cup and taking a mouthful. It was cold and over-stewed. It tasted like copper. Tilly shook her head.

"Try the bread and butter," said Anne, although she sniffed hers and put it back on the plate. Rancid again. It turned Elizabeth's stomach.

"Here," said Elizabeth. "I'm eating the oatmeal at least." She stuck her spoon into the mess and filled her mouth. The oatmeal tasted of nothing and the molasses was so bitter her eyes started to water. A mouthful of tea, terrible as it was, was preferable to that. Anything was preferable to it. She scraped the butter from her bread and forced it down.

"You must eat, Tilly," urged Anne once more, scraping the butter from her and Tilly's bread.

"Later, perhaps," was the only answer she'd give.

Upstairs after breakfast, Elizabeth again refused to undertake any chores. She sat with Tilly, who rested her head on Elizabeth's shoulder and appeared to fall asleep. Nurse Grupe stood in front of them with her hands on her hips for what felt like a full minute, presumably weighing up whether or not to create a scene, but before she could get started there was a commotion in the hallway. Nurse Grady and Nurse McCarten bowled through the double doors with an old woman writhing and struggling in their grasp. They half-dragged her to an empty bench and forced her to sit down. She rocked back and forth, weeping and crying. It was the woman Elizabeth had heard in the night.

"What are you doing with me!" she shouted. "I'm so cold!" She rubbed her thin calico dress. "Why can't I stay in bed?"

She got to her feet and staggered. When she put both arms out in front of herself, Elizabeth realized the woman was blind. Her face was lined and her skin sagged from her bones. Her eyes roamed wildly. Nurse McCarten shoved her back on the bench so hard she hit her head on the wall.

That made her quiet. But not for long.

"What is her name?" Elizabeth turned her head slowly to avoid disturbing Tilly.

Josephine was on the next bench. "I'm not sure. Normally she sits near the door. I've seen Matty help her find her way around. But this is what happens to women here. They suffer in silence. Until they can't suffer any more."

The old woman grew even more agitated. She stood and tried to make her way across the hall. "I am going to my bed," she declared. "I am cold and I need to lie down and rest."

Nurse McCarten stepped forward to confront her, but with a wicked smile on her face, Nurse Grady caught her arm and pulled her aside. They let the poor creature stumble into tables and struggle and whimper until she was nearly by the doorway. Then they grabbed her by the arms and pulled her all the way back to the farthest bench from the door. One of her shoes fell off in the process. Nurse McCarten called Nancy, the hard-faced woman who had given Elizabeth her bath, to bring the shoe. A scuffle ensued.

"This is a disgrace." Elizabeth wanted to go and intervene in some manner, but Tilly clung to her arm like a limpet. Anne stared at the floor. Looking around the room, Elizabeth saw so many of the women were the same. All three nurses and at least three patients laid hands on the old woman, who kicked and cried and refused to wear her shoes. And yet half the room acted like nothing was happening. Finally, the old woman tired. Her heavy shoes were thrust back on her feet and laced up. She tried to lie down on the bench and called for a blanket and pillow, but Nurse Grupe sat down on her and ran her hands over the poor creature's face, down her neck, and even inside her dress.

"I'll show you cold, you stupid old bitch," she said.

The old woman was left to shiver in misery alone on the bench until Dr. Ingram entered the ward about half an hour later. As Dent had done the night before, he walked around the room, saying hello to various patients and asking how they were. Unlike with Dr. Dent, several women responded, and he stopped and chatted with one or two of them.

When he saw the old woman shiver, he sent Nurse Grupe to bring him a shawl and settled it around the patient himself. Elizabeth hoped to catch his eye and ask him to take a look at Tilly, but when Nurse Grady saw her lean forward, she stepped between Elizabeth and Ingram, making sure the doctor left without noticing her.

All morning, rain rattled the windowpanes. There was no walk. Several women muttered and complained about missing a ride on a carousel.

"Mary? Is there really a carousel here?" Anne asked the woman on the bench nearest to her. She was another that seemed sane to Elizabeth.

"There is. And Wednesday is our turn to ride it. But not in

that." They all gazed at the grey blankness that fills every window. Elizabeth tried to imagine riding on a carousel with these women. She imagined the fraught excitement of some, and the lost listlessness of others. She couldn't bear to think of it. Elizabeth hoped to be long gone from Blackwell's Island and Hall 6 before next Wednesday rolled around.

Dr. Dent arrived not long after Dr. Ingram's visit. He had another man with him, older and well-fed – a sight that annoyed Elizabeth now that she knew what gnawing hunger was. Neither so much as glanced in her direction, but she heard Dent tell Nurse Grady that he wished to examine Nellie Brown, and so she lifted Tilly's head from her shoulder and stretched out the tension in her neck.

His examination was as cursory as all the others. He felt her pulse and put a clammy paw against her forehead. There was something in particular that she disliked about Dr. Dent, but she couldn't yet put her finger on it. He had her stick her tongue out. What he was looking for there, she couldn't imagine. The rigmarole of these examinations wore on her nerves. She suspected that Dr. Dent was acting out a role for this other man, whoever he might be. At first, she answered only in monosyllables – Yes, when asked if her name was Nellie Brown; No, when asked if she remembered arriving in New York. Cuba was her answer when he asked where her family was. Confusion and shrugging were all the responses she offered to any other question he chose to pose. But then she thought of Tilly. Perhaps if he looked over Tilly, he'd see how ill she had become.

"I am cold, but not unwell," she volunteered, aiming for the lightest of Spanish overtone to her voice. "I wish I could say the same for others here."

They ignored her completely. When Dent completed his notes, he signaled that she should leave and then the two men followed her back across Hall 6. Seeing Tilly looking at her and knowing the doctor was right behind her, she gestured to her to stand up. Dent needed to look at her. If words didn't do it, perhaps actions would.

Tilly, thank goodness, got to her feet but she swayed as if

dizzy, and Elizabeth dashed forward to hold her steady before turning to call on Dr. Dent.

"What is this?" he asked, with a cold look on his face and both eyebrows raised.

"I'm just so fearfully cold, Doctor," said Tilly. "I have been ill and—"

He cut her off with a wave of one hand. "The nurses will do all that is required here." He tucked his arm in his companion's. "You see how confused these women are."

"Indeed," said the older man. "Although Miss Brown seemed quite lucid, despite her memory problems. Is hers truly a case of lunacy?"

Elizabeth was still supporting Tilly but leaned toward the door, trying to follow the men's conversation as they moved in the hallway.

"Not all lunatics have staring eyes or a rapid pulse, sir," Dr. Dent said. "I have my eye on her and have no doubt that she is in the right place. We will see her display evidence of hysteria soon, I am sure of it."

***

The bad weather took its toll on everyone in Hall 6, not just the patients. The nurses were cross all day and hissed or snapped at the least provocation. Nurse Grupe made a point of shoving into Elizabeth when they waited in the hallway before dinner.

"Why don't you tell the doctors I hurt you and see how far that gets you?" she said. "They don't care what you say. You're a crazy girl to them. A freak. You'll soon see."

Downstairs, once again, Tilly refused to eat. "Who was that man this morning with Dr. Dent?" she asked Elizabeth.

"I have no idea. He didn't bother to introduce himself, of course. Now that we are patients instead of people, even common politeness is forgotten."

"It must be nice to have a visitor," said Tilly, in a dreamy voice. Elizabeth and Anne exchanged a glance.

"Please eat, dear," said Anne.

"Perhaps later," was all Tilly said.

At four o'clock, word spread through the ward that a new patient was to be admitted. All around, the women brightened but Elizabeth missed the new arrival as she was called to the sitting room.

She had never been there alone before. At first Elizabeth sat down on a small settee, thankful to be sitting on something other than a hard wooden bench. The three doors caught her attention. One led back to Hall 6; one gave access to the doctor's office; and the third must lead to a different part of the asylum. She considered the door to the doctor's office. What if it wasn't locked? Might she find something there, some evidence, useful for her reports? She edged around the room until she sat in the chair nearest the door. Could she be seen from Hall 6? She didn't think so. The wall between the sitting room and the hall held a large window, but the glass was thick and she was seated. She reached for the door handle.

"Miss Nellie Brown!" The third door opened and Elizabeth snatched her hand back and stood up. "No, no, sit down, sit down." Dr. Ingram smiled kindly at her and she allowed herself to smile at him in return. He ushered in a man and a woman, both smartly dressed. The woman wore a fine velvet walking dress, and although her face was covered by a thin brown veil, it was clear that she was anxious. The man's face lacked expression, but when he saw her he breathed out heavily through his nose. The woman's hand was on his arm, but it fell away and her shoulders sagged.

"No." The man shook his head.

"You are sure?" asked Ingram.

"Quite." The couple turned to go and Ingram made to follow them, but Elizabeth stood and called his name.

"Yes?" he turned in the doorway and looked at her.

"Who are they?" she asked.

"A couple looking for their missing daughter," he said. He looked sorry for them; sorry that she was not their missing child.

"That must be terrible," she said.

"Indeed." He frowned a little. "But now you must return to your hall, Miss Brown."

He turned away. She heard the lock turn and put her hands to her cheeks.

She stared at the door, lost in thought.

Back in Hall 6, the new patient was being quizzed by the nurses. Other patients buzzed around trying to hear the conversation, or whispering gossip and speculation from bench to bench. Only Tilly wasn't paying attention. Her eyes were on Elizabeth as she walked back in and took a seat by her friend.

"Where have you been?" Tilly's sharp tone came as a shock.

"Only to the sitting room," Elizabeth said. "A man and a woman came, looking for their missing daughter. But they were not my family."

"Did they say so?"

"They did. Are you feeling quite right, Tilly?"

"Of course I am!"

Elizabeth sought to change the subject. "Who is the new woman? Did you catch her name?"

"No."

"She is called Urena Little-Page," said Anne, crossing the room and sitting next to Tilly. "The nurses are having fun at her expense already. I think it must be this weather. We are all out of sorts today."

"Of course we are out of sorts," said Tilly. "We are trapped in this horrible place forever." She rubbed at her temples. "And now I'm trapped here between you two talking, talking, talking, talking. And I'm so cold."

Before either Elizabeth or Anne could say a word, Tilly got to her feet and moved to a bench at the top of the room near the piano.

"She is becoming unwell," said Anne.

"She is," agreed Elizabeth. "And I have no idea what we can do to help."

They both fell silent and Elizabeth turned her attention to the new patient. The woman was odd, and that was putting it kindly. She was very tall and thin, with a long neck that seemed too slim to support her head and all her long black hair. Her pale blue dress – still her own, as she had yet to go through the bath-time ritual for new arrivals – was filthy, splattered in mud as if she had fallen in a ditch. It was ripped around the collar. Her face was red and bewildered. Elizabeth moved to a nearer bench.

"She says she is eighteen!" crowed Nurse McCarten, doubling over in laughter. "Just look at her face!"

Emboldened, five or six patients crowded round Urena, grinning and laughing. "She looks older than me! Thirty-three at least," cackled Nancy.

"You're not eighteen," said another, whose name Elizabeth did not know. She had a flabby face and ugly sores around her mouth. Urena cringed away from her but there was nowhere to go. "If you are eighteen, I'm twenty-one and a princess," the woman said, poking her finger at Urena's chest.

"I want to go home," Urena howled in reply. Her arms flailed and the women fell back a little. "You are so mean and heartless to a young girl!"

That set the patients and nurses laughing even more, and Urena was quickly in floods of tears. She began rocking on her heels and her mouth hung open. She sobbed, quietly at first, but then louder and louder until Elizabeth couldn't stand a second more.

"Isn't that enough already?" she said, approaching the nurses' table and trying to lead Urena away.

"Sit back down, Brown!" Nurse Grady shoved the women apart, and pushed her face into Elizabeth's. The Irishwoman was taller and broader than her. Despite herself, Elizabeth was afraid.

"You!" Grady turned on Urena and smacked her across the face. For a moment, the sobbing stopped. The nurse poked a finger into Elizabeth's collarbone. "You'll get the same and more unless you get your God-forsaken arse back on that bench this minute. Do you hear me, bitch?"

Elizabeth's mouth went dry. She felt a tug at her sleeve. "Come and sit," said Anne softly. Elizabeth allowed herself to be led away, tears filling her own eyes. She sat on a bench and turned her back on the room.

"Tell me what is happening," she said to Anne with a sniff. There were clear sounds of a scuffle. "I can't watch."

"They're all grabbing her," said Anne. "Oh, my goodness, it's quite dreadful."

The sound of the women struggling filled the hall. There was a moment of quietness and then a choking sound, and a muttering among the women watching.

"Good God, they're strangling her," whispered Anne. Elizabeth's shoulders heaved as more tears came. She could not contain them.

The hall doors swung open and closed.

"My goodness." Anne leaned back against the bench and rubbed her hand up and down Elizabeth's back. "I've never seen anything like that in my life," she said.

"I have," said Elizabeth.

She refused to say more to Anne, but remained dull and listless for the rest of the day. Urena reappeared a few hours later, subdued and quiet, but with her neck livid with fingermarks. The nurses screeched at her any time she tried to touch where they had marked her.

Threats were issued. Anyone aggravating the nurses would be taken to "the closet", as Urena had been. One woman, a Mrs. O'Keefe, to whom Nurse Grady was normally kind – perhaps because they were both Irish – was talking to herself as usual. Nurse Grady shouted at her to be silent, but Mrs. O'Keefe paid no attention. Being ignored infuriated the nurse.

Grady grabbed Mrs. O'Keefe, pulled her up by the hair, and dragged her over to Nurse Grupe and Nurse McCarten. Even as she winced at the pain on the woman's face, Elizabeth wondered at these three nurses and how low they were sinking in their treatment. They were as lost as some of the patients: more lost than some – like Anne and Josephine, who could keep their composure and seemed endlessly patient. Mrs. O'Keefe tried to pull herself out of Nurse Grady's hold but stumbled, stamping on Nurse Grupe's foot. That sent them into a fury. She was pulled kicking and screaming from the room.

A few minutes later, the three nurses returned looking hot and flustered. They sat down heavily at their table and silence fell in the hall.

***

Elizabeth ate her evening meal in silence, swallowing what she could, sharing what she could not, and wondering that so many of the women tolerated it. She swallowed a lump of grey, unsalted fish and gagged. Further down the table she saw Tilly and Anne. Anne was speaking, urging Tilly to eat, but when the poor girl did finally take a mouthful she retched and bolted from the table. A nurse followed her out into the hallway. They heard her scolding tones, and Tilly did not return. Anne stared down at the table and Elizabeth could not catch her eye.

There was no chance to speak with Anne later upstairs and Tilly was nowhere to be seen. Nurse Grady suggested Nellie Brown might like to play the piano, but she refused. She longed for her room, to be alone and to be asleep, but when the time came her mind was busy. She curled up, making herself as small as she could under the one thin blanket, but the window had been open all day and she shivered. She counted back the days since she had left Mrs. Tanner's boarding house. It was still less than a week.

Six nights ago, she had stared in her mirror and wondered what a mad woman looked like. Now she knew.

Eventually, she fell asleep. She dreamed of the sound of her mother choking.

Beatrice

June 1920

The day trip to Coney Island was heralded as a great success, particularly in *The New York Journal*, where Miss Bly described the entire event as perfect in every way.

We started at City Hall, assembling over 700 orphans. They devoured a breakfast supplied by the Nedick Company, and Mayor Hylan waved us on our way. He smiled and nodded but I was sure he was glad not to be going with us. 700 excited children make a heck of a noise. Ernest arrived but was so busy we barely caught each other's eye, and perhaps that was just as well. I'd a number of things on my mind and, besides, Miss Bly wanted me with her at all times. It wasn't that she didn't like me seeing him, she said, just not on her dime. I couldn't argue with that. We were all working flat out to give those poor kids a day to remember. The Manhattan Tourist Company provided their largest bus, and Brown and White sent us their whole fleet of one hundred cabs to drive the children and staff out to Brooklyn.

Dorothy was there, of course, and Miss Bly singled her out, holding her hand and taking her on ride after ride as if she were her own child, or grandchild. They were easy in each other's company, and it was wonderful to see Miss Bly so relaxed and ready to smile. As soon as she'd recovered from her last bout of bronchitis, she'd thrown herself into work on *The Journal*, writing numerous articles about a missing girl, Henrietta Bulte. Everyone had believed the girl had been kidnapped until Miss Bly started asking questions. She guessed the girl had run away to Hollywood, insisted on making inquiries, and Miss Bly was proved right. Henrietta returned home to her parents.

In just a few days, Miss Bly was heading to Chicago to cover the Republican National Convention. She had high hopes of a new band of women becoming active on the political stage. New pieces of her asylum story appeared on my desk, but less often. Sometimes I thought she'd stopped writing it altogether. Or that she was finding re-visiting it was too much. But perhaps there was just so much going on, she struggled to find the time. It was hard to tell.

What was clear, though, was that the trip to Coney Island was an oasis of pleasure in the midst of all her activity. For most women, organizing a day like that would be a major undertaking. For Miss Bly, the day out was a luxury. She reveled in it.

I was happy to see it all come together: for her; for Ernest; and for all the children. But I also wanted Ernest to see how much Miss Bly and Dorothy enjoyed each other's company; to see with his own eyes how close they had become. Miss Bly talked about Dorothy more and more. She'd even made enquiries with her lawyer about becoming an adoptive parent herself. She hadn't mentioned Dorothy specifically in that connection, but I was sure that was where her thoughts were leaning.

What worried me was Ernest's likely reaction. From all he had said on the subject, Miss Bly was far from an ideal adoptive parent. A married couple, young, financially stable: these were his fixed criteria. I selfishly dreaded another rift between him and Miss Bly.

These were the kind of thoughts that swirled in my head as Miss Bly and Dorothy went round and round on a carousel for the third time. I watched Miss Bly holding onto her hat and Dorothy's blonde hair whipping in the wind. There had been a carousel on Blackwell's Island. It seemed grotesque to me the idea of grown women – madwomen – riding round and round.

It must have been nothing like this. Dorothy was laughing, turning in her saddle and trying to wave at me, while Miss Bly called on her to hold on firmly and not fall off. It was hard to believe such an open-hearted and charming child had no proper family to care for her. Miss Bly had had news concerning Dorothy's mother, and that was another cause of anxiety. I had no idea if she planned to share it with Ernest or not. The Society had legal responsibility for Dorothy, and Miss Bly was duty-bound to pass on anything she knew. But when would she do that? I watched her with the little girl and wondered. Miss Bly's sense of right and wrong was very strong. It just didn't always accord with everyone else's.

I toyed with the idea of speaking to Ernest myself. I tried to see past the strong views of the two people I cared about most, and focus in on Dorothy. What was the best future for her? Her mother, assuming she could reform? Adoption by one of the rich families Miss Bly knew, or a more modest but vetted family of the kind that Ernest might find? I looked at the little girl – happy, healthy and enjoying her day at the seaside. I wasn't as knowledgeable as Ernest or as passionate and caring as Miss Bly. Who was I to interfere and choose her future for her? I had been lucky. My own upbringing was blessedly ordinary and dull.

Their ride on the carousel finished. Miss Bly lifted Dorothy down from the back of her horse and swung her around by her armpits. The girl shrieked, and as soon as she was on the ground came running over to me.

"Oh, Miss Alexander," she declared breathlessly. "This is the most wonderful fun. It's the best day I've ever had!"

"Is it truly, Dorothy?" Miss Bly joined us, walking slowly, but fast enough to hear the little girl's words. She sat down next to me on the bench and pulled the little girl onto her knee. "I'm so very happy to hear that."

I said nothing. I took in the warmth in Miss Bly's words, the softness in her eyes, the way she wrapped her arms around Dorothy and held her close. I wasn't sure that being with Miss Bly was in Dorothy's best interests, but being with Dorothy was certainly wonderful for Miss Bly.

Elizabeth
XII
September 29th, 1887, a Thursday

On their third full day in Blackwell's Island Insane Asylum, Tilly Mayard had a fit. One moment she was sitting quietly, the next her body was in convulsions. First, her back arched and her head hit the wall. Then a spasm shook her from her shoulders to her feet. Anne grabbed Tilly to try and hold her up. Elizabeth screamed for a nurse. Tilly's arms thrashed and her teeth rattled. Her knees jerked and her head rolled.

"Let her fall on the floor," said Nurse Grady, standing over them with her hands on her hips. She displayed as much emotion as a butcher's wife sizing up a pig carcass.

"How can you be so uncaring!" shouted Anne. "You are not fit to call yourself a nurse!"

As Tilly continued to jerk and twitch, Anne eased herself and Tilly to the floor. Elizabeth didn't know how to help and wished for it to stop. Tilly's eyelids flickered. Her mouth was open, her lips pulled back from her teeth, and her jaw so rigid that the tendons stood out on her neck. Saliva pooled under her chin.

"Will she bite her own tongue?" Elizabeth whispered.

"I don't think so," said Anne. "But make them move back."

Elizabeth turned and saw that most of the patients had gathered behind her to see the spectacle of poor Tilly writhing on the floor. She shushed them away and knelt beside Anne and Tilly.

"This should be over by now, shouldn't it? She should have come out of it by now?"

Anne shrugged. She bent over Tilly, stroked her hair, and whispered calmly to her, as she might soothe a child.

Her calmness did not work on Elizabeth, who got to her feet, determined to insist that the nurses do something.

Before she could begin, Nurse Grupe called her from the sitting room. "Brown! The doctor wants you."

A doctor! Even better. Casting a last glance at Tilly, Elizabeth scurried across the hall and went straight into the doctor's office.

"Tilly Mayard needs help! She was cold, oh so cold, and now she is on the floor in a spasm. Please go to her. Please! All this cold and no nourishment! It has broken her. She has been on the floor for so long and the nurses do nothing! I'm begging you!"

Both Dent and Ingram were present. Ingram moved first, but Dent frowned and put his hand on Ingram's shoulder. He nodded at Elizabeth and left the room, but too slowly. She couldn't contain herself any longer.

"Why doesn't he hurry? She is on the floor, I tell you! Thrashing around! She was ill before she came here and now look what has happened! It is all very well for those women – women who call themselves nurses but do nothing to deserve the name – to say that this is a public institution and we get no more than we deserve, but that is not fair or right! In fact, it is a disgrace! Tilly has been cold and hungry for days! And this is the consequence!" She burst into tears.

"Miss Brown." Dr. Ingram's voice was firm but calm. "Please. Take this." He handed her a clean handkerchief. It smelled very faintly of lavender. "Dr. Dent is an accomplished physician. He will look after your friend. It sounds as though she has had a seizure. There is every reason to believe she will recover completely. You have done all you can."

Elizabeth sniffed and hated herself for crying. The place was affecting her. She was better than this.

"We are too cold. And the food is an abomination. Can't you *do* something about it?"

"I shall," he said with a smile. "I will call Nurse Grady down here as soon as we have finished our conversation, and speak to her about finding some warmer clothing. How would that be?"

"Very welcome," she said, smiling back. She took a deep breath in. It was the first real conversation she had had in almost a week.

Dr. Ingram swallowed and took a moment to rearrange his papers on the desk in front of him. "Well, we are agreed then. But now we must talk about your case. Have you remembered any more about your family?"

"No." Elizabeth stared at her hands on her lap. For the first time, she simply wanted to tell the truth and be done with this charade.

"Nothing? We have several visitors coming today who believe you may be their relative. Let us hope that one of them is your family. In the meantime, I want to talk about your memories. Who do you remember loving most as a child? Parents? Your mother? Or father?"

"My father." This was true. Elizabeth thought of her mother. Yes, she loved her. But it was complicated.

"Tell me about your father."

She told him something like the truth. She told him that her father was an important man. He was a judge, she said, who had died when she was six, but she omitted the breakdown of the family that happened afterward, and the disastrous fighting over money between the children from his first marriage and her mother, Mary Jane. She said she had learned Spanish somewhere – she didn't know where, but not in America; that at least was true. She had picked it up easily on her travels in Mexico.

Did she have siblings? he asked. She said she thought so. Elizabeth saw Albert's face in her mind. "I'm not sure I get on with them all," she offered.

Was she married? No. Not courting either. She looked up. He wasn't watching her.

Had she ever worked? Here was the greatest lie. She said she'd never worked that she could remember. In truth, she barely remembered a time when she did not.

Dr. Dent slid back into the room and stood behind her. "Miss Mayard is resting now," he said. "Anything new?" he asked Ingram, talking as if she was not there. Her fingers curled into fists.

"No."

"Then you may go. Dr. Ingram told you to expect several visitors, though?"

"He did." She stood up and went to the door. "And you will speak to Nurse Grady, Dr. Ingram?"

"I will." He nodded, but her eyes were on Dent's face. As she walked back into Hall 6, she imagined him telling Ingram not to listen to the patients and to let Nurse Grady be. She did not know if Ingram was to be relied upon or not. He seemed so kind and considerate. But perhaps that was all an act. He wouldn't be the first man she'd met who proved to be not all he seemed.

Tilly was nowhere to be seen but Anne rushed to speak to Elizabeth.

"It was so terrible, Nellie. I am only glad you were not here to see it!"

"But what can you mean? I sent Dr. Dent. He said she was herself again."

"Herself?" Anne's normally placid face bunched in disgust. "She may never be herself again!"

"Anne! What do you mean? What did he do?"

But Anne could not even bring herself to describe it. In the end, it was Josephine who explained that Dent had knelt down and cupped Tilly's head in one hand while forcefully pressing the fingers of his other hand into her forehead, just above her eyebrows.

"It looked like he was going to crush her skull," the Frenchwoman said. "Nurse Grady held Anne back. She looked ready to pull him off her. Tilly's face turned purple. It was terrible. But then the fit ended. And they took her out."

"Dear God."

"I am not sure God is looking, Nellie," said Josephine.

"Don't say that," whispered Anne, rocking back and forth on the bench. "Please. Don't say that."

***

In the afternoon, Tilly returned to the ward, but she was given a chair near the doctor's office and the patients were told to leave her to rest. When Elizabeth was called for the first of Nellie Brown's visitors, she rushed to Tilly's side and asked her how she was. Bruises had appeared on her forehead. Tilly said nothing, beyond repeating that she had a headache. She didn't seem to know or even care who Elizabeth was.

When Elizabeth came back out of the sitting room, however, Tilly was different again. She was brighter, and called out to Elizabeth by name.

"Who have you been seeing, Nellie Brown?" she asked.

"A family. They were looking for their niece. She has gone missing from Rhode Island."

"Rhode Island?" Tilly's tone was indignant. "Why ever do they want to look at you then?"

Elizabeth was a little surprised, but put Tilly's harshness down to her headache. "I have no idea, my dear," she said. "Shall I sit with you for a while?"

"No." Tilly jerked back in her chair and Elizabeth feared the onset of another fit. But Tilly turned her head away, and Elizabeth, seeing how little she was wanted, made her way back to the other side of the hall.

Tilly's morning seizure had been interesting enough to occupy the minds of the women and nurses of Hall 6, but by afternoon, with the sky as grey and the rain as heavy as it had been the previous day, the same restless atmosphere seemed to spread through the women. Elizabeth was singled out twice more for visitors. One pair were nothing better than ghouls, there to examine a madwoman close up, and not really enquiring after a missing person at all.

The other women disliked the attention she was getting. She heard some of them muttering about her, and their eyes were on her off and on throughout the afternoon. Tilly, too, seemed to be offended by Elizabeth in some way. During the cold hallway wait until they were allowed to descend to the dining room, Elizabeth saw Tilly notice her and then quite purposefully move away. Perhaps she was tired and wished to avoid pointless conversation, or being encouraged to eat to keep her strength up. And yet Elizabeth knew there was more to it than that.

She was buoyed up, however, after their meal, when the nurses came through the hall offering shawls to anyone who was cold. Dr. Ingram had kept to his word and she was happy to see it. Watching some of the older women snuggle into their shawls made up for the meanness of Nurse Grady, who caught her by the arm in the hallway, pinched her skin, and whispered that she'd soon be sorry if she made a habit of running to the doctors with complaints. Elizabeth did not care what Grady thought. She nodded and tried to look crushed, but inside she relished the victory. It wasn't much, but in a sea of difficulty it was such a relief to think there was a person prepared to listen, someone who saw her as a person and not as a lunatic. Or at least, she hoped he did. She kept her eyes on the door all the rest of the day hoping that he would appear so she could at least say thank you. It also made it much easier to ignore the hard stares Tilly Mayard continued to throw her way.

"Is Tilly staring at you?" asked Anne, dispelling any hope Elizabeth had that she was imagining things.

"I don't know! I'm afraid I have offended her in some way, but in what way? I have no idea."

"Perhaps she still has the headache, poor girl. I have been praying for her ever since."

"I hope that's all it is. But I have felt it ever since she came back after this morning. She asked me why people were visiting me and was quite rude about it, if I'm honest."

"She told me she hopes her family will come for her."

"I hope your family comes and takes you away from here, Anne."

"You are kind, Elizabeth. But I am afraid it is my family that sent me here, and I'm not sure I see any way out for me. I try to imagine it. But I can't."

"But you should not be here! Look around you. Look at these women. You are nothing like them. Not crazed in the least."

Anne patted her hand. "Thank you for saying so. I think so

myself for most of the time. And then at other moments, I'm not so confident. For why would my nephew place me here if not for my own good? If I was managing out there," she nodded to the window, smeared with heavy rain, "then why send me here? Perhaps there's something I have forgotten. A reason for my being here that I no longer know."

"I highly doubt it," said Elizabeth.

A little later, she was called to the sitting room again. This time, her visitor was already there. To her horror, Elizabeth realized that she knew him.

With Nurse Grady right behind her locking the door to the hall, she stared at George McCain, her fellow journalist at *The Pittsburg Dispatch*. McCain was the *Dispatch's* man on the ground in New York, and he'd been angry when Elizabeth turned up in New York, angry enough to make it plain that she should not look to him for assistance. He hadn't liked her sending articles back to Pittsburgh for the last four months. She had encroached on his territory, she knew it, but what had she been supposed to do? Starve?

When he saw her, his face blanched. He started up out of his chair, his jaw falling open and his eyes wide. She put a finger to her lips and implored him with her eyes not to give her away.

"I do not know this man," she said, turning to Nurse Grady and trying to prevent the nurse seeing McCain and the evident shock on his face.

"She is right." His voice sounded strangled. "This is not the young lady I came in search of."

Nurse Grady muscled past Elizabeth. "You don't know her? Then you must leave." She waved to the visitor door and turned to unlock the other door to return Elizabeth to the ward. As she did so, Elizabeth had a sudden panic. McCain was at the other door. She called him back.

"One moment, Senor." He turned and moved back to stand near her. "Do you speak Spanish, Senor?" She leaned as close as she dared and said under her breath, "I'm after an item. Don't tell."

"No. No, I don't speak Spanish." He frowned and gave her the smallest of nods. Then he turned on his heel and was gone.

***

The episode weighed on her mind. If he'd said her name, she would have denied it. She hoped she had said enough to stop him dashing back to town and try to have her released. But that brought a more somber train of thought. She was relying on Cockerill and Pulitzer. What if they let her down? She allowed herself to think the unthinkable – that they might leave her here for weeks or even months. She couldn't even think about forever. What if one day she realized that this had been her one and only chance to escape? Nausea gripped her.

Elizabeth passed the evening standing by a window, looking out at the East River. She thought about the water beyond and the land beyond that. She thought about her family in Pittsburgh and her room on West Ninety-Sixth Street. What was her mother doing now? Clearing up after supper with Albert and his wife? Albert would not be helping, that was certain. He'd more likely be complaining about someone from work. Harry would also be home. He would not be helping around the house either, she supposed, but Harry's domestic laziness came with smiles and soft words and gentleness. Whereas Albert's? Well, Elizabeth had enough to think about without dwelling on Albert's failings.

She tried to focus instead on life after her release. She wrote some lines in her head and even smiled into her reflection in the window, thinking of some choice terms she might use to describes the three nurses and Dr. Dent. She wished for her notebook, but Nurse Grupe had snatched that away. Perhaps Dr. Ingram might be persuaded that she needed it back.

Ingram and Anne were the only bright spots she could find to dwell on.

Something swooped past the window. A bird or a bat. She imagined it soaring high over the asylum, flying down the Island past the alms house, the penitentiary, and the smallpox hospital. It would coast on the wind of the East River. It would fly free. She remained in the cage.

XIII
September 30th, 1887, a Friday

Elizabeth woke the next morning feeling better. At first, all the noise made by the night nurses checking on patients and locking and unlocking doors had made sleep impossible. Now she was becoming accustomed to the rhythms of the place. Her hunger had plateaued. She'd adjusted to her sleep being broken. Being locked alone in room 28 from 8.30pm to 5.30am was a blessed escape from the madness and cruelty. It gave her time to marshal her thoughts and remind herself that this was all temporary.

She thought a week was long enough. Cockerill and Pulitzer had not said they intended to have her out in a week in so many words, but that seemed to her to be a reasonable supposition. Tomorrow, Saturday, it would be a full seven days since she had been committed to Bellevue. She decided her release could come as soon as Monday.

With that in mind, she wanted to spend the day hearing more women's stories and questioning some of the doctors. Madwomen there were – and in numbers – in Hall 6. But there were also far too many women trapped in the place for the wrong reasons. There were women sent there by their own families because of squabbles over property or money. There were women who were unwell and branded hysterical. There were women who were simply foreign, poor, and unable to fight the system. They were inconvenient, these women, not insane. She needed to push the doctors on their methods. She thrust her feet into her shoes and went to work.

It was raining again. The nurses had found a new target for their boredom in a pretty young woman named Sarah Fishbaum. Elizabeth had been unable to get much of Sarah's story, as she spoke an East European language, and although she seemed to understand well enough, she could barely string a sentence together in English. Her reason for being in the asylum was quickly spelled out by the behavior of the nurses.

"Sarah, wouldn't you like a nice young man to visit you tonight?"

"A young man?" Her face lit up, and she rubbed her hands up and down her arms. "Yes, yes."

"Or one of the doctors?" Dr. Ingram chanced to walk through the hall at this moment, and Nurse Grady pulled Sarah over to the nurses' table.

"Isn't he handsome, Sarah? Shall we ask him to kiss you?"

Sarah nodded eagerly and Nurse McCarten burst out laughing. "Or do you prefer Dr. Dent, Sarah?" she said. "He's so tall, dark, and handsome. I could put in a good word for you, if you like."

"You are disgusting to tease her in this way," Elizabeth called out from her bench.

"Who asked you for your opinion?" said Nurse Grady. "Shut it now or you'll be visiting the closet. I'll talk to this filthy whore any way I like. Lord, when a woman's own husband has her locked up because she can't keep her stinking hands to herself, then she deserves all she gets. It's a disgrace, so it is."

All morning, the nurses were up and down dispatching patients to the doctor's office, handing out sewing tasks, and breaking up any small disputes. Tilly Mayard spent the morning singing by one of the windows, despite Nurse McCarten chiding her to stop or at least to vary her repertoire. Elizabeth smiled at Anne but chose to sit by a fair-haired, older woman who always appeared calmer than most, sitting each day on one bench or another with her hands clasped on her lap and a stoic expression on her face.

"You never seem to be disturbed by all the fighting and upheaval," Elizabeth said to her gently. "I have been watching you and thinking I should do well to cultivate half of your patience."

"It is kind of you to say so," she replied. "But to be honest, I have little choice in the matter."

"How so?"

"To move is agony to me. I have a skin complaint, see." The woman rolled back her sleeve. Her forearm was raw – a mess of red sores and broken scabs mixed with tiny patches of normal skin. "It is on my legs, on my back, everywhere."

"But why are you not in hospital? Do the doctors know?"

"Only about my arms. I cannot bear the idea of showing them more. And so I sit and wait for it to get better."

Elizabeth struggled for words. "What has caused it?"

"I was sick. I could not work. It was a difficult time. I had a problem with my father. I could not stay at home any longer. The streets were a safer place. It started then. My skin broke out in sores, I scratched them in my sleep. I wanted to go to the poorhouse. I thought I'd be safe there."

"But this is the madhouse, not the poorhouse. Were you sick mentally?"

"Not at all. I am not now. I am simply in pain. They brought me here and bathed me, never mind that I told them it was the one thing I was not to do. Every inch of my skin became inflamed. I feel like I am on fire."

"This is terrible. How can you tolerate it?"

"Ha. You are young. You have not been tried yet. We can all bear a great deal more than we think we can."

Elizabeth surveyed the room. So many of the women seemed cast in shadows and confusion, their hope and confidence lost. Tedium and lethargy, and no outlet or occupation to lift the spirits, opened the door to malicious thoughts and violence, large and small. These were the great city's abandoned women: women too sad, or too loud; too lascivious or too emotional; too stupid; too hysterical; too unreliable; or too ill, to be looked after by anyone but three base and semi-illiterate women who treated their charges like livestock. Those who were not ill, would likely become ill. The sane would become mad. It was yet another aspect of the inherent unfairness of the world in its treatment of women.

"Visitor for Nellie Brown!" Nurse Grady barked out her

order and disappeared into the sitting room. Elizabeth rolled her eyeballs and stood up. Stiffness cramped her back and legs. The inactivity of asylum living had physical consequences, too.

She was surprised to find Tilly on her shoulder as she reached the doorway.

"Were you also called for Tilly?" she asked.

"Who is this visitor?"

"I have no idea."

"I don't believe you."

"What do you mean you don't believe me?"

"Brown. Get in here." Nurse McCarten was at the door. She dismissed Tilly with a wave of her hand, and Elizabeth, bewildered though she was by Tilly's odd behavior, had no choice but to do as she was told.

Inside the sitting room, a familiar scene played out. This time it was a couple in their late fifties, richly dressed and highly agitated. They saw her and knew at once that she was not the girl they were looking for. It made her sorry to see their shoulders sag. The husband's hand went to his wife's shoulder.

"Have you tried the newspapers to find your missing loved one?" Elizabeth asked. "They can do a great deal these days, you know."

The man threw her a look that made her face color. It was dismissive, scornful. It said, what are a lunatic's words to me? She was stung, and for once thankful, as Nurse McCarten was quick to usher them out and send Elizabeth back onto the ward where she made a beeline for Anne.

"Tilly was extremely odd just now," she said. They both looked at their friend. She was back at a central window, swaying back and forth, her arms cradled, lightly singing *Rock-a-bye Baby*. "Has she lost her mind so quickly?"

"I don't know. Perhaps she is just trying to keep warm?" Anne's words sounded hollow, as if she wanted it to be true but knew it was not. "She did mention you this morning."

"And?"

"She said she doesn't trust you."

"Why ever not? Did she say?"

"You won't get upset, will you Nellie?"

"Upset? What on earth did she say? Tell me at once."

"She said she doesn't believe you have lost your memory." Elizabeth saw Anne's eyes on her, watching for a reaction and realized that Anne too must be having her doubts. She knew a moment of wild temptation to tell Anne her true story, but crushed it down.

"But why should I make up such a thing?"

"Exactly what I said to her," Anne breathed out heavily. "I said no one would do such a thing.

"Unless they were mad," said Elizabeth, her lips twitching, hoping to prompt a smile from Anne. She was well rewarded. "Did that answer?"

"Only for a moment. I think it is your visitors that distress her."

"I am not to blame for that. There was a reporter at the courtroom when I was sent to Bellevue. He wrote about me in *The Sun*. And now every poor, sad creature that is missing a loved one is boarding a boat and dashing to Blackwell's Island to see me for themselves. That's not any reason to take against me personally, though. Honestly, just now I thought she wanted to hit me."

"It's certainly not your fault. But I think perhaps she hopes that someone will come for her, and as each day passes she grows more agitated. I fear for her, truly. She has changed so quickly."

Although it saddened her, Elizabeth made sure to avoid Tilly, sitting as far away from her as possible at meal-times and making sure to keep her distance in the bathrooms or on the stairs. In Hall 6, she spent some time with Matty and with Josephine, talking about their lives before Blackwell's Island and the food and warm clothing they longed for. They all longed for fresh air, however cold it might be, but the steady rain kept everyone indoors. The walk that Elizabeth had found so distressing now seemed intensely desirable. Knowing that civilization and normal life was so close, yet to be unable to smell the river and see how short a boat ride they were from the world, was painful. A glimpse or two of Manhattan Island might sustain her, like a burst of oxygen to a tired brain, but instead they were trapped indoors waiting for the nurses' next outrage or the next woman to begin raving or take a fit, or attack herself or others. And the benches did not get any softer to sit on.

In the afternoon, Dr. Ingram spent several hours in his office interviewing patients. Elizabeth hoped to be one of them, but when she was finally called in and seated opposite him, she was disappointed that he only wanted to ask her the same, tired questions about her family, her origin, and how she had found herself in New York all alone and with no trunks.

"Is lack of memory, then, enough to make a woman mad?" she asked.

He looked across the desk at her and put down his pen. "No."

"Then why am I here? I am as sane as you are. What do you see your job here as doing?" She had caught his interest. He leaned forward on the desk, crossing his arms over his papers.

"I am here to take care of patients and test their sanity."

"Test mine then. Test the other women. There are several of them out there as sane as I am."

"All the women here have been thoroughly assessed, Miss Brown.

"By whom? How many doctors work here?"

He sat back in his chair, thinking, she suspected, to humor her. "Sixteen."

"Sixteen. And yet, excepting yourself, I have never seen one exert himself over his patients in any way. No one listens to their complaints. They are barely conversed with. One doctor in particular walks through this ward and says good morning only to the air. He makes no eye contact in case someone might ask him for help. He interviews people in here in the most perfunctory manner. Checking that a woman has eaten and slept amounts to doing no work at all. And that's before we come to the question of whether these nurses are even capable of accurately recording their patients' behavior. When I was first in this room, Nurse Grupe could not even read off my height when I was measured."

"Perfunctory?"

"Excuse me?"

"You said perfunctory. It seems an unusual word choice for someone who we have been thinking speaks Spanish at home."

She bit her lip. "I can't explain it."

"Just as you cannot explain where you are from and how you got here." He smiled at her suddenly. "You are a mystery to me, Miss Brown."

His smile was charming. It knocked her off course. She had been in the middle of pressing him, and now she was afraid she was blushing.

"I am merely asking questions," she said. "I am concerned that there are women here who are in the wrong place. Anne Neville. Josephine Despreau. And there are others."

"A woman may appear quite sane, Miss Brown. Even as you yourself appear so now. But we have records, multiple doctor examinations, referrals from doctors at Bellevue and other hospitals all around the State. Many suffer from delusions but have learned how to keep things hidden. I assure you, we are doing our very best."

The conversation was over. There was a hint of pride, she thought, in his last answer and she supposed that was to be expected. He was a conscientious man and a professional. Men – people – did not like to have their methods questioned or their motives challenged. Dr. Ingram was blind to some of the problems in the asylum – the failings of Dr. Dent being one that sprang quickly to mind – but he was the one person in the place that any woman could rely on. She wondered how he'd react when he read the articles she planned to write for *The World*. What would he think of them? And of her?

Late afternoon brought another visitor for Nellie Brown. This time, she met a gentleman on his own, and was left in the room with him when Nurse Grupe was called back into the hall by Nurse Grady.

"You are a pretty young thing," he began. The hair on the

back of her neck rose. He was a short man, in a brown check suit that looked respectable enough. She noted his high collar and tie, and a clean, new-looking hat on the sofa beside him. Perhaps she was rushing to judgment. Still, she chose not to reply. "I'm looking for someone," he continued. "Do you think it might be you?" He gestured to her to sit in the chair opposite him. He had thin hair on top but a thick moustache that swooped across his cheeks to join his sideburns.

"I'm afraid not, sir," she said. "I don't believe I know you."

"Of course you don't!" he said, lowering his voice and looking at the door. "Look, that nurse woman will be back in a moment. Here's my offer. I'll say you're my daughter and sign you out of here. I'll put a roof over your head and buy a nice pretty dress for you."

"And why would you want to do that?" She kept her face still and her eyes wide.

"Why do you think?" His face turned ugly, and he ran his eyes up and down her body. She looked at the door. In that moment, he lunged for her, crushing her in her chair and pressing his face against hers. His hand went for her breast.

"Get your filthy hands off this patient!"

Nurse Grady lifted the man by his jacket collar and propelled him to the door. She pushed one thick finger into his chest and whispered into his ear. Whatever she said was enough for the creep to stand quietly while she unlocked the door and sent him on his way. When she turned back to Elizabeth, it was as though nothing had happened.

"Get back in the hall, Brown," she said.

The moment she returned, Tilly sat down next to Elizabeth and started asking questions.

"Who was your visitor? What did they want?"

"A man. No one I knew."

"Who was he looking for?"

Elizabeth sighed. "No one."

"You are lying!"

Elizabeth twisted round. "I am not. He was not looking for any one here. He wanted something else entirely. I don't really want to talk about it."

"Oh. You don't really want to talk about it." Tilly took a firm hold on an inch of skin on the back of Elizabeth's upper arm and twisted. "You don't want to, but you will. I know what you are up to!"

"Tilly!" Elizabeth slapped the other woman's hand away and rubbed her arm. She opened her mouth to call a nurse, but thought better of it. She could handle this. "The man was horrible, Tilly, if you must know the truth. He wanted me to pretend to be his daughter and go and live with him. You may imagine why."

"That's ridiculous. Do you think I'm a fool?"

"No, I don't, and it's not ridiculous. Tilly, why are you so concerned? What are you thinking?"

"Tell me the truth!" Suddenly, Tilly was on her feet and her hands were in Elizabeth's hair. She pulled her from the bench, smacked her across the face, and knocked her to the floor. "You hate me don't you! You hate me!"

Elizabeth tried to get to her feet, but Tilly shoved her back. Elizabeth glanced at the nurses' table long enough to see they were watching but not making any move to intervene.

"Tilly, stop it!" she screamed as a sharp kick landed on her ribs. Elizabeth scooted back on the floor, trying to escape the next blow while Tilly ranted.

"They want to see me, not you! They are looking for me, coming to take me away from this hell-hole, not you!" She kicked Elizabeth's legs and ribs. "You shouldn't have told them you were Tilly Mayard. You lied to them. They keep coming and you keep lying!" She kicked her again and again. "You won't tell them the truth because you hate me! I was kind to you. I liked you. But you hate me and want to keep me here in misery, rather than let me leave. You are like a devil!"

On this last scream, she reached down, pulled Elizabeth's hair, and banged her head against the wooden floor.

Finally, Nurse Grupe and Nurse Grady pinned Tilly by the arms and dragged her back. Elizabeth lay panting and weeping on the floor. The nurses slapped Tilly twice about the face and manhandled her from the hall. Nurse McCarten stepped over

Elizabeth on the floor, as though she wasn't even there. She shouted at the other patients to sit back down.

"Can you stand?" It was Anne. She helped Elizabeth to her feet, and they sat back down on a bench in silence.

For the first time, Elizabeth knew that being in the asylum might break her. Her ribs ached. And her scalp. She was afraid. She sat with her arms wrapped around herself and stared at the floor. What reward could be worth this experience? How stupid had she been to bring herself to this place? Arrogant. Foolhardy. Naive. Tilly was demented. And yet in Bellevue, Elizabeth had been so sure that the girl was every bit as sane as she was. Well, she had been wrong. Wrong. For years she had prided herself on her judgment. She had known that her stepfather was no good, long before Mary Jane had. She had seen it all coming – the arguments, the thieving, the beatings, the choking, even the gunshot. None of it had really surprised Elizabeth, as terrible as it was to experience. But here, she was truly out of her depth. She knew it. She needed out.

But the way out wasn't in her hands and she cursed herself silently again, seeing how her ambition, her desperate need to succeed in New York, had compromised her judgment. No one had made her do this. She could have said no to Pulitzer and Cockerill and simply walked away. Instead, she had put her life and her safety into the two men's hands. Her safety in a man's hands. The one thing she had sworn never to do. And now, when she was desperate, who did she look for every time the hall door opened? Dr. Ingram. She was pathetic. Her ribs ached.

In the afternoon, more new patients arrived, but Elizabeth studied them with none of her usual curiosity. One, called Carrie Glass, was obviously an idiot. It could be seen in her slack face, the way her mouth hung open and her eyes swung around like empty lanterns. The other girl, another German, seemed more sensible of her situation. She sniffed back tears and looked around in alarm. Elizabeth didn't have the appetite for her story, and was glad when the girl sat far away from her.

She was devoid of energy and hope. Her morning optimism seemed laughable. She thought about laughing out loud, about how mad she could be if she just let go of herself.

Dr. Ingram had said they were all mad, all of them. She looked at Matty talking to her reflection. At Mrs. Fox weeping silently at the piano, even as she played a merry tune. At Anne staring at her hands, and Josephine crammed on a bench with four other women, leaning her head back against the wall and keeping her eyes firmly closed. And she thought of Tilly. She would surely be taken to the Lodge where all the violent patients were kept securely. Tilly's face as it had become in madness, filled her mind's eye.

At night, she could not sleep. Tilly's face did not leave her. Being locked in alone was no longer comforting. She wanted her family. Her brother Harry. Her mother. Even Albert. Her mind darted. And then she thought she smelled smoke. She sat bolt upright and sniffed. The smell was there, caustic, burning, acrid, catching her throat. She threw away her blanket and ran to the door to knock.

"Is there a fire? Let me out! Fire! Fire! Let everyone out!" She pounded the door with her fists. The nurses came.

"What is this nonsense?"

"A fire! Can't you smell it?"

"Are you dreaming? There is nothing."

"I smelled it. I'm sure of it."

"It was nothing. Get back to bed."

Elizabeth saw that the nurse meant to leave and lock the door again. It was intolerable.

"Don't lock me in here. I'll die in the fire."

"There is no fire!" The nurse turned away, but Elizabeth grabbed at her arm. "Here! Take your hands off me!" She called for help and two other nurses rushed in. Elizabeth was slapped in the face and pushed back to the bed. While she struggled, one nurse disappeared only to return moments later with the young doctor who had first examined her in Hall 6.

"Hold her down," he said. Elizabeth saw he had a glass bottle and a spoon in his hands.

"You can't make me take that."

"I can and I will," he said, leaning over her. "You will take this and sleep."

"I won't."

"You will, if I have to go and find a needle and stick it in your arm. You will take this dose and give us some peace."

The thought of the needle stilled her. "I'm afraid there is a fire," she said in a small voice.

"There is no fire," he said. "And it is time you submitted."

She opened her mouth and took the dose.

Beatrice

October 1920

She was sick again; this time, sick enough for Mary to call in the doctor. Miss Bly was admitted to St Mark's Hospital straight away. She insisted on working, though, and we took it in turns to take a cab down Second Avenue to Twelfth Street, taking her letters to read and carrying away pages of handwritten answers, draft articles for *The Journal,* as well as correspondence with lawyers about all manner of issues. She could not stop. She never rested. Even when her body fought her, her mind resisted any desire to rest. The challenge she must have faced in the asylum wasn't lost on me. She wasn't made for inaction. All those dull days indoors in Hall 6; the experience must have driven her nearly mad. She caught me staring at her sometimes and scolded me for fretting over her, but I was as much fascinated as I was concerned. I believed I knew her as well as anyone, perhaps better. And yet I wondered if I knew her at all.

One day, I asked the taxicab to follow me when I left the hospital. I put my papers on the seat and hurried down the sidewalk. The place I was looking for was only seven blocks south. I strode down the streets with purpose, trying to imagine what she must have felt almost exactly thirty-three years earlier. The wind was cold on my cheeks. Heavy clouds threatened rain. The driver surely thought I was some new form of fool, but he followed me closely until I stopped outside 84 Second Avenue.

The building had changed. It was no longer a boarding house. The first floor was a grocery store, although the dingy windows and leaves and trash blowing around the front steps suggested that business was slow. I crossed the street so I could have a better look. There was no mistaking it. The green paint, the diamond pattern near the roof; this was the house where she had so successfully feigned madness. She had changed the newspaper world forever. But where did it get her? I looked back up Second Avenue and pictured her in her room in St Mark's, propped up in bed, or in the rocking chair by the window, or writing furiously at the small round table they had put in there at her demand. I had no answer to it. She was driven, that was clear enough, but by what and to what end?

She hadn't given me any more of her story recently. I was afraid her enthusiasm for the task had waned and I might never truly understand what she went through. Of course, I'd read the two articles in *The World* that she published on her release. I knew the story as she had chosen to tell it then. But the public story wasn't the same as the private one. In the newspaper, events were glossed over. The story she was writing for me was different. I decided to stop waiting. I'd ask her to keep going. I'd push her to see it through.

I looked up once more at the windows of 84 Second Avenue, and tried to see Miss Bly's face up there, tried to picture her looking out. It was foolish perhaps. I had no knowledge of which window had been hers, or if she had even stood at it.

I shivered.

And then I took the cab back up to the McAlpin Hotel.

***

The next time I went to visit her in hospital, a week or so later at the most, she had a visitor. Miss Bly looked angry when she saw me at the threshold and I stepped back in surprise, but as soon as I saw her visitor, I understood.

During the summer and into the Fall, Miss Bly had corresponded with Dorothy's mother through an intermediary she called Mrs. H. I never saw the letters or told Ernest a word about it. Everything I knew came from Miss Bly's phone calls and meetings with her lawyer. She could be secretive in some ways, but with every door always open and her tendency to speak passionately, I was able to follow the story. Dorothy's mother had fled New York after pleading guilty and receiving a suspended sentence for shoplifting. Miss Bly heard through this Mrs. H. that Grace was acting in a small company of players, travelling around New England and trying to save money. She had not managed to pay Dorothy's board, and was afraid that she would be thrown in jail if she returned to New York to try to claim her daughter. Miss Bly instructed her lawyer to ask the judge for leniency, hoping to bring Grace back to the city, but this was refused. For some time she had heard nothing, at least not as far as I knew.

"Beatrice!" For a moment I thought she meant to send me packing, but then her expression changed and she beckoned me inside. "Grace, this is my assistant. She has met your lovely daughter and is wholly discreet and trustworthy. With your permission, I will have her take notes about your story."

Grace Harris barely glanced at me. She was tall and graceful, thin as a willow. She might have been beautiful once, but she was obviously sick. Her face was all angles, her skin horribly pale, and her eyes sunk so deep in her face it was like looking at her skull. In contrast, her auburn hair was bright, too bright, but I could see what she had been, and understood why the stage might have attracted her, and how she must have attracted men. Miss Bly was propped upright in her bed while Grace sat by her side in the rocking chair.

"Mrs. Harris is unwell, Beatrice. She has been admitted here already. But she has sought me out to talk to me about her life and Dorothy's, and discuss her wishes regarding her daughter's future care."

I nodded and took a seat at the small table. The woman was dying, and they wanted me there to bear witness to their conversation. Miss Bly's comment on my discretion was not lost on me, but I was soon busy listening to Grace Harris's story.

"I had a simple upbringing," Grace said. "I went to school and helped my mama at home and went to Sunday School every week. My parents died of tuberculosis when I was twelve, Miss Bly. My sister and I were orphans. When I was fifteen, a rich boy sweet-talked me. He...he pressured me into doing what I shouldn't have done."

"And the result was Dorothy?" asked Miss Bly.

"Yes. I tried to look after her. I even married Clarence to try and give her a name and a better life."

"Your husband is an actor?"

She nodded. "A travelling man. He has a vaudeville act. He sings. I danced. He said I could be the next Eva Tanguay."

"But you separated?"

"We fought. He said I was unreliable. He wasn't wrong. I made some bad choices. Some days I couldn't lift my head off the pillow. Worries crowded in on me. He wanted a wife to cosset him. I didn't do that. I did try. At least sometimes. He kicked me out in the end. That's when Dorothy and me came to New York. It's hard to be a woman alone. Harder with a child in tow."

"It is only after one is in trouble that one realizes how little sympathy and kindness there is in the world," I said. Miss Bly smiled and Mrs. Harris turned her eyes my way.

"That sounds like you are quoting someone," she said.

"I am." I tipped my head toward Miss Bly.

"She is quoting me, Grace dear," Miss Bly said. "Something I wrote a long time ago and stand by because it is true. And even more so for women than it is for men. You will find no judgment here. All I wish to do is help you. And Dorothy."

"What will happen to her?"

There was so much unsaid in her question. The word "after" hung in the air.

"She will be well cared for," said Miss Bly. "You have my word on it."

I walked over to Mrs. Harris and handed her a handkerchief. She didn't make a sound, but her shoulders shook and tears streamed down her face. She was so painfully thin that the joints in her fingers appeared swollen out of all proportion.

"I haven't seen her since the day they arrested me," she said. "She will have grown."

"Taller every time I see her," said Miss Bly. "She is healthy. Happy. Friendly. She's a charming child. A child you can be proud of."

"Does she remember me?"

"Of course she does! She knows that you love her. She knows that you are not well."

"I only picked up the doll because I wanted it for Dorothy. I was going to pay."

She meant the doll she had been accused of shoplifting. The cashier had called the police. "I had money on me," she said, sniffing. "It was less than three dollars. Why steal something like that?"

Miss Bly and I exchanged a glance. It was impossible to know the truth. Whether it was true or not, Mrs. Harris certainly believed now that she had never meant to steal the little doll.

"We believe you, my dear," said Miss Bly. "Do not concern yourself on that count."

"And I only pleaded guilty because my lawyer told me to!" She was worked up, retelling the story. Words spilled out. "The cocaine was given to me by a friend. I wasn't well. I needed it. I needed to work to support my girl, and the drugs helped. I only ever took the smallest amount. I was careful. I pleaded guilty so that I could get home to Dorothy. But they took her. They took her from me anyway."

I thought back to the letter Miss Bly had received from the woman in New England and discussed with Ernest in his office. Mrs. Love-Beauregard had been kind enough about Grace Harris, describing her as a well brought-up girl who had experienced misfortune. But she also described her as a drug addict and a prostitute.

"What will happen to her?" she asked Miss Bly again.

Miss Bly let out a long sigh. She patted the bed and Mrs. Harris slowly got to her feet and went to sit by her. Miss Bly gathered her hands into her own. "We will find a wonderful family for her. I was thinking she might do well somewhere in the country. Somewhere with fresh air and wholesome food. What do you say?"

Mrs. Harris was nodding.

"But first, we need to establish certain legal questions. Let me ask you first. What is Dorothy's religion?"

"I'm a Methodist."

"So your child is a Protestant. She has been in Catholic care. The first thing that will happen is that she is transferred to an institution supported by her own faith. That is the law."

Again, Mrs. Harris nodded.

"Do you have any family who could take in Dorothy?" asked Miss Bly.

"None."

It was heart-breaking, really, to look at this woman, so ill and so alone.

"Have you written a will?"

"Never."

"Beatrice will call my lawyer. He will visit us here. In the meantime, you may consider what your wishes are for Dorothy."

"My wishes?"

"Yes. At the moment she is in the legal care of the Society for the Prevention of Cruelty to Children."

"And are they good people? Will they look after her? Find her a family."

Miss Bly did not look my way. "In the main part, I'd say yes," she replied. "They are people of good conscience, trying to do the best they can." It was faint praise. I heard her reservation plain and simple. So did Mrs. Harris.

"But?" she asked.

"They will find a home for Dorothy, I have no doubt. A good home. Whether it is the best home…that's a matter of opinion."

"What do you suggest?"

"I have done some work in this area, as you know. There are wealthy families, people with connections, looking to adopt children but reluctant to go through the kind of invasive scrutiny a body like the Society insists upon."

"She should be with a family like that! She's an angel. She deserves the best!"

"I agree." Miss Bly patted Mrs. Harris's hands. "I have tried to put forward more than one family. Details have been lodged with the judge in Dorothy's case. But the legal standing of the Society is so much greater than my own."

"But I trust you! I can't think of anyone better to take care of her. There must be something we can do!"

"Perhaps." Miss Bly shifted in her bed, sitting up straighter against her pillows and brightening. She looked better than she had for her days. "Let's call in my lawyer, today." She turned to me and lifted her eyebrows.

"I will see to it at once," I said.

***

As she had known he would, Miss Bly's lawyer advised Mrs. Harris that her only way to give Miss Bly control over Dorothy's future was to appoint her as the child's guardian. She did so happily. Grace Harris signed an affidavit confirming that Dorothy was of the Protestant faith, made Miss Bly her guardian, and willed to her daughter her only possessions – a battered brown suitcase and one cheap, ten-dollar dress.

Ten days later, Grace Harris died.

Elizabeth
XIV
October 1st, 1887, a Saturday

"I heard you had a difficult day yesterday, Miss Brown," said Dr. Ingram.

"I did. And I am concerned that today will be no better."

"Why do you say so?"

She swallowed. "Miss Tilly Mayard keeps glaring at me. You know what happened?" He nodded. "I do not wish her ill, but she frightens me. What will happen if I have another visitor? What is to stop her from attacking me again? I don't feel safe."

Dr. Ingram put his elbows on the desk and interlaced his fingers. "You did nothing to provoke her?"

"No!"

"What caused it then?"

"She thinks I am stopping her from seeing her family. She thinks all these visitors asking for me have been deceived. She thinks they are her family and that there is a conspiracy to keep her here. A conspiracy led by me!"

"Might any of these visitors have been Tilly's family?"

Elizabeth thought of the man yesterday and gave a hollow laugh. "Definitely not."

"What is it? Why do you say definitely not?"

"It's nothing. I was just thinking of something else. Nothing important." He was frowning at her, but she could not help that. He believed she was mad. What else should he expect? "I have a headache," she said.

"I notice that they gave you a dose last night."

"Was it laudanum? It didn't smell like laudanum."

"It was chloral hydrate. A sedative.

"It doesn't agree with me."

"Why did you need it?"

"I didn't."

"That's not what the doctor's record says. It says here that you thought the building was on fire."

"What if I did? Have you ever thought about a fire here? About what would happen? About how many women would die?"

"What do you mean? The nurses are trained to evacuate the building."

"In the day, perhaps. But what about at night? Think of all those doors to unlock. You are expecting the nurses to put their own lives at risk for a group of patients they despise. Besides, even if they tried, they couldn't open them all in time. If I were a nurse, do you know what I'd do? I'd open the rooms with the most women in and get them out. Why save one woman alone in a room, when you can save six in the same amount of time? Many women would burn to death. Many."

She had the small satisfaction of watching him at a loss for words.

"You should do something about it," she said.

"But what?" He looked truly concerned, and again she thought what a good man he was, what an oasis in a desert of unkindness. "What do you suggest?"

"The locks must be changed," she said. "There is a system that I have seen in some places, where the locks can all be turned at once, using a crank. Locked or unlocked. That gives us some chance of escape. Now there is next to none."

She looked at him, expecting him to approve of her suggestion, but instead he was frowning and opening his folder of papers.

"Nellie Brown. In what institution did you see such a system? You said you saw locks like this. I thought you had never been in an institution before."

He looked truly anxious, bewildered almost, and she hastened to reassure him.

"None. I've been nowhere." She gave a half-laugh. "Unless you count boarding school."

He wasn't amused. "But where did you see these locks then?"

She had seen them on a visit to the new Western Penitentiary in Pittsburgh, on a job assignment from her editor, but the truth would not do. "Oh...somewhere I went once. Only as a visitor, you understand."

"Nellie Brown, there is only one place that I know of with such a locking system, and that is at Sing Sing." He raised his eyebrows, asking a silent question.

"No! I have never been in prison, far less in Sing Sing. Nor have I visited the place ever." She laughed heartily but could see he was far from convinced by her denials. Another long note was entered into her file.

"The best I can do for you is to see if you can be moved to a room with other women. Then you may rest better, less afraid of being left behind during any fire. Not that there will be one, but still, peace of mind is important."

"And what about Tilly Mayard?"

He chewed on his lip a little and then put down his pen. "Miss Mayard requires further evaluation before we decide where she will be best looked after," he said.

"Please don't send her to the Lodge."

"I will not. But I do think that you will both make better progress if you are separated. I will have you moved to Hall 7 this morning."

Nurse Grady took Elizabeth and Anne, whom Dr. Ingram had also reassigned, upstairs, grumbling the whole time about Elizabeth's inability to remember anything about where she came from on the one hand, and her ability to complain to the doctors about every little thing the nurses did on the other. She called her a damned hussy, and said she was glad to see the back of them. Then she stomped off back downstairs.

***

At first glance, Hall 7 proved to be remarkably like Hall 6, not least because the new ward was positioned directly above the old one. But there were subtle differences. There were many more pictures on the wall, attractive landscapes, and a view across the river toward New York. Hall 7 also had a square piano, but an altogether finer instrument with a softer stool and piles of sheet music, suggesting it was in regular use. Elizabeth soon learned that there were four nurses in charge of the ward – odd, given that the patients here were notably less unruly than those downstairs. But although they were less coarse and unnecessarily cruel than their Hall 6 counterparts, small meannesses – name-calling, pinching, and occasional slapping – soon proved to be as much a feature upstairs as they were down below.

The first task of a new patient in Hall 7 was to change clothing. Elizabeth was unimpressed by the pink checked dress she was asked to wear, and said so.

"Look how short it is," she declared to Anne, who was also changing. "I look like a schoolgirl. My mother used to always dress me in pink, but I've never thought it was my best color." She turned to the nurse, a small sandy-haired woman with a plain face and a downturned mouth. "You don't actually expect me to wear this, do you?"

"Where do you think you are, a city café?" the nurse said. "No one cares what a crazy asylum girl looks like."

"Women should always care what they look like," said Elizabeth. "Even here. Perhaps even more, here."

The nurse frowned. "Even more here? Why, I thought you were quite sensible, but it seems you are as silly as the rest."

"Perhaps you could let down the hem?" said Anne. "The bottom of the dress doesn't even reach the top of her boots."

"Let down her hem?" The nurse put her hands on her hips. "What do you take me for? A lady's maid? There are no ladies here and no maids. And the sooner you realize that the better it will be for you both."

She scooped up their discarded dresses and ushered them into Hall 7. There were fewer women in this ward, and a quieter atmosphere reigned. Several were busy sewing, and an older woman with a round face and kindly expression was giving piano lessons. Anne and Elizabeth headed for an empty bench, but the nurse called them back.

"We won't have you two sitting whispering sweet nothings to each other all day, thank you," she said. She pointed to one bench and sent Anne to it, and then pointed to another, as far from the first as it was possible to be.

"What is your name?" asked Elizabeth.

"Nurse Finney." For a moment, the two women looked at each other. Elizabeth had had enough of being pushed about by ignorant women and didn't hide her contempt. Nurse Finney flushed. "Just go and sit down and keep quiet," she said.

In truth, Elizabeth was ready to be quiet for a time. She'd been giddy arriving in Hall 7, happy to be away from Tilly Mayard's staring eyes and the gross cruelty of Grupe, McCarten, and Grady, as well as thankful to have the continued company of Anne. Rain lashed at the windows. It was the first of October. She wondered how many of the women in the room were even aware of the date. It was only too easy to lose track in such a place. The routine was intended to keep the patients orderly and calm, of course, but the monotony dulled their wits. It was happening to her. She imagined a piece of paper, beginning to blacken and curl when held too near a flame. Her mind felt like that. Imperiled. Fragile. Precious. She knew she should be talking to the patients and gathering their stories. She tried to look around at the women and interest herself in her surroundings. Perhaps it was the chloral they had given her. Perhaps it was thinking again and again about Tilly and how quickly she had changed. Perhaps it was tiredness, or just the constant, constant rain at the windows. Elizabeth was never cast down. She never lacked energy. She always had drive. But not today. She spent her first afternoon in Hall 7 speaking to no one and staring at the floor. She looked every bit as mad as any other woman in the ward, and she knew it. She just didn't care.

The women on Hall 7 ate in a different room than those of Hall 6 – a larger room, shared with the women of Hall 8, who looked to Elizabeth's jaded eyes just as miserable and anonymous as the women in every other part of the building. The food was as unpalatable as ever, and Elizabeth did not even have the pleasure of sitting with Anne. She suspected Nurse Finney had spread the word among the nurses that she and Anne should not be together. True or not, the fact was that Anne was sitting again as far from Elizabeth as possible, and was in deep conversation with a tall, somber-looking woman who Elizabeth noticed leading a long prayer at her table before anyone began to eat.

The trouble began when the women were ordered to retire to bed. The night nurse for Hall 7, Nurse Conway, was a large-boned, grey-haired woman with ruddy cheeks and nose. A drinker, Elizabeth thought, something of her normal curiosity returning. Nurse Conway directed the women into the hallway and shoved them, sometimes bodily, toward different doorways, much as a farmer might order his dairy cows to be milked. Elizabeth saw once again that her friend was nowhere nearby, but found herself next to the woman who had been with Anne at dinner.

"I saw you with my friend, Anne Neville, earlier," she said. "My name is Nellie Brown."

"Miss Doyle." The woman had a faint Irish lilt to her voice but none of the friendliness Elizabeth associated with most Irish men and women she had met.

"Miss Neville and I have been together since we were at Bellevue," Elizabeth said. "I had hoped we might share a room."

"You would do better praying for your salvation," said Miss Doyle.

Elizabeth's eyebrows shot up, but she had no time to respond as Nurse Conway was barking out orders. All around her, the women started taking off their clothes.

"What is this?" she asked. "What are you doing?" No one answered her, and so she crossed the corridor to speak to Nurse Conway herself. "Why are these women undressing in a public space? I want to undress in my room!"

Nurse Conway, busy sorting through a pile of cotton

nightgowns, barely lifted her eyes from her task. "You will do as the others do or you'll be sorry. Get yourself back where you are supposed to be and strip."

Elizabeth looked down the corridor. There were up to twenty women in various states of undress, folding their clothes, even taking off their undergarments and standing shivering and naked in groups outside each doorway. It was degrading. It was unnecessary. Her face colored. Even as she recognized it as a tactic to suppress, as another way to take the patients' dignity, their individuality and their self-respect, she knew she had to succumb to it. Naked, they were all the same, all of them: young; sick; bent; dark-skinned or pale; skinny or plump. She didn't want to look, but there was no way of not seeing what was before her.

"They will stand there naked until you join them," said Nurse Conway.

Elizabeth walked back to the door and undressed. Nurse Conway stood watching. All the women stood watching. Only when she was as naked and cold as the rest of them, did the nurse finally begin handing round nightgowns.

"See how your vanity costs us all our dignity?" hissed Miss Doyle in her ear.

"What?" Elizabeth's face burned, and her eyes were on the floor as she waited for a gown. "My vanity? You know nothing of me."

"I know enough. Miss Neville has told me."

"She would not speak badly of me. You are lying."

"I am a daughter of God. I do not lie. I will pray for you. I will pray for you all night."

"I won't sleep in this room with this woman," declared Elizabeth as she struggled into her nightgown. "I will sleep on this corridor first!"

Nurse Conway stopped in her tracks and turned back. She looked Elizabeth up and down, pulling in her lips and making her chin bulge. She looked cross for a moment and then amused. She called across the hallway. "Brooks. You can exchange rooms with Brown." Then she turned her back and moved on.

Elizabeth gave Miss Doyle a parting glare and crossed to her new doorway, following six other women inside. Nurse Conway's smile made her suspicious but at this point, anywhere far away from Miss Doyle seemed like a good place to be. This was the first night she had spent in a room with someone else since Ruth Caine in the home on Second Avenue. That seemed an age ago now. She hung back while the other women lay down, waiting to see which bed they left for her. Of course, it was the one nearest the door, the one where she would be the most disturbed by the night nurse doing her checks.

She sighed and laid down. She didn't plan to draw any more attention to herself tonight. The chloral experience wasn't something she cared to repeat, but it was not long until she wondered if chloral was not exactly what she needed.

Four of the women settled down to sleep very quickly, but the other two did not. One, young and painfully thin, lay shivering and moaning, complaining that her face was cold, that her hands were like ice, that her feet hurt, that her head hurt. There was soon no part of her body that she had not listed in her wailing. She fell silent for the odd moment and Elizabeth hoped it was over, only to be disappointed when she started up again, listing the same complaints time and time again. Elizabeth could not settle. She sat up against the wall with her knees pulled up and peered around in the small amount of light that slid in under the door from the hallway. The woman in the bed nearest her, on the other side of the door, seemed to sleep. Although she twitched and thrashed, her head never left her pillow. The other five beds were lined up across from them, under a high window. In the two directly opposite Elizabeth, the women were asleep, or at least pretending to be. The woman suffering from the cold was next to them, under the window. Elizabeth could see her squirm and shift as she tried to get warm. The beds in the far corner were harder to see in the dark. As her eyes adjusted to the light, she stared over. Gradually she could make out the woman in one of them. She was sitting, exactly as Elizabeth was, with her back against the wall and her knees pulled up.

Slowly, Elizabeth slid down her narrow bed and turned on her side, facing the sitting woman. She could still see her, even when lying down, and she concentrated on keeping her breathing steady. There was no reason to panic. She probably looked just as threatening from a distance. The woman would lie down any moment.

She did not.

As Elizabeth watched, the other woman peeled back her covers and put her feet on the floor. Bent over like an old crone, the woman started moving about the room, in and out between beds and then over to the door.

"Where are you, bitch?" she whispered. "Are you in here? I think you are."

Elizabeth watched in horror as the woman bent over each bed in turn.

"When I find you, I'm going to hurt you," she said now, turning Elizabeth's way and sniffing the air like a dog chasing a scent.

Elizabeth closed her eyes.

"Bitch? Can you hear me, bitch?" The woman was close now. Elizabeth was sure she was leaning over her, and she stilled every muscle, desperate to keep her breathing steady and slow. A smell washed over her, a smell of stale breath.

"You know I want you," came the whisper. "I'm looking for you, bitch. Don't you worry. I'm looking."

The smell and the sound moved away.

Elizabeth opened her eyes and saw only blackness.

The woman on the other bed began wailing again about her cold fingers and the pains in her legs. The creeping woman completed a circuit of the room and continued her threatening whispers and strange and angry search.

Elizabeth found herself praying after all.

XV
October 2nd, 1887, a Sunday

"I was hoping I could have my notebook," she said.

"Notebook?" Dr. Ingram looked up from his papers.

"When I arrived in Hall 6, I had a notebook and a pen. Nurse Grady took them from me. I'd like them back. I thought I might try and write things down. That it might help."

She had planned to say the notebook might help her remember where she came from, but it was difficult to lie to Ingram. She dealt with the other doctors differently. She refused to speak to Dr. Caldwell of Hall 7 in any language but Spanish, and Dr. Dent, since his assault on Tilly, she didn't speak to at all.

"I will see what I can do. How did you find sleeping in a shared room? Did that calm your fears of a fire?"

"It did." She opened her mouth to describe the events of the previous night but shut it again without saying a word. If he asked for her to be moved, she was sure he would hear that she had already insisted on being moved away from Miss Doyle. It was a story he could live without hearing. Tomorrow was Monday. She was convinced that she'd be released. The last thing she needed was another set of nurses complaining about her.

"How is Tilly?"

"I can't discuss another patient with you."

"Can you tell me that she is no worse, at least?"

He smiled at her. "Your concern does you credit. Yes, I can tell you that much."

This room was the mirror of the doctor's room downstairs, but with the advantage of height, it held a view of the East River and the buildings of New York. She gazed across.

"Do many women leave here? So many of the women I've met simply long to be released."

"Many do, Miss Brown. Many. I think you might be pleasantly surprised."

"Will Mrs. Cotter?"

"I've just said I can't discuss other patients."

"Hypothetically then."

He smiled again. "Hypothetically. Another unusual word choice for a Cuban girl."

"Maybe there is more to me than meets the eye." She smiled.

"I think that's already well established."

They gazed at each other for a moment and Elizabeth struggled to remember where she had been driving the conversation. She forced herself to focus.

"Let me give you an example then," she said, "of a story a patient told me this morning. She is a pretty woman, with fine features and good skin. She's not tall. Certainly shorter than I am. I'd call her lady-like, perhaps delicate. She looks remarkably like Mrs. Cotter, in fact. Although of course, she is not her, or we could not discuss her case."

"As you say. We could not. But this unknown woman? What is her story?" He sat back with his arms folded, smiling at her once again.

"She came here because she wasn't coping at home. She had a breakdown, she does not deny it. She believed she was in danger of being murdered in her own home. She couldn't sleep. She told me she got up in the night and checked all the windows and doors were locked. Then she would lie down and be still for a little while, but the sensation always returned and she was up and checking every window and door all over again, even though she'd already done so. One night, her husband tried to stop her. When he put his hands on her shoulders to guide her back to bed, she attacked him. She scratched his face. He wasn't rough with her and she loves him, yet she lost all self-control. She agreed to see a doctor. And the doctor sent her here."

"Such experiences are not uncommon. Rest and routine will

often help a troubled mind greatly. If she is able to be rational, there's no reason why she will not be sent home in time."

Again, he smiled. Elizabeth was reluctant to pursue the story, for what she had to say next might not please him, but Mrs. Cotter had described experiences to Elizabeth that she could not in all conscience ignore. She needed to know if what the woman had told her earlier that day was true. And if it was, was Dr. Ingram aware of it?

"Why might a woman be sent to the Retreat?" she asked. He frowned but answered quickly enough.

"The Retreat and the Lodge are two wards for patients who we consider to be a danger to themselves or others. There are more nurses in those wards, and fewer patients. We are better able to take care of some women in more supervised conditions."

"The woman I was describing, she told me that one day when she was walking with the women of her hall, as is customary, she saw a man that she believed was her husband. She left her place and ran to him. That got her sent to the Retreat."

Elizabeth looked at Ingram. His face was unreadable.

"Her treatment there has ruined her health," she continued. "She cried and complained, and was beaten with a broom handle for her trouble. She showed me a dent in the back of her head. She said they tied her hands and feet and threw a sheet over her head, twisting it about her throat. She said they put her, like that, in a bath of cold water and held her under. She thought she was going to die." Elizabeth paused. "I thought perhaps it was not all true."

"If it is true, I was not aware of it."

"She said they pulled her hair out at the roots. There are patches where it has not grown back."

He sighed audibly. "We often see patients here who are suffering from hair loss. There may be other medical reasons that account for any bare spots you were shown."

"But she may also be telling the truth."

"She may. I really can't discuss it any further." He looked acutely uncomfortable.

She wanted to reassure him, but the woman's story had been wholly convincing.

"She told me, this woman, that when her husband visited and saw the condition she was in, he insisted she was removed from the Retreat. If not, he threatened to go the papers. After that, she was brought to Hall 7. Might not something like that be in her records?"

"There is nothing like that in her records."

His troubled expression made her feel guilty. "I'm sorry," she said.

That got his attention. "Sorry, Miss Brown? Don't be sorry. This is a hard place, and not everything that happens here is either known to the doctors or approved by them."

"And yet someone heard the husband's complaint and moved the woman."

"Allegedly."

"That is true."

Ingram got to his feet and walked to the door. He held it open for her, smiling politely yet making it clear that their conversation was over. Without forethought, she squeezed his arm on her way out.

"I do not suppose that you are involved in any wrongdoing in the place, I hope you know that. You are the finest of all the doctors I have encountered. Easily the finest."

He was taller than her. She looked up, saw surprise in his face and dropped her head before he could see her face redden.

She walked away, but not before she heard him say, "And you, Miss Brown, are the most unusual of patients."

***

Setting aside Miss Doyle and her appropriation of Anne Neville, Elizabeth found Hall 7 vastly more pleasant than Hall 6. She made sure to keep her distance from the woman who had prowled their bedroom all night, and to be fair, the woman showed no sign of madness during the day but sat quietly sewing near the piano. Patients deemed to have been well behaved during the week were allowed to leave for an hour or so to attend a church service. There were also more visitors allowed, and not only visitors wishing to inspect the pretty Cuban girl who had lost her trunks. Here there were visitors for other patients, concerned family members allowed to spend time in the hall itself, giving Elizabeth hope that for some women, the Blackwell's Island Insane Asylum was a place to get well, rather than a prison by any other name.

One woman arrived to visit her sister and held in her arms a baby, only a few months old. She had the exhausted look of so many mothers of newborns, with the added concern for her sister, and so the woman was more than happy to hand off the child to a sensible-seeming patient who said she missed her own children and wanted to tend to the baby. The sisters talked while the other woman walked up and down the ward, rocking the baby and singing him songs. But when the visit came to an end, everything went awry. The patient did not want to hand back the child. Nurse Finney and two other nurses had to force her to give him up to his mother. Both sisters were in tears. The patient grew hysterical after the child and his mother hurried out. Her crying seemed to infect the other patients. Other mothers remembered how long it was since they had seen their children. Several younger women began to wail that they would never be mothers, because they would never escape the asylum. The noise and commotion upset everyone else and soon there were women screaming at each other to be silent, and the nurses' slaps and threats were not enough. It took the arrival of Dr. Dent and Dr. Caldwell to bring the situation back under control.

Elizabeth sat back from it all, watching closely how the hysteria spread through the women.

"You don't want children yourself, then?" asked the woman next to her.

"I hardly know. I have not thought of it."

"That's hard to believe, if you don't mind me saying. Most women your age have at least an idea about it. Isn't it what young girls dream of? Husbands? Children?"

Elizabeth looked at the woman. She was heavy-set, with a square jawline and a low hairline, which would look better if she wore bangs. Her lips were cracked and dry, but her eyes were bright, and she sounded quite rational.

"Do you have those things? A husband? A child?" she asked.

"I do not. Nor will I. My past, present, and future are all here. In this hall. If I am lucky."

"If you are *lucky*?"

"This is the best berth in the place. And I should know."

"How do you know?"

"I've been in them all, the best and the worst."

"The worst?"

"I began in Hall 6, as we all do. But I did not get on well with Nurse Grady. She took a dislike to me, fellow Irishwoman though I am. Let's just say I gave as good as I got and leave it at that. She had me sent to the Retreat."

Elizabeth turned. "I have heard terrible things. I heard they half-drown people."

"All true." The Irishwoman leaned back on her bench and crossed her legs at the ankle. She could have been talking about anything from baking to the weather. Her air of calm made what she had to say even more alarming. "I was on the 'rope-gang' in the Retreat, tied up to lunatics from morning till night. When I complained, I was beaten and pulled across the room by the hair. They covered my face and held me under water until I choked. The nurses stationed a patient on watch, so they knew when the doctors were coming. No one dared tell on them. We believed they'd kill us if we did. One day, I broke a window."

"What happened?"

"They sent me to the Lodge."

"I am almost afraid to ask what it is like."

"Worse than you can imagine. The women there are too violent to be touched. The nurses are afraid. They can't wash the patients, so they never bathe. The stink is unimaginable. The women won't clean up after themselves and the nurses do not care. In summer, the heat, the smell, and the flies are unbearable. I fought it and they broke my ribs. Then one day, a pretty girl was brought in. She was a fighter, though. And what language! She drove the nurses wild with her cursing. They beat her, held her down in a cold bath until she nearly drowned, and then left her naked on a bed for the night. In the morning, she was dead. That took the fight from me. That beat me down. I worked hard to be allowed to come here. It is the best I can get."

Elizabeth found the story all too believable. "But you don't hope for release?" Elizabeth pointed at a girl on the other side of the room, the one who had cried in her bed all night. "That girl there, she told me this morning she dreamed of her mother last night. She thinks it is a sign, and believes her mother will come for her sometime today."

"She has had that dream every night for months. No one comes. She has been here at least four years."

"Four years!"

"There comes a point when it is harder to leave than to stay."

"I don't believe it."

"Give it time. You can believe anything, given time."

The woman fell silent, and Elizabeth thought over all she had said. The idea of either the Lodge or the Retreat terrified her. She believed herself to be brave, she prided herself on it even, but here was her limit. The thought of another night in a room being stalked by a madwoman was bad enough. Her reports on those two wards could not be eye-witness accounts. And besides. Tomorrow was Monday. Her time here was nearly up. She wanted out.

Beatrice

December 1920

Ernest did not take the news of Miss Bly's legal involvement with Dorothy Harris well.

Her case had finally come before Judge Levy again. Miss Bly and her lawyer appeared in court on Dorothy's behalf, providing the affidavit where Grace Harris confirmed her daughter was a Protestant. The Society's first point of action was to find a different orphanage to house the child, but when Miss Bly approached Ernest on the steps of the courthouse to discuss options, he was tight-lipped.

"The Society will determine a suitable new home for the young girl and transfer her immediately, Miss Bly," he said. I was right behind her, but he did not so much as glance my way. "If you wish to maintain contact with the girl and her case, you have the telephone numbers you need, I believe. My staff will be able to advise you of Dorothy's whereabouts when her move is complete."

Miss Bly's jaw stiffened and her eyebrows rose. "I had rather thought we might meet and discuss Dorothy's options. I want her in an institution for as little time as possible."

"What you want, and what is in Dorothy's best interests, are not necessarily one and the same."

She drew in a sharp breath.

"That's not fair!" I said, but he continued to ignore me, and Miss Bly held up her hand to stop me from saying more.

"I will not debate the point in the middle of the street, Mr. Coulter," she said. "But we will most certainly discuss Dorothy's case further. Either in person, or through our lawyers."

She turned on her heel and marched away. I gave him a moment to look at me and say something.

Nothing.

He put his hands behind his back and stared off across the street.

What could I do? I stamped my foot in frustration with him and then, of course, I followed Miss Bly.

"He reminds me of someone," she said much later on, when we were back in the McAlpin and after she had disappeared into her room for an hour or two. She handed me the pale beige folder that always contained the next chapter of "Elizabeth's" story and made a point of raising her eyebrows. She was gone again before I had the chance to speak.

She could only have meant Ernest. Ernest Coulter and Frank Ingram. But what was I supposed to make of the comparison?

Elizabeth
XVI
October 3rd, 1887, a Monday

Finally, the weather improved. Elizabeth took it as a good omen and after breakfast positioned herself by a window, watching the boat traffic on the East River, assuring herself that one of those vessels was bound to bring her rescue. By mid-morning, no one had come, but her natural optimism kept her buoyed-up and expectant. When the women were told they were taking their first walk in days, Elizabeth rushed to Anne to try and secure some time with her friend. All the previous day, Anne had spent with Miss Doyle, but with the tall woman distracted by a nurse, Elizabeth hoped to get Anne to herself, perhaps for this one last time.

It was not to be.

"Brown. Go and stand by the piano."

"Why should I?"

"Because I am telling you to," came the answer.

"But I want to walk with Miss Neville."

"I want doesn't get."

After another night locked up with six crazy women and barely able to sleep, Elizabeth had no patience for the nurse's rudeness.

"I am not a child and don't need to be spoken to in such a manner. In Hall 6, we walked with whomever we liked. You are simply being unkind."

"We do things differently here," said another nurse, called Kroener. "We like our ladies to look their best when outdoors. We pair you according to your dress."

"You are not serious?" Elizabeth did not hide her disgust.

"I am entirely serious, and you will do as you are told or

you will not walk. Your dress is dark pink, Miss Neville's is much paler. You will not be walking together while you remain in this hall."

With two frowning nurses standing before her, Elizabeth had no choice. More than she wanted to be with Anne, she desperately longed for fresh air. She took her place in the line without further argument, but her anger festered.

She found herself paired with Bridget McGuiness, the Irishwoman she had spoken to the day before, and the pair fulminated together over the indignities of asylum life.

"Imagine thinking that by walking in matching shades of dress, they add to their reputation for running the best hall," announced Elizabeth loudly as Nurse Finney walked near them. They were outside by now, turning past the end of the asylum building and taking the pathway running south, so near to East River and New York that Elizabeth had the mad thought that if she just dived in, she could swim her way to freedom.

"What fools these nurses are," she declared.

"Shut up, Brown," said Nurse Finney.

"Or what?"

"Nurse Kroener!" Nurse Finney called to the senior nurse at the back of the line and grabbed Elizabeth's arm, forcing her and the women behind her to stop.

"Get your hands off me!"

Nurse Kroener steamed up and pointed her finger in Elizabeth's face. "Enough of this nonsense, Brown. Walk quietly or you will walk with me instead."

"You can't make me!"

"Can't I?"

"No!" Elizabeth snapped. She seized Nurse Finney and pulled her arms behind her, pinning the nurse in front of her own body and holding her tight. "See!" She held fast, even as Nurse Kroener tried to pull her arms and free Nurse Finney. "Don't think I'm afraid of you," she spat at them. "Try and beat me and I'll beat you instead. Try it. You are no match for me."

"You are one, Brown, and we are many." Nurse Kroener's

face was red. She couldn't get Elizabeth to let go of Nurse Finney, but she still could threaten. "Let go and walk properly or it will be the Lodge for you. Do you hear me?"

"Let her go, Nellie Brown. Sweet Jesus, girl, it's not worth time in the Lodge!" Bridget implored Elizabeth with her eyes.

Elizabeth's temper fizzled away. She let go of Nurse Finney but wanted the last word. "Touch me and I'll jump in," she said, nodding her head toward the brown, grey water behind them. Wind blew around them, whipping up fallen leaves.

"You'd die of cold and drown," said Nurse Finney.

"Not a chance. I'm an excellent swimmer. Before you knew it, I'd be in New York and you'd never see Nellie Brown again."

"Ladies!" From the top of the line, another nurse called, anxious to get the walk back into progress.

"Just behave yourself, Brown," hissed Nurse Kroener. "Or I'll tell the doctors you are suicidal, and what will they do with you then?"

Elizabeth opened her mouth to retort, but Bridget shook her head and she thought better of it. She stepped back into line and they moved on.

***

Later, she saw Miss Doyle and Anne clearly talking about her. Anne's head was down, but Miss Doyle stared over at Elizabeth as she dripped her poison into Anne's ear. At lunch they sat together, their heads bowed in prayer again before eating. Elizabeth saw Anne smile at her new friend, and her heart sank. She had arrived on the Island confident that in Tilly and Anne she had two sane companions to help her face whatever the asylum threw at her. Now, neither wanted anything to do with her. Tiredness made her head ache. Her actions earlier, on the walk, seemed outlandish and frightening in retrospect. What had she been thinking? She spent the afternoon alone, waiting for word of her release, imagining what form it might take. But no one came for her.

In the evening, the piano was in full use. Miss Matilda

Morgan, a patient who had previously worked in a music store, held a recital with the patients she had been teaching to play and sing. Several doctors attended, including Dr. Caldwell and Dr. Ingram. Elizabeth stayed away from the crowd around the piano, too dull and too anxious to join in. One woman, a Polish girl called Wanda, sang beautifully, but to Elizabeth it was painful and unnatural, like a canary in a cage singing for its supper.

After the singing ended, Miss Matilda offered to play a waltz or two for anyone who wished to dance. Elizabeth watched Dr. Ingram dance with poor Mrs. Cotter, and wondered if he singled the woman out because of the conversation they'd had about her the day before. She hoped for a moment that he might ask her to dance. Was he looking for her as he stepped and turned, moving up the hall so gracefully? She looked at his face and saw only goodness in it as he talked and danced with Mrs. Cotter. It was impossible not to be drawn to him. But next he chose to dance with the girl who dreamed of her mother coming to collect her and waited in vain every day. Elizabeth experienced a pang of something she didn't want to call jealousy. To be jealous of a mad girl? That way madness lay.

She sat up straight and turned her eyes away, watching instead the antics of a stout middle-aged woman who sat every day holding a piece of newspaper and reciting stories and plays as if from the paper before her but obviously from some vault of memory.

Elizabeth listened to the words but still heard the music stop. She kept her gaze on the woman telling stories, reluctant to watch the doctor's choice fall elsewhere.

"Miss Brown, would you care to dance?" His voice was light. Her ears grew hot.

"I should like that very much, Dr. Ingram," she managed to say.

It was only a dance, she thought later.
Only a dance.

XVII
October 4th, 1887, a Tuesday

On her ninth day in the Blackwell's Island Insane Asylum, a baby was born.

The women were in the basement eating bread without butter and trying to cut fist-sized lumps of tough beef with their spoons. Elizabeth sat with a quiet Mexican woman whose broad white smile and gentle manner comforted her. Elizabeth's knowledge of Spanish meant they could talk to each other, even if only in the most superficial fashion.

It started with a weak cry. The women nearest the door heard it first, and a whisper ran along the benches, like the wind rippling a still pond. Complete silence fell in the room. The nurses stopped what they were doing and gazed at each other. The cry came again. One of the nurses went to the door and looked out. With the door open, there could be no mistake. There was a baby crying in the hallway.

"It cannot be a visitor's. It's too early in the day." The whispers grew louder now, the women turning to one another and sharing their common thoughts.

"No one is here except patients and nurses."

"It sounds like a newborn."

"Whose can it be?"

"It can't be a newborn. The doctors must have known."

But the doctors had not known; that became apparent as the day progressed. The crying lasted only a few minutes before the child was taken elsewhere, but the women of Halls 7 and 8 had all heard it. There was something primal in it, Elizabeth thought. Women who were normally dull and vacant shook themselves alert. Chatterers stopped their chatter. The fog that clouded so many minds suddenly lifted. Anger, disgust, and concern brought a collective clarity and a need for answers, and the women refused to settle again.

Talk of the baby overtook everything while the women were outside on their walk. Was there anyone missing? If a patient had given birth this morning, she could not be walking now, surely. Who was not where they were supposed to be? Different names were bandied around; no one Elizabeth had heard of. She was paired again with Bridget, who doubted any patient was involved.

"It's a nurse," she said. "I'd bet my life on it. I've seen this kind of thing. A stupid girl, taken advantage of by some man – by some boy even, sometimes. She barely knows she has done the deed, she doesn't understand the changes in her body. She puts on weight. No one cares about her. No one notices. And then the baby. Somewhere around here there is likely a baby without a mother, and a mother in a state of shock." She shook her head.

Elizabeth looked at the asylum. It looked so clean and sterile. The walls were smooth, dappled grey, almost marbled-looking. It appeared stately and honorable, perched on the narrow tip of the Island, surrounded by manicured lawns, neat walkways and trees, in sight of a somber lighthouse that guided boats through the rocks in the East River. What rottenness lay inside.

Dr. Dent arrived in Hall 7 after the women returned from their walk. Several women were on their feet at once, clamoring for information. He was angry, although trying to hide it, smiling through gritted teeth, holding up his hands, swallowing rapidly. He claimed the noise had not been that of a child at all, but of a young patient weeping uncontrollably. The women would have none of it. One laughed in his face. He made a show of retrieving some papers from the office at the end of the hall and quickly left. For once the nurses were on the side of the patients, not the doctors. Nurse Finney had heard that a patient from Hall 4 was missing and stood gossiping with a group of patients as though they were neighbors in a New York tenement, rather than staff and patients in an asylum. But then the woman who had been hysterical two days before over the visitor's child leapt to her feet.

"What about the child, you stupid bitches!" she screamed, climbing on a bench, her face a mess of snot and tears. "Where is the baby? They have taken it and killed it! That's why we can't hear it anymore! It's dead. Murdered!"

Two nurses laid hands on the woman and dragged her from the room. Nurse Finney laughed and then put her hand over her mouth. Elizabeth went up to her.

"You should find out what they did with the baby," she said quietly. "Find out where the baby is and where the mother is. If it is possible, they should be helped to stay together. If you have any decency, or humanity, you will do this."

Nurse Finney turned and glared. "If the child belongs to one of your lot, then it is better off dead."

Elizabeth frowned at her. "If you believe that statement, then you are more lost than I imagined. Dr. Ingram at least will see that both are looked after properly."

But that set Nurse Finney laughing. "Miss Brown is sweet on Dr. Ingram," she said, looking her up and down and smirking. "Nurse Kroener!" She turned her back on Elizabeth and walked away toward her fellow nurse. "Another one in love with Dr. Ingram," she declared loudly. "If I had a dollar for every patient in love with Frank Ingram, I'd be rich woman and retired from this hell-hole, that's for certain!"

Elizabeth shrugged off the insults and went to listen to Miss Matilda teaching the piano. The sound of the baby crying, coupled with yesterday's visit from a mother, had certainly upset a large number of women. Most affected were those with their own children, but some younger girls cried all afternoon about never having children of their own. Elizabeth thought of Tilly Mayard downstairs somewhere – she would almost certainly not be released. Family, children, a home; all of these things, out of her reach now. She glanced over at Anne, deep in prayer with Miss Doyle. She hoped all this godliness was giving Anne some peace of mind at least, even though she still felt her defection keenly. Anne would make a wonderful mother. If she had the opportunity, that was.

Her thoughts circled back to herself. What was in her future? What did she hope for beyond her immediate desire to be rescued by *The World*? She was ambitious, but then she needed to be. Her family depended on her. But would there be marriage in her future? Children? It was hard to say.

Dr. Ingram's face swam into her mind, and along with it, Nurse Finney's laughter. Elizabeth half-smiled to herself. The nurse, callous and hard-hearted though she was, was right to scorn the idea of a doctor and patient falling in love. He saw her as an interesting patient, little more. Did she find him attractive? Of course she did. But she was still herself enough to realize that the asylum was not like the real world. In the real world, where she was Nellie Bly, she and Ingram had nothing in common. Except perhaps a bent toward honesty. That was something they shared. Yet what must he think of her honesty when he found out she was a journalist? Anyway, no doctor wanted a wife like her. And being a wife had not served her mother.

Elizabeth was not a creature of introspection. It was self-indulgent. Time-wasting. A form of narcissism, that she claimed to despise. But the thought of the squalling infant weighed on her. She was struck by the unfairness of it all and the terrible start to the child's life this was – if it still even lived at all. Being in the asylum weighed on her. The future, her work, her family responsibilities; her thoughts became heavy, physical weights on her shoulders. Where were the baby and its poor mother? She was powerless to find out. Her words about Ingram to Nurse Finney had been fine and brave but she doubted he would tell her a thing about it, even supposing he knew. She was tired. Disgusted by the world. Defeated.

"What is wrong, dear?" Elizabeth looked up as a woman sat down next to her, the older woman, Mrs. Rebecca Farron, who recited stories all day long. She had long, white hair that seemed to float around her soft face; a face for baking and knitting, or sitting reading to a grandchild before tucking them up for the night. A kind face. Elizabeth's shoulders relaxed.

"I am thinking too much, I expect," she said with a half-smile. "I'm not used to so little occupation. I'm dwelling on things. It's silly, really."

"Never call yourself silly, my dear. There will always be others ready to do that for you. Believe in yourself. Nothing that troubles you is unimportant."

"Do you really think that?"

"Of course I do."

"How do *you* cope with your troubles?"

"With my stories. My troubles are simple, though. I am safe here. A little cold, a little underfed, but safe. I have no family left. No one needs me. My greatest trouble is passing the time with no books to read. That is all. So, I remember stories instead. I tell them to myself and to anyone who cares to listen."

"You're not insane?"

"Insane?" Mrs. Farron smiled. "Who is to say what I am? I'm alive. I'm not unhappy. I don't want to leave here. Maybe that means I am insane." She gave a gentle laugh. "But I can keep a secret." She tilted her head and lifted her eyebrows. "Why don't you tell me your story?"

To even think about telling this woman about herself was madness. She knew that. But who could say who was mad and who was sane? She had already been wrong about that, very wrong. Perhaps she was going mad, too. Why not? After nine days locked up, short of food and sleep, afraid of the future, shaken by this unknown child and mother, Elizabeth could imagine going mad. It might be easier to be crazy than stay sane. But to confide in this woman? Madness.

And yet. Where was the harm? She was simply one mad woman confiding in another. Elizabeth moved closer to Rebecca Farron and began to talk.

"I am not what I seem to be," she began, hearing how crazed she sounded but plowing ahead regardless. "I am a writer. My name is Elizabeth Cochrane. I pretended to be mad so that I could live here among the mad and then write about it for *The World*." She wanted to giggle. It was preposterous.

This woman could tell the whole room that Nellie Brown was really an undercover reporter, and not one of them would believe her.

"I had to take the assignment. My mother and brothers live in Pittsburgh. Money is tight. My brother Albert is a wastrel. There, I've said it. He can't hold down a job to save his life. Thank goodness, he and his wife have had no children yet. Charles and his wife have a son. They get by. And my younger sister Kate has a daughter. Her husband, though? I cannot warm to him. My brother Harry is too young to earn much yet. And then there is Mother. She has no one to look after her but me."

"She can't look after herself?"

"Oh no, she can. Well, at least in some ways. Just not in others. It's a long story."

"I love a long story."

Elizabeth took a deep breath. "I love my mother. I truly do. But I think, sometimes, that she let us down. Not deliberately. She made some poor decisions."

"A good story has a beginning, a middle, and end. You sound like you're making a list, not telling a story."

Elizabeth smiled. "I'm a reporter, not a novelist."

"At least try. I'm not in a rush." She patted Elizabeth's hand.

"I'll try." She thought for a moment or two and then began again. "Mary Jane Kennedy was born in Somerset, Pennsylvania, in 1828. How is that for a beginning?"

"Better. Now add some detail."

"She came from a good family and grew up to be an attractive young woman. She enjoyed reading and sewing. She always looked neat as a pin. Does she sound dull?"

"A little. But we are early in the tale. She may develop."

"She does. In her early twenties, she was married to a man name Cummings. They weren't blessed with children, but it is believed that they loved each other dearly."

"Only believed?"

"She does not talk of him. He died when she was twenty-eight, but I don't know how. Would you wish for me to make something up?"

"No, no. If he is dead in the story, he is dead. I'm done with him. What happened next?"

"She returned to live with her parents. Mr. Cummings had left a little money, but not much. Mary Jane wanted her own household. And children. She needed to marry again. In due course, she was drawn to a man, Judge Cochran – an upstanding member of Armstrong County society, and recently widowed. He had ten children from his marriage, six of whom were still at home and one – Mildred, aged only seven – vastly in need of a new mother. Mary Jane was a natural fit with the younger children, although some of the older Cochran children were less than impressed. Their father was nearly fifty yet here he was hitching himself to a woman almost twenty years his junior, a woman who was soon pregnant with the first of her five children."

"That was Albert? The wastrel?"

"Yes, it was." Elizabeth found herself chuckling. "His mother loves him, though. In her way, she loves us all. But back to the story. The marriage was a happy one. Judge Cochran was a successful man and an industrious one. The family was touched by the Civil War – what family was not? – but the older sons, who fought for the Union, came home safe and sound. Mary Jane had another son, and then a daughter Elizabeth. Everyone called her Pink."

"Pink? And this is you, is it? This Pink?"

"It is. Everyone called her Pink in the family because her mother dressed her so particularly finely. She wore pink dresses instead of grey or brown, and white stockings instead of black. She still likes fine clothes. Although she lacks the resources to purchase as many as she wants."

Mrs. Farron's lips twitched in amusement.

"The family continued to grow," said Elizabeth. "Kate was born two years later, and Harry followed – when Pink was nearly six. She doted on her younger siblings, preferring them to Albert and Charles, and was always happiest when in her mother's company. Mary Jane was content. They moved to a fine new house in Apollo. Mildred, all grown up now and married, lived nearby."

"I sense a turning point. All this happiness. It's not good story material. What happened next?"

"Judge Cochran died. It was sudden. Wholly unexpected." Elizabeth paused as tears threatened. She had only been six years old. Her memory of the event was vague, but her sorrow had been fixed and real. "He was not a young man, but he was healthy and fit. Mary Jane was devastated. Harry was only a few months old. The judge had not written a will."

"Ah. Money troubles. Good. You can't give your characters too easy a time of things."

"I won't, don't worry! This was just the beginning. The judge's sons from his first marriage petitioned to have lawyers decide how the estate should be shared. Everything had to be accounted for. The beautiful house, the family mill – all was sold. Mary Jane received a widow's third, and moved with her young children into a much smaller house and tried to live in a much smaller way. She did not find it easy."

"I imagine it was extremely difficult. Let me guess. She married again?"

"Three years later." It was interesting, telling her mother's story this way. How old had Mary Jane been when she remarried? In her early forties. Elizabeth struggled to imagine herself in twenty years' time, in her mother's shoes. "She married a man called John Jackson Ford. It was a mistake."

"He was cruel?"

"Cruel. Drunken. Angry. She tried to tell us it was the war that made him so. That he had nightmares. It may even have been true. Of course, he moved into our home and changed everything. He took her over. He took everything over. They had not been married long – I don't remember exactly – I heard them arguing one evening and crept downstairs. He was ranting. Staggering. But able enough to grab her by the neck and try to choke her."

"That's a terrible sight for any child. How old were you?"

"Nine. Perhaps ten. I still dream of it."

"And then?"

"Difficult years. Arguments. Food thrown. Broken plates.

Foul language. Tears. Money was tight. They opened a grocery store for a time. Mama made ice cream. Albert tried to help. More arguments followed. Ford hated Albert, and Albert hated him. He shoved his gun in Albert's face one night."

"What happened after that?"

"Nothing. Albert left home for a while. But he came back again soon enough. Are you ready for the ending?"

"I'm not sure I'm ever ready for a story to end."

"Let's not think of it as an ending then. Perhaps it is only the end of the beginning."

"I like that idea." Mrs. Farron nodded.

"Things came to a head one New Year. Ten, no, nine years ago now. I was at least thirteen by then. Mother had taken us all to a party in the Odd Fellows' Hall. It was organized by the Church and was a dull affair, to be honest, although I remember being very excited before we went. Ford wasn't with us; there had been an argument about going and he had forbidden us to attend, but Mama defied him.

"Ford burst into the hall, waving his pistol. He was drunk, raving drunk; a disgrace to himself and to us all. He threatened to kill Mother and had to be wrestled to the ground by Albert and two other men. Mama was hysterical. She fled to a friend's home and we were parceled out to neighbors for the night. The shame of it was unbearable. But still she took him back."

"What else could she do?"

"There was talk of divorce."

"Divorce!"

"I know. Not a common step. Mama wasn't brave enough for it quite yet, and besides, they were soon reconciled. A kind of tense peace reigned. He kept his temper, moderated his drinking, made some effort to be civil to her...but it didn't last.

"What happened?"

"He went on a drinking spree that lasted for days. He'd disappeared – we'd actually started to wonder if he had run off for good – but then he crashed back in one evening while we were eating supper. He was clearly drunk but denied it entirely. He knocked his plate to the floor and then blamed Harry, cuffing him about the head. That set off Mama. She told him to go and sleep it off and leave us all in peace. Harry was crying on the stairs. Ford and Mama were shouting, both on their feet. Charles and Kate huddled together by the stove. Albert and I went and stood by Mama. Ford tried to grab at her across the table, and when he couldn't he picked up his chair and threw it at her. When that missed, he tried to come around the table for her, staggering into her rocking chair and sending everything flying.

"I remember he stumbled into a pile of freshly-ironed clothes, and for some reason that distracted him. He grabbed them by the armful and hurled them into the backyard and the pouring rain. In those moments, Charles and Kate grabbed Harry, and the three of them ran for the front door. Albert and I tried to drag Mama out, but she was crying about her rocking chair – it had been her mother's – and screaming that he had gone too far. It was a mistake. He turned on her. He grabbed the joint of meat we had been about to eat, and threw it at her. When she threw it right back in his face, he went wild. Out came his pistol. Albert and I tried to reason with him. We told him he'd have to kill us both first.

"Somehow, we managed to get between Mama and Ford and move back toward the front door. He was screaming the place down, calling her a 'black-eyed devil and a whore'. I have never been so frightened, and hope I never will be again. He came round the table toward us but stumbled on the fallen chair. His gun fired. We turned and ran."

"No one was killed?"

"Lord alone knows how, but no. We ran to a neighbor's house while Ford destroyed our home. He pulled down drapes, destroyed furniture, ornaments, dishes, almost everything we owned. Then he boarded the door from the inside and nailed the downstairs windows shut. For a week, he went in and out of the house using a ladder from the second-floor window. I expected to be homeless forever. But after a week, he left town again. Friends helped Mama recover what she could from the house, and we rented a new home as far away across town as we could. She had to divorce him after that."

"How did you feel about it?"

"Happy! Albert and I both gave evidence in the court case, as did many of our neighbors. All I wanted to do, all I want to do, is see my mother comfortable and happy. Ford nearly killed her. He nearly destroyed her peace of mind. I was afraid for a time that she might even end up in a place like this."

"You are protective of her."

"I suppose you might say so. I certainly vowed that neither she nor I would ever be so bound to any man ever again. My mother believed that a husband protected his wife, but she found that not all husbands are created equal."

"Do you blame her?"

"Blame? No! I blame Ford. He was not worthy of her. And sometimes I have thought to blame my father. He should have provided for her. And us."

"But you disagree with her choices. You said she had let you down."

"Yes, but not on purpose. She believed in Father. She believed in Ford. I just wish…" Her voice trailed away. What did she wish for? That Mary Jane had been stronger when left alone with five children to bring up? That she had coped better with the divorce and leaned less on her children, particularly Elizabeth, who had to take on so much care for the siblings and household while Mary Jane mourned her marriage to Ford and let her regrets and self-pity fester so that she could barely get herself out of bed and dressed some days?

Those dark days had not lasted forever. Her mother was herself again. And with Elizabeth to protect her, Mary Jane must remain so.

"What do you wish? That things had been different?"

"Yes." Elizabeth let out a long sigh. "Although they could have been worse." She blinked and shifted her thoughts out of the past and back to the present. "I don't think I'll ever forget the sound of that infant crying this morning," she said. "Think of it – a little innocent babe, born in such a chamber of horrors. Nothing I have known compares to it. I can imagine nothing more terrible. Nothing.

"At least I had parents who loved me. At least I do still have a mother. Children need parents who love and care for them. Don't you think?"

Beatrice

January - February 1921

I typed up the latest section of her story with tears in my eyes. The abandoned baby explained so much. I thought about the sense of powerlessness she had experienced in the asylum, coupled with her all-consuming drive for action. I thought about her mother, and mine, and Dorothy's, and the unknown mother of the baby in the basement. In different ways, I wept for us all.

***

Although Ernest and I continued our friendship, we never spoke of Miss Bly or of our work. That made me unhappy; I suspected it made us both unhappy. Yet we loved the same things. We saw *The Kid* with Charlie Chaplin, the day after it came out, and went to see Sophie Tucker's amazing routine in Reisenweber's three times. We liked dancing in the clubs in the Tenderloin and finding new places to eat. We met each other's families. He threw ball on a Sunday afternoon with my nephew Thomas, and I knew that I loved him. He was the best man I knew. My mother considered me all but engaged, and I struggled to make her understand that although that was what I wanted, and what I hoped Ernest wanted, too, there were things we needed to discuss and difficulties that I wasn't sure were surmountable.

Miss Bly was unconventional, he wasn't wrong about that. But when he suggested on the courthouse steps that she did not have Dorothy's best interests at heart, I'd instinctively defended her, and I didn't regret it, despite having similar doubts myself. I just wished he could know her better. She was one of a kind. She continued to write her story of Elizabeth in the asylum, and I saw the imprint of the experience on the woman she was now. Institutions were abhorrent to her, and for good reason. When I thought of the story of her childhood, I felt defensive. Especially given her mother and brother's treatment of her now. And then there was the baby. That was the worst moment for her, worse than Tilly's madness even. I went back to her clippings and re-read her second column, the one where she wrote about her days in the asylum. So much of what I was reading now was either glossed-over or missing altogether. The abandoned baby wasn't mentioned, nor was Mrs Farron, or that the doctors sometimes danced with patients in Hall 7.

More than once I thought of showing Ernest the story so that he might understand Miss Bly as I did, but how could I betray her confidence? Or maybe I was simply a coward. I loved him and wanted to be with him. It wasn't perfect, but I was afraid to lose what we had.

Miss Bly, in the meantime, continued to crusade on a range of issues. She added to her long-running focus on fallen women, failed marriage, orphaned children, women's equality, and passionate support for the American maritime industry. She was a fierce patriot, demanding that American companies hire American workers, particularly seamen, who were unemployed in large numbers. She even formed an Association to support their cause.

Beyond all that, she also found time to ruminate in her column, almost philosophically, on life and the pursuit of happiness. I tried to adopt her advice on the latter most particularly. *Don't be a grouch, and waste life*, she wrote. *Don't be disgruntled and dissatisfied; don't be a growler; don't be a crank.* She had a talent for speaking directly to her readers – whether that was me, sitting in her hotel suite, or a woman on a streetcar, reading her column on her way home from work. But I also suspected that she was sometimes preaching to herself, or sending a message to the family that she had severed ties with – most notably, her mother and her brother Albert.

When her mother died in February, Miss Bly barely stopped to take in the news, and that worried us all. Pauline, Mary, and I talked about her when she was out, and watched her like three frowning hens when she returned.

Elizabeth
XVIII
October 5th, 1887, a Wednesday

Elizabeth woke on her second Wednesday morning in the asylum with a sense of dread. Her chest was heavy with it, too heavy to lift from the mattress almost. Her head hurt. Thoughts of the outer world, of simple things – brushes for her teeth and hair – were enough to bring tears to her eyes. She wanted to talk to Anne Neville. Anne had been in Bellevue with her – in the mad pavilion, yes, but still in New York, in the real world. In Bellevue, Elizabeth had been silently exultant at the success of her madness-feigning enterprise. She'd been sharp, ready to train her journalistic eyes on every aspect of the asylum. If she could just talk to Anne now, she would be more herself. More that girl again. Not a girl that slept the night in fear of a creeping madwoman and tormented by dreams of abandoned, starving infants. She just needed a chance to find Anne when Miss Doyle was not around. Perhaps during the morning wash and combing. Or downstairs in the breakfast room, she thought.

But the chance did not come. Miss Doyle was glued to Anne's side at every moment, and when the women returned to Hall 7 after another meal of hard bread, prunes and cold tea, Elizabeth was called to the sitting room to see a visitor. She found Dr. Dent in the room with a tall, thin man dressed in a high collar and tie and long coat. She noted his fine hat, his shiny leather attaché bag, and some papers and a pen spread out on the table beside him. She held her breath.

"This man is a lawyer, Miss Brown," said Dr. Dent. "He has a proposal to make to you. Mr. Hendricks?"

"Miss Brown. My name is Peter Hendricks. I am a lawyer

for a family that knows you well. Dr. Dent here is naturally concerned for your protection. The family I represent wish to offer you accommodation in their home in the city, but we can only arrange your release from this institution and into their care with your consent. Dr. Dent has advised me that you have been experiencing memory problems. I am hopeful that when I tell you that the family, the *Bly* family, has only your very best interests at heart that you will sign the documents that permit me to take you to them."

Heat rose in her cheeks.

"Yes!"

"Miss Brown, I must caution you," said Dr. Dent. "Is the name Bly familiar to you? Think carefully."

Think carefully!

She grinned and enjoyed watching Dent's expression change in response.

"I am entirely positive, thank you, Doctor. I suspect that with a good meal inside me and friends who know me, I'll be recovered in no time at all. Mr. Henricks. Where do I sign?"

She was a different person walking back into the ward. She was on the verge of release. The men had not told her when, but it was enough to know that Pulitzer and Cockerill had not forgotten her. Her stomach growled at thought of real food, and her scalp itched to be properly washed. In the center of the room, she hesitated for a moment. Then she located Anne and Miss Doyle, and walked straight up to them.

"Anne," she said, ignoring the Irish woman. "I will not disturb you, but wanted to say that I was thinking of you this morning and how grateful I was to have had you as a friend in our early days here."

Anne's face grew pink. "Nellie Brown. You are very kind to say so."

"You have a kind heart, I believe. I have always believed you were as sane as the next woman and did not belong in this fearful place."

"Miss Neville and I are talking, Miss Brown." Miss Doyle shifted on the bench, as if she was about to stand, but

Elizabeth forestalled her.

"I am nearly done, Miss Doyle. There is no need to disturb yourself." She turned again to Anne. "That's all that I wanted to say to you, really. Just that I wish you well. With all my heart."

She turned and walked quickly away before her emotions could get the better of her.

Her release came quickly. They were walking in line, Elizabeth looking across the East River in anticipation rather than wistfulness, her mind busy with thoughts of *The World* and the sheer exhilaration of being able to put her mind to work. They were just passing the Lodge when a woman fainted, causing the lines of crazy women to halt and much noise and muttering to erupt. Elizabeth craned her neck to see how the nurses behaved toward the woman, given they were all outside and shivering, so that she failed to hear Nurse Finney call her name and was surprised to be tapped on the shoulder.

"You need to come and get changed, Miss Brown!" Finney said. "It seems you are one of the lucky ones."

A few of the women turned and stared. Elizabeth's hands flew to her cheeks. "I'm coming at once." In a fluster, she turned and said goodbye to the women around her, before following Nurse Finney back to the asylum. In a small room she was given back her own clothes and, wonder of wonder, her own boots to wear. She was exuberant, grinning wildly, and with a bubble of excitement rising in her chest.

"Don't you want to say goodbye to the doctors?" asked Nurse Finney as they walked to the door.

"The doctors?" Elizabeth's eyes had been on the carriage outside, on Peter Hendricks and – oh, the rush of joy at the sight of a known face – Walt McDougall waiting for her. But she stopped, just at the bottom of the curved staircase of the asylum's central octagon.

"Dr. Ingram. I will say goodbye to Dr. Ingram."

"You can't. He's not here. But Dr. Dent is in his office. I can call him if you wish."

Elizabeth's eyebrows rose up. "Dr. Dent? I've no time for Dr. Dent." She didn't hide her disdain for him, either in voice or expression, and she enjoyed seeing surprise in the nurse's eyes. "When you see Dr. Ingram, please tell him Miss Brown was sorry not to take her leave of him. But the rest of them? No. I cannot see the back of them or this place fast enough."

She marched out with her heart thumping and her hand on her hat; her own battered and terrible sailor's hat. She had laughed at herself in that hat only ten days previously. Now it was a treasured possession.

Walt McDougall bowed her into the carriage as if she was a Fifth Avenue socialite, a Vanderbilt or an Astor, and within a minute they were on the way to the boat.

"Annabel insists that I bring you straight to our house, Nellie, that you may wash and dress, or sleep if you need to."

"How wonderful that sounds!" Elizabeth let her head fall back and closed her eyes. "In this life, I swear I will never be as hungry, or tired, or as badly, badly dressed as this ever again. Who said, 'apparel oft proclaims the man', Walt? Whoever it was, certainly knew what he was talking about."

"I have no idea!" he declared laughing. "You have a story for *The World* then, I take it? I can hardly imagine what you have been through. We saw the women walking while we waited for you."

"The walk is the best of it, Walt." She shook her head slowly. "Oh, I have a story, you may be certain of it. Many stories. I can't wait to get to work."

This boat, the one used for visitors to the Island, was a far superior and significantly cleaner vessel than the one that had taken her there. The thought caused her euphoria to slip a little. Elizabeth had intended to keep her eyes firmly on the city during the short crossing, but against her own instincts she turned and stood in the rear of the vessel, regarding the Island she was leaving behind. Cold wind whipped her cheeks. She saw that the leaves must soon turn color and fall from the trees that made a pastoral scene so at odds with the human stew that the city was hiding in plain sight. She closed her eyes and saw inside the grey asylum walls. She saw the women, the misery, the boredom, the underlying threat of violence that colored every moment, and felt a great sweep of guilt. She thought of Tilly Mayard, and of the day-old infant that might be alive or dead for all she knew, or would likely ever know.

And then she turned her back on it. She looked at Walt and the buildings growing nearer.

She thought of food and sleep and clean hair and skin.

She was only human, she told herself.

She was free.

Beatrice

Spring 1921

Miss Bly had barely written any of her story for months. When the folder appeared again, I was elated. It was only a short chapter, but I was with her on that boat to freedom. For a day or two, I worried that she intended to conclude it there; that the asylum story might just end, as it had in the newspapers so many years earlier. I nearly asked her, but we'd never discussed a word of it. She knew where I was if she wanted to talk.

Most days now, she was agitated and preoccupied. She spent more time alone in her room and Mary, Pauline, and I shrugged our shoulders at each other and shook our heads in dismay. Mary thought she was falling ill again. Pauline said it was grief. There was certainly something weighing on her mind.

***

Sometimes she took me with her when she went to see Dorothy but sometimes she didn't, so I thought little of it when Miss Bly ordered a car to drive her out to the Leake and Watts Orphan Asylum on May 20th.

The little girl's adoption was still a great cause with her, and she continued to exchange letters with Ernest's Society and the Superintendent of Leake and Watts, debating who had the best grounds to select an appropriate family to take the child. She had written about Dorothy and several other girls she hoped to find families for in a column for *The Journal* at the beginning of the month. Her praise for Dorothy was effusive – the little girl was a "princess", a "darling" and a "dainty little lady" who came from "old New England stock". There was no hint about the ugliness of her early life with Grace Harris, and only a nod to the fact that the child's mother had died a year ago.

I should have seen it coming.

After all, I prided myself on our closeness, on my special knowledge and understanding of her. Being privy to the personal story she was writing, I should have made connections and thought more on her own words to me when she talked about letting people down. I should have thought more about Tilly Mayard and Anne Neville and the baby in the basement. I should have thought more about how she'd written about being free.

But all of that only came to mind afterwards. Afterwards, when she returned to the McAlpin that bright May day with Dorothy's hand in hers. They both wore smiles as broad as the Brooklyn Bridge.

"Dorothy has come to stay! I've kidnapped her," Miss Bly announced, unpinning her hat and picking up the seven-year-old girl to swing her around.

"For good?" asked Mary.

"For the foreseeable future," said Miss Bly.

As soon as I could leave without her wondering why, I put on my hat and coat and took the subway all the way up to the Society for the Prevention of Cruelty to Children. It was long past time I talked to Ernest about Miss Bly.

He surprised me.

"It could be worse," he said.

My brows snapped together. "I thought you'd be furious."

He smiled then and came round his desk to pull me into his arms. I thought my heart must crack my ribs open. Instead, I burst into tears. Thank goodness Ernest was not the kind of man who ran away from a weeping woman. He gave me one long look and then started laughing.

"And I thought you'd be happier!" he said, pulling me in again.

I pulled away. "I am happy!" I insisted.

"Then stop with the crying!"

I tried. I smiled. I stopped crying. It felt good.

A little later, we went for a stroll together in the Central Park and talked, finally really talked, about Miss Bly.

"It's her methods that I disapprove of, not her motives or her character," he explained. "She's a maverick, a one-woman show, a law unto herself even, but not a bad person."

"She's a good person, I'm sure she is. Her heart is kind. She sees the best in people." We were holding hands. Laughter bubbled up. "Well, apart from the English. She dislikes them intensely. I've no clue why."

"Really?" He pressed his lips together and then shrugged. "How odd." We walked past a line of vendors selling hot dogs, candied apples, and peanuts. "I'm not sorry to see Dorothy out of that institution, good though it is."

"I think that was Miss Bly's aim, above any other consideration. Particularly after what happened to poor little Harry Lisa. She promised Grace Harris that Dorothy would have a family. I think – that is, I suspect – that she wants to adopt Dorothy herself."

"She's too old. And not healthy enough."

He didn't say it callously. And besides, it was true. She had a weak chest. Who was to say she wouldn't have to be hospitalized again? She didn't look after herself either. I suddenly hoped that for her sake Dorothy had good table manners. Miss Bly, when she did remember to eat, always ate out.

"And what kind of a home could a hotel be for a child, anyway?" he went on. "No. This will turn out to be a good thing, in my opinion. Dorothy will be well-cared for and Miss Bly will soon realize, without you or I ever sticking an oar in, that Dorothy needs more than your Miss Bly can possibly provide, however warm-hearted she may be. If not, it won't end well. That is my one reservation."

I tucked my arm in his and we walked on in silence. There were things I thought about saying. I almost told him about her story – or Elizabeth's story, as it seemed to me to be. Perhaps that had been my mistake. I had got lost in the story of Elizabeth Cochrane and overlooked the fact that it was always also the story of Nellie Bly. All her urgency, all her drive to do good and help others. That crusading spirit didn't come out of nowhere. It started with her mother, but it flourished because of Blackwell's Island.

"I wonder why she and her husband never had children," said Ernest. "Seems to me she would have embraced motherhood."

Again, I thought of speaking but held my tongue.

"Mind you, in some ways," he continued. "I'm surprised she didn't do it sooner."

"Do what sooner? Take Dorothy sooner?"

"Yes. I mean, the mother gave her guardianship in October. Her will was clear. Miss Bly's guardianship was established in the courts by Christmas. Why wait until now?"

This time, I did answer him. "Her mother died in February," I said. "She left everything she had to Miss Bly's brother, Albert. The family had been split into two camps for years. And now it is too late. She doesn't talk about her mother's death at all. I'd believe she felt it less if she talked about it more. Instead, there is this silence. Dorothy will fill that silence. She needs her. I've always thought Miss Bly needed Dorothy."

"She's a puzzling woman."

"One of a kind."

"For which I am thankful!"

We walked on a little. I decided to take the plunge. "But you don't object to my working for her?" I asked.

He stopped and turned me to face him.

"Is that what you think? That I'd try and tell you where you may work and for whom?"

For a moment, I feared I had offended him. "There are men…" I began.

"There are men who want meek wives to stay at home and mend clothes and wash dishes all day long," he said. "Or at least, who think they do. But I want someone with spirit. With independence and a mind of her own. This is the twentieth century, after all!"

"Well, I hope I do have spirit," I replied. "Although perhaps not quite as much as Miss Bly. I'm not sure I know of a woman with more."

"She has enough spirit for ten women," he declared, laughing again. "She really did have a husband in the past, though, did she not? Some brave fellow he must have been to marry the woman who survived the madhouse and took herself around the world in how many days?"

"Seventy-two."

"Seventy-two. Well, if she has more spirit than you have, I think her husband must have had more than I do, too," he said.

I thought of what little I knew of the man and of all I had read about Frank Ingram in Miss Bly's story. There had been so much between them in the asylum. What had happened after she was free?

"I don't think you are listening to me," Ernest was saying. I closed my eyes and put Miss Bly out of my mind. When I opened my eyes again, I looked and thought only of him. "That's better," he said. "For we were talking of the qualities a lady looks for in her husband. And I was hoping that the question might be of some interest to a spirited – but not too spirited – young lady like yourself."

"Why, sir, you are most thoughtful," I answered. "Do you have someone in mind for the role?"

"As a matter of fact," he said. "I do."

Elizabeth
XIX
October 1887

Walt took her home to Annabel and, hungry though she was, even before food came the luxury of a warm, private bath, the chance to wash and style her poor hair, the pleasure of proper clean undergarments and clothes that fit. It was like gradually returning to her own body, her mind slipping back into her skin, living and breathing normally, instead of watching and waiting, divorced from reality and imprisoned. She touched everything: the cool porcelain basin; the soft expanse of pink towels; the warm metal radiator; the rippling fringe of tablecloth; the McDougalls' slender, elegant flatware and cold china plates. There had been such sensory deprivation on the Island; she only realized it now that she was free. She had so much to be grateful for. The thought brought tears to her eyes.

After they had eaten, Walt called a hackney carriage and they drove down to *The World* together.

"Are you sure you want to go today? You must be exhausted."

She threw him a tight smile and said nothing of the burning sensation behind her eyes, or the ache in every limb. "I mean to finish where I began it, back at work. I want to meet with my editor and agree to terms." Pride warmed her voice. Her editor. Cockerill. *The World*. The success. She needed to make it real.

And real it was.

The newsroom rose and gave her a standing ovation as she walked in. Cockerill was there, in amongst the men, waiting for her and clapping with all the rest. She took a bow – not a curtsey, thank you – and had the pleasure of being shown to her own desk. Her smile did not waver, and any fatigue chasing her was completely forgotten. Soon, Cockerill drew her upstairs to his office and pelted her with questions. They agreed on a two-part report – one on the Sunday in four days' time, and a further article exactly one week later. How many columns could she fill? How many did he have to spare? Could she shock their readers? She could. She talked through her experience from gazing in the mirror in her own little bedroom to listening to Bridget McGuiness's tales of abuses in the Lodge. As she spoke, she refashioned events in her mind. She recounted much of what she had seen, but said little of how she had felt. That was her job, after all. That was why she had agreed to go in the first place.

"McDougall will illustrate it," said Cockerill. "I want every reader's eyes glued to your column. He will need the text by Friday, or you can work with him here as you go along."

"I'll report to my desk in the morning," she said. "I won't let you down."

"See that you don't," said Cockerill. "It is one thing to find the story. It's another to write it for *The World*."

She nodded. He was all business. She expected no less.

Elizabeth left *The World* building as night was falling. She had a check in her purse from Cockerill and coins pressed in her hand from Walt, who said she must not take the streetcar back to her lodgings but take a hackney cab instead. She was glad of it. In the dark comfort of the carriage, she was properly alone for the first time since she knocked on the door of the Temporary Home for Women on Second Avenue. She pictured it now and the women there. Was Mrs. Stanard still shaken by her experience with a mad guest who raved about her missing bags? Elizabeth's thoughts moved to the Bellevue Pavilion and then inexorably over the East River and into the halls of the asylum. She heard the bells of the Episcopal Church opposite Chelsea Park mark six o'clock as her coach rolled past. In Halls 6 and 7, the women were sitting staring at black windows, waiting for another dull day to drag to an end.

Perhaps Miss Matilda was playing the piano. Perhaps a doctor or two was there. They might be dancing. She pictured Dr. Ingram dancing with a patient, and shut her eyes to push the sight away. She thought of the baby, alive or dead. She hadn't heard if it was a boy or a girl. Tears, unbidden and unexpected, rolled down her cheeks.

Lights flickered between the trees in Central Park. She composed herself for her arrival, anticipating a few words with Mrs. Tanner, some quick lie about her lack of luggage and a swift escape to her own room and sleep. But when she walked into the parlor, her plan was turned upside down.

"Pink!"

Her mother. The child in her wanted to burst into tears. The woman in her wanted to cry also, but for a whole other set of reasons.

"Mama," she said, looking from Mary Jane to Mrs. Tanner in the parlor. The landlady looked tight-lipped, and as Elizabeth hugged her mother she threw a querying glance over her shoulder.

"Mrs. Cochrane has been here for six nights now, Miss Elizabeth," said Mrs. Tanner. "I have made her welcome as best I could, of course."

Elizabeth read between the lines. Mary Jane could be exhausting. She never wanted to be alone and always gave any companion a running commentary on her every thought. Mrs. Tanner expected her guests to keep to their rooms after the dinner hour unless invited to her parlor. Mary Jane, oblivious to that, had doubtless been a thorn in the landlady's side for days.

"Let me look at you," Mary Jane said. She pushed Elizabeth back and held her by the shoulders. They were of a similar height and build, although Mary Jane liked to say that she had had an even tinier waist than Elizabeth's – until her children came, of course. "You look horridly tired and pale. Wherever have you been?"

Elizabeth opened her mouth to answer but her mother had already moved on.

"But where shall we sleep?" She turned to Mrs. Tanner

expectantly.

"I've no free rooms."

Elizabeth saw the set of Mrs. Tanner's chin, and her temper snapped. Her narrow bed was too small for her and her mother.

"We will go to a hotel." She thought rapidly. "To the Clarendon. Mrs. Tanner, please ask Ned to find us a hansom cab? Mother, come with me."

She stalked out of the room and up the stairs. Waves of tiredness made her nauseous. Her mother clucked around her, whispering unflattering remarks about Mrs. Tanner, the quality of her food, her linens, and her company. She kept it up all the way to the Clarendon Hotel, even into their room and the large bed they shared.

Elizabeth blocked it all out. She fell asleep the moment she closed her eyes.

XX

The World newspaper, October 9th, 1887:

> *BEHIND ASYLUM BARS*
> *The Mystery of the Unknown Insane Girl*
> *Remarkable Story of the Successful Impersonation of Insanity*
> *How Nellie Brown Deceived Judges, Reporters, and Medical Experts*
> *She Tells Her Story of How She Passed at Bellevue Hospital*

On October 10th, Elizabeth dined out at Café Brunswick with her mother, John Cockerill, the McDougalls, and a friend of Walt's, James Metcalfe. She picked at the food, hoping no one would notice. Her Southern-born editor charmed Mary Jane to the point where Elizabeth grew anxious, but then she was herself distracted by Metcalfe. He was clever and a quick conversationalist. Somehow, she knew he was a Yale man without recalling a moment when he actually declared himself so. He was a writer, a theatre lover, manager of the American Newspapers Publishers' Association, and he carried himself with an air of sophistication and self-confidence that she wanted for herself. Metcalfe wasn't handsome. His hair was receding, his face a little too round and too studious-looking for her taste. But he was interesting. She wanted to hear what he had to say. Not least because he predicted a glittering future for Elizabeth, although Cockerill had some strong, and less palatable, opinions on the matter of his new reporter's success.

"She may be the toast of the town this week," he said, licking a drop of wine from his moustache, "but to remain so is the harder task. We have the story of her days inside the asylum for next Sunday, yes, but what will come after that? There may be room for Nellie Bly in our Sunday paper, but what will she find to fill it?"

"I won't have any trouble."

"Here's to Nellie Bly!" declared Walt, raising his glass and offering her a toast. "May her career go from strength to strength."

"Thank you," she said. "And here is to Mr. Pulitzer and Colonel Cockerill for giving a lady journalist her shot. Here's to *The World*."

"Which is now your oyster," Metcalfe said to her in a whisper.

"I do hope so!" she whispered back.

***

The Sun newspaper article came out a few days later, on Friday. Elizabeth, at her desk at *The World*, going over her second piece about the asylum – the actual gritty details of those ten miserable days – was quickly surrounded by other reporters reading sections out loud and shouting questions at her. *Playing Mad Woman*, she read. *The Sun finishes up its story of the 'pretty crazy girl'*.

"*Its* story! *Its*?" She was furious. "This is my story. No one else's." And yet there it was on paper in front of her, two days before her scoop, her hard-won – very hard-won – scoop was to appear in print on Sunday morning.

The Sun, irritated no doubt when they discovered the truth about "the charming waif" whose story they'd reported on from incarceration to release, had sent reporters to the Island to find out everything about her time there. The level of detail shocked her. They reported on her appetite, on her objections to the asylum dress, on her refusal to speak any language but Spanish. As she read, she felt physically sick. It was a theft. When she reached a section headed *The Unhappy Night Ending in Chloral*, indignation overtook any other reaction.

"This is false!" she declared, getting to her feet. She'd a strong urge to put on her hat and coat and march along to Dana's office right there and then. And she had thought the editor of *The Sun* was such a gentleman only a few months ago. She had different ideas now.

"Nellie Bly!"

She was called up to Cockerill's office. He surprised her by rubbing his hands together.

"This is excellent," he said. "Everyone will want to read our Sunday edition now."

"They will?" She thought for a moment and nodded slowly. "They will. To hear my side of it."

"Exactly. I take it your perspective is different."

"It is. There are nurses and doctors quoted here. They're obviously lying to protect themselves. Did you see that Nurse Kroener calls me rude and saucy? I was not in any way. And threatening suicide! I never did anything half so dramatic. I will need another column to rebut these slanders."

"*The World* will respond tomorrow. I'll have Philips write it, but you talk it through with him. We can re-hash *The Sun's* version and cast doubt upon the witnesses. Let's tee it up so that everyone knows the real story is yours on Sunday."

"I'd rather write it myself."

"You will make no more noise about *The Sun* until after *Inside the Madhouse* has gone to the press. Then you can go after *The Sun* piece as hard as you like. If I like what I read, we can print it on Monday. Agreed?"

Elizabeth agreed. But that night in her hotel room, she read *The Sun* article time and time again, brooding on how she could pay them back for trying to steal a march on her. She turned down the offer to eat at Gilsey House with James Metcalfe, and ignored all Mary Jane's requests for her to brighten up and be more fun.

"There is nothing to be lighthearted about after spending the day reading lies about yourself in a newspaper, Mama."

"Nonsense. It all adds to the interest in your story when it comes out. You said so yourself earlier."

"I suppose so."

"But you won't mind if I don't read it, do you? I don't like to even think about such places, far less my own daughter in there."

Elizabeth bit her lip. This was her mother. Always one to shy away from realities. Always serving her own interests first. Always frivolous. Loving and kind, yes, but disappointing, too.

"Mr. McDougall said the other day that they might make a book from your adventures, though. Wouldn't that be something?"

Adventures? She let it go. "It has been mentioned."

"And will that pay well? I imagine it will. Perhaps we can bring the rest of the family to New York. Albert and his wife. Charles and Sarah. I would love to see more of my little granddaughter. What do you say? If I am busy with family, I will be less of a burden to you, perhaps."

Did she say that in an honest desire to be less of a burden, or was she simply laying on emotion to serve the end she had in mind? It was so hard to tell with Mary Jane.

"What do they pay you for a book, do you suppose?" her mother asked.

"I have no idea."

"You should find out. As soon as possible." Her mother clapped her hands and stood up, starting to get ready for bed. "I'm so proud of you, my dear. And just know you will look after us all! So talented and clever. And so caring of her family. A mother could not ask for more."

Elizabeth said nothing. She turned her eyes back to *The Sun*. There were quotes from several of the doctors and nurses she'd encountered in the asylum, but nothing from Frank Ingram. The reporter had described him, though. Under a subheading that made her wince.

HOW SHE DECEIVED DR. INGRAM

Dr. Ingram is another handsome man, of a type directly opposite to that of Dr. Dent. His hair is fair, his light brown eyes are clear, and no expression except a kindly one seems able to find a place in them. His light moustache and sidewhiskers complete the pleasant effect of his appearance. Like all the officials of the institution, he was very much interested in Nellie's case.

She sighed and put the paper to one side. Did he think kindly toward her? Or was he so appalled at her deception that she'd never see his handsome face again.

She had no way of knowing.

Beatrice

Summer 1921

Ernest came to visit Dorothy and Miss Bly at the Hotel McAlpin. Brisbane rushed to his old friend at once and Pauline and Mary followed, fussing over my prospective husband and generally giggling like the two schoolgirls they must once have been. Miss Bly and Dorothy were in the little sitting room and did not immediately stir.

"She is telling a story," I told him. "Dorothy is enthralled. Stand at the door. You'll hear." We couldn't see them, but when we fell silent, Miss Bly's voice floated out to us.

"There were four oarsmen," she said, "who took us from the cruise ship to the shore. They were all terribly thin, all black fellows, but with the whitest teeth you ever saw. Can you guess how they kept their teeth so white?"

"Brushing them!" Dorothy sounded excited.

"Yes, my dove, but brushing them with what? Not a toothbrush, as you and I do, but something else. Can you guess?"

"A hairbrush?"

Miss Bly's laughter rang out and Dorothy laughed, too. There had been so much laughter in the suite these last few months.

"Not a hairbrush, you goose, although something almost as crazy. I will tell you if you promise to tell no one. I'm thinking of starting a business, you see. I'm going to import the thing that they used and sell them across America. We will make a fortune!"

"But what is it? What is it?" urged Dorothy.

"Sticks!"

"Sticks?" I could imagine the little girl frowning at Miss Bly.

"Special sticks from a special tree. They scrape away the bark and then rub the sticks against their teeth until the stick wears away to nothing. Then they use a new stick. I tried them, too."

"Did they work?"

"They did. So just as soon as we can pack our bags, shall we take a ship to Aden and buy them up? We could soon be rich as Croesus!"

"Who was Croesus?"

Ernest seized the moment to knock at the doorframe. "I believe you are talking of the King of Lydia," he said.

"Mr. Coulter." Miss Bly and Dorothy came to the door. "How kind of you to visit. Dorothy, do you remember Mr. Coulter?"

The little girl tilted her head to one side and screwed up her eyes. "Nope." She shrugged her shoulders and grinned, making us all burst out laughing.

"Are you here to talk business, Mr. Coulter, or is it a purely social visit?" Miss Bly smiled at him and then looked pointedly at me.

"Purely social," he replied.

I doubt any of us believed him, but I was happy he said it.

"Dorothy is blossoming, and Miss Bly seems as content as I have ever seen her," he said later, when we had left the suite.

"But?" I knew him. I could hear the reservation in his voice.

"It won't last forever. It can't. Does she know it yet?"

"It's hard to say. She talks about schools for Dorothy. She's arranged piano lessons and German lessons. She teaches her reading and writing herself. She loves her."

"The Superintendent of Leake and Watts has a family in mind for Dorothy. A good family."

"Not yet," I pleaded. "If you can, Ernest. Tell him not yet."

Elizabeth
XXI
October 1887

Elizabeth's second and concluding article about the asylum completed Nellie Bly's transformation into an instant celebrity, known across New York and beyond. Her name was in the headline, her signature in the paper at the end of the story – an honor for a newcomer. She not only wrote the story, she *was* the story. Her success excited comment and controversy beyond the plaudits for her bravery. Across the country and into Canada, newspaper columnists wondered at her audacity and questioned a system that could be so easily taken in by a young woman with no special knowledge, who was not a trained actor and who, most evidently, was not in the least bit mad.

Cockerill accepted her follow-up piece, *Untruths in Every Line,* where she responded to *The Sun* with Frank Ingram very much on her mind.

I cannot give too much praise to Dr. Ingram, she wrote. *He really is the right man in the right place.*

Cockerill read it, nodded, and told her to get back to work on something new before she was forgotten about. His semi-indifference was salutary, but the moment she returned to her desk downstairs and found it drowning in letters, she was back riding high on the wave of success.

Many of the letters were from women. There were women who had been incarcerated and released – women who described recovery from illness, yes. But there were others who swore that they, like her, had never been mad at all. They declared themselves victims of poverty, illness, or of their own families. Their stories were heart-rending. A good number of women applauded her daring. A few declared she was a disgrace to her sex. There were also letters from men. She received several proposals of marriage, as well as invitations to meet unknown men in dubious locations. There were offers of employment, speaking engagements, and requests for interviews. There were insults, too; attacks from members of the medical profession, and men who thought her behavior at best unbecoming, at worst a betrayal of all womanhood and femininity. Those ones just made her laugh.

But there was also, late in the week, a letter from Frank Ingram. She hardly knew what to make of it.

Dear Miss Bly,

I hope you will forgive the intrusion. I have followed your story in the newspapers, since you left the asylum, with many emotions: from interest, to concern and some astonishment. Your kind words about my work in Monday's edition of The World encourage me to write to you now in the hope that you will consider a meeting to discuss your experience, your commentary, and the impact – both actual and potential – of your reports on the future workings of the institution. I can be reached at the address above, and can call on you at any place or time of your choosing.

Frank Ingram

They met on a damp Monday lunchtime in McGown's Pass Tavern in Central Park. It was a genteel choice, and she arrived in an optimistic mood, despite the foul Fall weather which had stripped the trees of leaves and laid a blanket of low grey clouds overhead.

She'd had some difficulty escaping Mary Jane. Her mother's ideal was to pass every day in a bliss of mother-daughter shopping expeditions to the Ladies' Mile around Broadway and Sixth, but Elizabeth was learning that if there was one thing her mother respected, it was her daughter's ability to produce an income. When Elizabeth said she had to work, with a strong enough emphasis, then Mary Jane settled down with her periodicals or some stitching and let her daughter be. Today, on the back of a written offer to publish her asylum articles as a book called *Ten Days in a Madhouse*, she told Mary Jane to start looking for a home for them to rent and shot out of the door before her mother could say another word.

Dr. Ingram looked exactly as she remembered him. She hoped she looked rather different.

"Miss Bly." He shook her hand and took a seat. "Thank you for seeing me."

"I am glad of the opportunity," she said quickly. Too quickly. She forced herself to draw a breath. "I'm sorry I had to lie to you."

That seemed to disarm him. She wondered what he had expected. A completely different person?

"Thank you," he said. He fumbled with his menu card and then put it down and looked her in the eyes. "I'm sorry I didn't realize you were sane." He shook his head. "Now there is something I thought I'd never say." His mouth formed a rueful smile, but she saw behind it and knew that she had hurt him.

"Some people call me malicious," she said. "They think I made fools of everyone. But it wasn't the people I was trying to expose." Some of the nurses' faces swam up in her mind. "At least not all of the people, and certainly not you. It was the system. The system is deeply flawed." He nodded but said nothing. "How is Tilly? Tilly Mayard? And Anne Neville?"

"You must know I can't answer that kind of question."

He sounded pompous. She was reminded of the first time she encountered him in the little room beside Hall 6. It had been the second day. He'd treated her like an exhibit in a freak show. He wasn't perfect.

When their tea arrived, she tried again. "You could tell me, at the very least, that the women I knew are well."

"They are well. I know of precious few changes – at least in our patients' health – since you left."

"There have been changes then?"

"Oh yes! What? Don't you think that people that work on the Island have read your story? They are 600 yards away, in the East River, not the other side of the Atlantic."

"Every word I wrote was true."

"It was the truth as you saw it. Some things you were wrong about."

"Such as?"

"Such as Anne Neville." He thrust his hand in his pocket and pulled out a folded newspaper article.

It was from the previous week. October 15th. *The Sun*, again. The headline pulled no punches: *Annie Neville was Insane.* Elizabeth swallowed, threw Ingram a glare, and read the short article. Anne, it said, although it called her Annie, had previously been a patient in an asylum in Utica. The details given were painful. Doctors there described her as raving and incoherent. They said she was very much disturbed. Elizabeth knew all too well what a simple phrase like that might mean in practice. Staff at Utica believed Anne had fallen into illness after having relations with a man who afterward deserted her.

"Do you think this is true?" she asked Ingram. "Does this fit with the Anne you know?"

He nodded sadly and her heart fell. Elizabeth read until the end, hoping to find some fact that might suggest this was a case of mistaken identity, that there might be another Anne Neville – it called her Annie, after all – whom *The Sun* journalist had uncovered, but the last paragraph ended all that. The Utica Asylum had heard from a Sarah Neville that her sister was ill again but was working in New York, at the Buckingham Hotel. It was from there in September that Anne had been committed to Bellevue.

"In their article the day before – *Playing Mad Woman* – they said she had religious delusions. She didn't have religious delusions. She believed in prayer. But that doesn't make her mad."

"You are not seeing it, are you?"

"Seeing what?"

"That the question is complex. That the lines between insanity and sanity are finely drawn. That a person may be crazy and recover. And people who appear sane," he paused and looked at her, "may not be."

She sat back in her chair. "Are you showing me this to make the point that I was wrong about Anne, or that you were not wrong about me? Or both? She seemed sane to me. I seemed crazy to you. Is that it?" She looked at him more closely. "Dr. Ingram, why we are meeting?"

He surprised her by laughing. Her anger vanished.

"You are the same woman, but at the same time, another person altogether!" he said. "What you did was truly staggering, you know. Fooling so many people. Myself included." He smiled ruefully and she warmed to him again. His pride had been hurt, she thought. That was it.

"But did you come here to berate me or applaud me? At the moment, I can't tell which." She raised her eyebrows, and his eyes went to her lips. She found herself staring at him.

"I came here to enlist your help," he said.

Her articles, he explained, had caused major upheaval. Some improvements had been made already, but more were needed. He talked about the food, the bathrooms, and the fire hazard posed by all the locked doors that she had so eloquently pointed out to him.

"You thought I had been in prison in Sing Sing."

"Well, forgive me for not realizing that you were an intrepid reporter! I have met rather more women criminals than reporters in my time, I'll have you know!"

They both burst out laughing. An elderly couple at a nearby table frowned, and that made Elizabeth laugh even more. But in a moment or two he was serious again. He certainly had come with a purpose in mind.

"In early October," he said, "on the very day you were released, in point of fact, the Department submitted their budget requests to the Board of Estimate."

"The Department of Public Charities and Corrections?"

He nodded. "They are asking for an additional million dollars."

"For the asylum?"

"If only it were. No. It is for the asylum in part, but also for the prison, the hospital, the workhouse, and the almshouse."

"How will it help the women?"

"Improvements to the kitchen and bathrooms. Separate accommodation for nursing staff." He saw her eyebrows shoot up. "We might attract better staff if their conditions are also improved. Then there is the question of fire safety. And work on the Lodge." A wave of distaste crossed his face. She had never been inside, but he surely had. What she had seen of those inmates while out walking still made her shudder.

"What can I do?"

"Keep the story in the public eye. There is to be a grand jury inquiry. Testify. Insist that the jury visits the asylum. Accompany them."

"Accompany them?" She had been nodding, but the idea of returning made her breath catch.

"Would that be difficult?" He reached out and touched the back of her hand. She stared at his fingers, trying to compose herself.

"No. No, I will do it. Of course I will." She spoke rapidly. "I want to help. I don't want to be the kind of reporter that creates a storm and then leaves without a backward glance."

"I can't tell you how relieved I am to hear you say so," he said with another wide smile. "I was afraid you would be too busy with new assignments."

"Not at all. By which I mean to say that I am busy, yes, but not too busy." She smiled at him again and tension rose between them. It was flirtatious and exciting. But his next remark inspired a different set of emotions altogether.

"That's wonderful. Truly it is. To be honest, when I first sat down and saw you looking so…well, very pretty, obviously, but also so fashionable – if you don't mind me saying so – well, I was worried that you were the kind of girl – or I should say woman…" He threw her an apologetic glance and she nodded, but yet still knew he was about to say something she did not want to hear. "I was afraid that you were someone who was more interested in the fine things in life, in her own fame and prosperity, rather than someone who believed in hard work and service. As I do."

She thought for a moment before responding. "You don't think that fame and prosperity can be derived from hard work and service, then? Are the two things mutually exclusive?"

"In my experience, yes," he said.

Beatrice

Fall 1921

Superintendent McClain – from the Leake and Watts Orphanage where Miss Bly had kidnapped, rescued, stolen, or liberated Dorothy, depending on one's point of view – wrote to her at the end of August, just as we were all looking forward to fall leaves and a drop in the temperature. I read the letter when I typed her reply and filed them both away for her. He had found a wonderful home for Dorothy and wanted to call on Miss Bly at her earliest convenience. She replied that her diary was entirely full for at least the next two months.

Around that same time, Pauline and Mary were busy overhauling our archives. There were thousands of letters in our keeping, pinned to carbon copies of her typed replies and handwritten scrawls where she had replied by hand. They grew nostalgic, those two, calling Miss Bly out of her sitting room to remember individuals and causes she had applied herself to over the past two years or so. One struck a particular chord amongst them – the story of a woman who had written to Miss Bly, a few months before my time, describing her dire financial circumstances and asking Miss Bly if she should give up her two-year-old son.

"*Don't let him get away from you.* That's what you wrote, Miss Bly," said Pauline, scanning the reply that had been published in *The Journal*. "*You brought him into the world. On you rests the responsibility of his future.*"

Miss Bly sat down on Mary's office chair and rested her chin in her hands. "I had interviewed O'Brien, just the week before I received that letter," she said. "He weighed on my mind. Still does."

"Who was he?" I asked.

"Edward O'Brien. Seventeen years old. He was a clerk in a Wall Street firm." She shivered as she remembered him.

"What did he do?"

"Killed his employer with a hammer. I interviewed him in prison. Such a damaged creature. He never had a father. Never knew a real home."

She passed me a folder containing the article she had written about him for *The Journal*. It was passionate, persuasive. Pauline leaned over my shoulder, reading it with me. The details of the murder were chilling.

"He was a danger to society," she said.

"True." Miss Bly got to her feet. "Although society let him down first. Children need families. That's what I told the woman who thought of giving up her son." She looked around at all the piles of correspondence to be sorted and at the pile of typing I had amassed on my desk. "I am unwell, ladies," she said in a more subdued voice than normal. "I think I'll retire for a while. Could one of you look after Dorothy when she returns from her lessons?" She walked slowly from the room, and we all shrugged our shoulders.

***

The realization that something had changed in her grew on me gradually. She spent more time alone and threw herself into her hours with Dorothy with less enthusiasm, although she was never less affectionate or generous, just somehow calmer and more thoughtful in her interactions than she had been before. Her writing changed, too. I thought it was grief for her mother, finally taking hold. And perhaps it was, to some degree.

In September, I typed up a miserable article about family breakdowns, questioning the value of "ties of blood". She wrote that she had "known mothers who abhorred the very presence of their daughters", and "daughters who despised their mothers". She slid the papers onto my desk and hardly glanced at the article in print when *The Journal* published it.

The Miss Bly who called the editorial desk and complained vociferously if she didn't like the placement of her column, became a distant memory. In October, she worried me more, writing a reflective piece about regret that I was sure was prompted by her unaddressed grief. "Before you are unkind and ill-tempered to anyone," she wrote, "try to think what you would do if that one was forever removed from your life." Was she regretting the break from her mother? When I considered her story from the asylum and understood her mother's second marriage, I could see why she was so conflicted.

At the same time, Albert, her brother, continued to be a thorn in her side. In October, she was back in St Mark's again, complaining that the change in temperature had sunk into her lungs. But one day the hospital called us out of the blue. Miss Bly had disappeared and taken one of the nurses with her. I took a taxicab downtown straight away, only to meet her on her way back in. She had been, she told me breathlessly, to meet the police at her mother's house. Albert had been holding an auction, including things Miss Bly claimed as her own – souvenirs from her round-the-world trip, for example – and so she had had her own brother arrested for theft. She appeared buoyed by the effort she had gone to, exhilarated even. But it cost her an extra week in bed, at the very least.

I took Dorothy there to see her and they were as cozy together as ever, but surely Miss Bly herself saw now that the challenge of caring for Dorothy long-term was beyond her. I left them alone for a while, so I didn't hear their conversation, but Dorothy was an open child who loved to ask questions and share what was on her mind.

"Miss Beatrice," she said to me in the taxicab back to the hotel. "What do *you* think of the name Dorothy? Do you think it's nice?"

"Of course I do," I said. "Nicer than Beatrice."

She smiled at that, as I'd intended, but she was still chewing it over. "But there are nicer names than Dorothy, don't you think?" she said. "And if a girl had a new family, they might want for her to change."

"They might, I guess. I don't know. Would you like me to ask Mr. Coulter? He knows all about new families for children."

"Sure," she said. She was quiet for a little. It was dark outside, and I watched the street lights stream like water as we drove by. "What about Elizabeth?" she asked. "Do you think Elizabeth is nicer than Dorothy? For a girl like me."

In the darkness of the back seat, I reached for Dorothy's hand and held it tight. "Did someone suggest the name to you? Maybe Miss Bly?" I held my breath.

"Oh, she calls me Elizabeth all the time now, Miss Bly does. She says she likes it. So long as it's Elizabeth. Never Lizzie."

"And what do *you* think, Dorothy? It's your name, after all."

She shrugged and I could see her teeth. She was smiling, not concerned about the oddity of Miss Bly changing her name one bit. She was curious, that was all.

"I don't mind. It makes Miss Bly smile. She has an old face, you know, but I'm always happy when I see her smile."

"It's funny you should say that," I said to her. "I'm happy when she smiles at me, too."

Elizabeth
XXII
October 1887

Was she in love with him? She thought she probably was. If love was measured by the number of times one person thought about another on any given day, then Elizabeth Cochrane surmised that she was very likely in love with Doctor Frank Ingram. The problem was, she wasn't sure she ought to be. Mary Jane certainly didn't think he was the man for her daughter – or she would not, had she so much as known about him – because Mary Jane had settled on James Metcalfe as her future son-in-law.

Mr. Metcalfe enjoyed sending flowers. It seemed to Elizabeth that every time she returned to their hotel room, Mary Jane was arranging a fresh bouquet of something very expensive and out-of-season looking. Elizabeth never gave them a glance. But she did long for more space, and urged her mother on in her search to find them a proper apartment. Elizabeth also loved to go shopping. She worried she was too frivolous for Frank Ingram, and struggled to see herself as any doctor's wife. Or any man's wife, for that matter.

The night before her return visit to the Island, she slept badly. She didn't care for the reactions of the doctors or nurses – she stood by her words, and even looked forward to looking some like Nurse Grupe and Nurse Grady, Nurse Finney and Nurse Kroener in the eye, not least because she'd be there in her own clothes and her own shoes, with her hair shiny and styled and her cheeks freshly-powdered. But what would the patients think? Did they even know her story? Would she see women she had known and talked to? And if she did, would they even recognize her?

She dreamed she was walking in the line, much as she had been that last day, three weeks earlier. But in the dream, every woman she tried to speak to stared at her in horror, broke free of the line, and threw themselves into the river. Elizabeth called for help, but everyone ignored her. She ran to the river's edge and saw the women struggle to swim while their heavy skirts threatened to pull them under. None of them stood a chance. In the dream, she grew frantic. She screamed and screamed for help, but behind her the rest of the women walked away, back into the asylum. As the women in the river flailed and drowned, she woke up with tears streaming down her face.

***

All of the twenty-three men on the Grand Jury made the short trip to Blackwell's Island. Having heard her evidence earlier in the week, many of them nodded toward her in a friendly manner and made sure she was assisted on and off the boat, but otherwise they talked among themselves and left her with her own thoughts. It was impossible not to contrast this visit with her arrival from Bellevue with Anne, Tilly, and the others. Now she knew what to expect.

She walked the halls of the asylum every night when she closed her eyes. She saw the women's faces in her dreams. The cries of the baby abandoned in the basement returned to her again and again, waking and sleeping. It said everything to her about how life was unfair. She bit her lip and reminded herself that she'd be back for a matter of hours only. She could keep her emotions in check.

The Grand Jury visit was intended to surprise the doctors and nurses in the asylum, but it was immediately clear that they had been forewarned. She had been vague with Frank Ingram about the arrangement, but someone else had not been so scrupulous. The Commissioner of Asylums, Dr. MacDonald, received them in the central hall of the asylum, at the bottom of the grand stairway, and led them into Hall 6. The room had been cleared of patients, and chairs were set out to accommodate the men of the Jury and Elizabeth. Dr. MacDonald – one had to give him credit for trying to make something good come out of the scandal – was prepared for every question the Grand Jury threw at him, and had members of staff on hand to answer any questions.

Elizabeth remembered little of what was said afterwards. Nurses she had known, as well as several she had not, were brought before the Jury. Nurse Grupe and Nurse Grady glared at her when they arrived, but left with their heads down. They were questioned about the bathrooms, the food, and their physical abuse of patients. Nurse Grupe might have gathered some sympathy – she characterized the women in their care as dangerous and threatening, outnumbering and intimidating the nurses, and she was young enough and pretty enough for that version of events to be almost believable. Not so Nurse Grady. Her anger at having to submit to any questioning at all was obvious. She answered in monosyllables and kept her arms crossed at all times. The women deserved no better, she seemed to imply. Where Nurse Grupe colored up and looked shamefaced when challenged over women bathing in old and filthy bathwater, Nurse Grady was defiant. She even told the men that if they thought they could manage better, she'd be happy to have them work with her on Hall 6.

"Was it true," asked one gentleman, "as Miss Nellie Bly wrote, that you spat into one of your patient's ears?"

"What if it was?" the Irishwoman shrugged. "If I did, then the woman was asking for it. They all are. Every one of them."

Dr. Ingram wasn't present, but Dr. Dent was, and Elizabeth enjoyed his discomfort when it was his turn to be questioned. No, he could not say how often the bath water was cold or how many women were bathed in the same water before it was changed. Yes, it was likely that such practices were injurious to patients' well-being. Yes, he was aware that some of the meals were substandard, but as he understood it that was a financial issue, not a medical one. Yes, he agreed that a healthy diet was important for patient health, and so perhaps, yes, if he was aware of deficiencies in the kitchens he should have been more vocal about raising his concerns. No, he could not promise that the nurses were uniformly kind to their patients. Possibly, acts of cruelty had occurred without his knowledge. Yes, all the doctors were competent, although given the low wages on offer, he could not promise that they attracted the best men, or managed to keep those few good doctors in their employ.

While he spoke, he frequently directed his answers to Elizabeth, even though she asked no questions or participated in any way. She imagined he'd enjoyed seeing his name and work abused in the newspapers no more than she had – but if that was the case, he should have given her nothing to criticize. He remained outwardly calm, she gave him credit for that. His smooth civility only slipped the smallest amount when one of the gentlemen of the Jury asked if they could question some of the patients specifically mentioned in Nellie Bly's reports in *The World*. Dent looked to his Commissioner Dr. MacDonald. They had no choice but to comply.

There was a break in proceedings while a patient was summoned. When she realized it was to be Anne Neville, Elizabeth hastened into the hallway. Even on her best day, Anne would shrink from appearing before such a crowd of gentlemen. Elizabeth hoped her familiar face was reassuring.

"Anne," she said, stepping forward and embracing her as she reached the bottom of the stairs. "Anne, it's me, Nellie Brown. Do you recognize me?"

Elizabeth pulled back but still held her elbows as the two women looked at each other. Anne was much changed. Her face was grey, and her hair greasy, combed flat against her scalp. Her eyes were wide, though, her pupils enlarged, and her lower jaw worked back and forth as she stared back at Elizabeth.

"Nellie Brown." She nodded slowly. "Have you been in a different hall?"

"I have been away, Anne. But I'm back now. I'm trying to make things better. Are you well? You seem different. Have they given you something? Have they given you some medicine?"

"Yes."

Elizabeth pulled Anne back into her arms and kissed her cheek. "I am trying to make things better, Anne. And I hope you can help me. Can you come and tell some gentlemen how we came here together? And how we were in Hall 6 and then Hall 7 together. Can you remember it? Can you help?"

Anne nodded, although when she saw the number of men in the room, she baulked and began to tremble. In the end, Elizabeth sat with Anne before all the Jury and doctors, and held her hand while the poor creature did her best. Haltingly, she acknowledged that Nellie Brown, as she knew her, had been in the asylum with her and corroborated her report of poor food and cruel treatment. Things had improved since Nellie Brown had left, said Anne Neville, before her head dropped. She whispered to Elizabeth that she'd like to go back upstairs.

The last part of the visit was a tour, and Elizabeth saw improvement upon improvement in the familiar halls, bedrooms, and bathrooms. Walls had been painted. New basins had been installed in bathrooms. Beds were made, and extra blankets sat in neat piles in every room. The kitchen was clean and the sight of loaf after loaf of fresh bread sitting cooling had Elizabeth's eyes out on stalks. There were even two large barrels of salt, near the door.

But it was what was missing that left Elizabeth most concerned. Anne Neville she saw, yes, but where were Miss Doyle, Bridget McGuiness, Miss Matty the pianist, old Mrs. Farron, or Josephine the Frenchwoman? Nurse Finney was at work in Hall 7 and she stared straight through Elizabeth as if she were made of glass. In Hall 6, Elizabeth asked Nurse Grupe where Josephine was, and was told she was in the Island hospital, dying of paralysis. Hall 6's patients, it seemed, had changed almost in their entirety in the short weeks since she had been there. Only Tilly Mayard remained, standing beneath a window with her back to the visitors. She was singing *Rock-a-bye Baby* and did not turn around.

Dr. Dent caught up with Elizabeth just as they were about to leave.

"I'd like to take the opportunity to thank you, Miss Bly," he said, in a carrying voice. "If I had known your purpose when you were a patient here, I'd have aided you myself. We had no means of learning about many of the problems you identified. But now that we know of them, I think you will see we have already made remarkable progress. The nurse, for example, whom you described keeping watch at the Retreat, so they could hide their worst excesses of behavior from my doctors? She has been dismissed."

"If you want me to be impressed, Dr. Dent," she said, "I'm afraid you will be disappointed." She let her voice drop to a whisper. "You can blame all the deficiencies you like on a lack of funds, Doctor, but a deficiency in kindness and humanity is something no amount of money can change. Good day to you."

Beatrice

Winter 1921/22

We agreed that Ernest would not intervene in any way until after Christmas. Miss Bly, released from hospital in November, was consumed with the concept of Christmas for Dorothy and, besides, she was under fire from other quarters.

The Catholic and Protestant Sisters organizations had both had enough of her. Her private adoption arrangements had never been popular. Ernest might have come round to her ways and peculiarities, but many in the charitable world believed she cut corners and lacked transparency. They weren't wrong. Miss Bly was frequently contacted by young women who had "fallen". It was understood that if a girl sought her assistance, Miss Bly could make arrangements. The girl's reputation was shielded, and she was properly cared for in a hospital. Families were able to adopt the children born in these circumstances in complete privacy and without fear of any further correspondence or inspection.

I have spent years studying this subject, she railed in *The Journal* after receiving a letter complaining about her methods. *I have been in close contact with these unhappy girls and they are not to be molested, bullied or nagged by anyone. There is no reason for any baby to be abandoned so long as I live*, she declared.

***

Christmas came and went. Ernest and I talked of marriage plans, but I think we both knew there was a crisis brewing in the suite in the McAlpin Hotel, and that only when the puzzle of what to do with Dorothy was resolved, would we really be free to move on with our own plans. Miss Bly must decide to give her up, he said. The time was coming. She needed to find the girl a proper home, as she had promised.

"You were there, weren't you," he said one day, after coming to the suite to collect me and admire the Christmas tree Miss Bly had thrilled Dorothy with, "when Grace Harris told Miss Bly her wishes for the child?"

"You know I was."

"And she promised her Dorothy would have a life in the country. You heard her. I know you did."

I nodded somberly. "She did. I believe she meant it, too."

"But now?"

"But now, I don't know. I will speak with her. She's finishing her story. Making plans for the New Year. I just need a little more time."

Elizabeth
XXIII
December 1887

Ten days in a Madhouse was published by Ian L. Munro in December, and sold for twenty-five cents a copy. Inside the front cover, an advertisement for *Madame Mora's Corsets (a marvel of comfort and elegance!)* promised comfort for ladies of a fuller figure and no need for breaking-in. Elizabeth wrote a brief introduction explaining that the book was a response to the enormous popular interest in her experience in Blackwell's Island Insane Asylum. The two articles she'd written for *The World – Behind Asylum Bars* and *Inside the Madhouse* – were reproduced with some careful tweaks. There were also new sections: a closing chapter describing the Grand Jury investigation and another, near the end, that she called *Incidents of Asylum Life*. There, she wrote about the baby in the basement for the first time, and mentioned that the doctors sometimes danced with patients in Hall 7. Her words were poor, small things, conveying facts but hiding the truth.

In addition, there were two articles Elizabeth had written for *The World* since her asylum triumph. The first, *Trying to be a Servant – My Strange Experience at Two Employment Agencies,* had appeared in the paper on October 30th. Cockerill had liked it and she'd uncovered some sharp practice among agencies that supplied servants without any proper references. Posing as a girl seeking work in a factory had developed into the other article, with her own name in the headline: *The Girls who Make Boxes – Nellie Bly as a White Slave.* Elizabeth had a newfound respect for the kind and gentle girls she had encountered working in unsafe conditions and for very meager pay. None of them had heard of the Cooper Institute where they might learn for free, or the Knights of Labor, or any number of new groups she told them were springing up to support women at work. She hoped her words had impact.

"Working girls," Cockerill had said. "That's your audience, that's *The World*'s audience." But he'd been less delighted, although he'd published it, with the article she was most proud of, that had come between those two.

To gather information for *What Becomes of Babies – Hundreds and Hundreds of Little Ones Given Away Yearly*, Elizabeth had pretended to be an unmarried mother with a child she wanted to find a new home for. With Blackwell's Island and the abandoned baby always prominent in her mind, both waking and asleep, she had tackled the story with her heart in her mouth. The women she found who were taking babies "full surrender" had sickened her. Full surrender meant that the babies' mothers agreed to never know what happened to their child – the infants could be abused, neglected, or murdered, for all anyone could tell. It had distressed her, but she had not let a sniff of that seep into her write-up for *The World*. She was sure she hadn't. Nevertheless, Cockerill had pressed his lips together and looked gloomy. Worse, he gave her column for a week to Fannie Merrill.

Fannie Merrill!

Fannie Merrill was a perfectly nice girl, already working at *The World*, writing the kind of society and fashion pieces that Elizabeth had been so keen to avoid. Suddenly Cockerill was talking to Fannie Merrill and running her piece on the life of a cigarette girl in the Sunday slot that Elizabeth had hoped to… never mind hoped to, had already been calling her own.

She was incensed.

Elizabeth sought reassurance. She wrote to Q.O. in Pittsburgh, regaling him with all her successes. That cheered her. She quizzed Walt, her mother, James Metcalfe, really anyone who was prepared to listen, on whose writing was better, whose style was most effective, whose point of view was keener: Nellie Bly's or Fannie Merrill's. Everyone backed her up.

Everyone except Frank Ingram.

They met again at the same McGowan's in Central Park. She had wondered at that. After the Grand Jury was complete and extra funding secured for the asylum, she'd hoped he'd ask her to dinner. It didn't need to be Delmonico's; she'd be happy to be taken somewhere halfway as fine. Instead, they met in the same rather stuffy old venue. At least she was happy to see a copy of her book lying under his gloves. Really it was seeing the book that set her off talking about Fannie Merrill. She hadn't meant to bring it up at all, and yet she found herself regaling him with her views on Merrill's theft of her hard-earned column, on her determination to produce better and more entertaining scoops, and to keep hold of her hard-won fame.

He didn't like it.

She saw his back stiffen and his smile fade. His gaze grew cool. He licked his lips and looked like he was about to speak, but then said nothing.

"What is it?" she asked.

His fingers drummed on his copy of her book. "Are you happy with this?"

"Yes. Immensely. Why?"

He picked it up and opened it. From the introduction, he read: "*I am happy to be able to state, as a result of my visit to the asylum and the exposures consequent thereon...*" He shot her a pointed look. "*...that the city of New York has appropriated $1,000,000 more per annum than ever before for the care of the insane. So, I have at least the satisfaction of knowing that the poor unfortunates will be the better cared-for because of my work.*"

She opened her mouth to speak, but he put up a hand and flipped through the pages. She knew what was coming.

"*I have one consolation for my work*," he read. "*On the strength of my story, the committee of appropriation provides $1,000,000 more than was ever before given, for the benefit of the insane.*" He paused and raised his eyebrows. "Neither of those statements are true."

"They did get a million. There's no falsehood there."

"Not for the insane, they didn't."

"There's been a substantial increase in funds for the Department of Public Charities and Corrections. The Mayor himself mentioned my work when recommending the increase."

"But only $60,000 will go to the asylum directly."

"I can't believe you are doing this. What point are you trying to make? You asked me to help and I did so. I returned to that awful place, only because you asked me to. So, *The World* has claimed some credit, *I* have claimed some credit for improvements. Why not? Things are improved. And will get more so, now there are more funds available."

He leaned back in his chair and looked at her. "You returned only because I asked you to?"

"Yes! My God, I hate the place. I have nightmares. I dream of that infant in the basement. I wake up thinking Tilly Mayard is pulling my hair out by the fistful. I thought you, of all people, understood what I went through to get that story."

He sniffed a little and closed his eyes for a moment. When he opened them again, he looked so sad that her breath caught in her throat and her heart stilled in her chest.

"I do," he said. "I do. It was extraordinary. I don't think another woman in one thousand could have pulled it off." He didn't smile. His eyes looked dark and flat.

"But?"

"But it was only a story for you. You have said so yourself. You are like a lighthouse, Nellie Bly, shedding light and moving on. Useful in a crisis, with flashes of brilliance, yes, but remote. And not constant."

"That's what you think of me?" Tears threatened. She wanted to walk away.

A shadow seemed to cross his face; some thought that made him angry, although he kept his voice controlled. "I mean, who are you anyway?" he said, leaning forward. "The paper said Nellie Bly is not your real name, no more than Nellie Brown was. I have no idea who you really are."

There were so many things she could have said.

That her name was Elizabeth Cochrane.

That she was an independent young woman who had lived

some hard years in a home with an abusive stepfather and a mother in fear for her life.

That she was a loving sister and daughter who was doing what she had to do to support her family.

That she believed in equality but also wanted to dress well and buy expensive hats.

That she was a journalist who found and wrote stories that people, many people, wanted to read.

That her asylum exposé had cost her more than anyone knew. Even him, although she had hoped it was otherwise.

She said none of that.

"My name is Nellie Bly," said Elizabeth.

And then she got up and walked out.

Beatrice

January 1922

"So, she didn't marry Frank Ingram?" asked Ernest.

We were standing at the end of Fifty-Ninth Street, underneath the ironwork of the Queensboro Bridge, looking across at Welfare Island, as Blackwell's Island had been renamed a few months earlier. There was a trolley stop on the Island. I thought maybe I'd take it over one day and just go and see what was left of the asylum, but decided today wasn't the day. If I went, I'd go alone. For now, I'd told Ernest something of the story; not too much, but enough so that he might understand her a little better.

"No. They wrote to each other, I believe. She met up with him once, a few years later. But then he died, she said, very young."

"It was the other one, she married then? The one her mother approved of?"

"James Metcalfe? No, not Metcalfe either, although I think she thought she might have, at one point."

"Then who?"

"A millionaire called Robert Seaman. He was much older than her. Forty years older."

"Forty! Four-o?"

"Yes."

Ernest was frowning. "She married for money? I can't believe it."

"Not so much money as security," I replied. "I think he was a father figure. And she always had this immense sense of responsibility for the rest of her family. She told me she went to great lengths when she married him to make provision for them. For her mother in particular."

"Her mother. The woman who she spent the last few years battling in the law courts."

"Yes. Over how Mary Jane and Albert ran Seaman's business while Miss Bly was overseas. They were never reconciled."

"Well," he said, leaning over and kissing me on the cheek, "here's to a life with no fame, no millions, and no lawsuits. What do you say?"

I nodded and smiled. "Yes, please."

***

Before Christmas, I had asked Ernest for a little more time for Miss Bly and Dorothy, but as it turned out, not much more time was needed.

On January 9th, I typed up her last column for *The Journal*. She sat in the office and petted Brisbane, watching while I worked. Pauline and Mary went home for the night. Dorothy fell asleep in her little cot in the sitting room. It was another philosophical piece and I wondered what had prompted it. I wasn't aware of any letter she had received that might have made her so reflective, but then, none of us had ever known everything she was up to, had we?

This last story was of two women whose life had begun in similar, testing circumstances. Both had fathers who deserted the families, and both went on the stage to try and make their fortune. I almost mentioned Grace Harris to her then. I certainly wondered if she was on her mind. If Ernest had been there, he'd have spoken up at once. That was the time to talk to her about Grace's wishes and Dorothy's future. I ignored his voice in my head.

Miss Bly's eyes were fixed on me, but she stayed silent and I continued typing. Both the women she claimed knowledge of in the piece got married. One became rich and her son gained a position in Washington during the war. He did well for himself. The other woman's husband gambled away their savings. Her son fell in France. Miss Bly asked her readers what made the difference between their two histories. Why did one succeed, while the other suffered? What shapes our lives? she asked. Are we the product of our choices or at the mercy of fate?

"And what is the answer?" I said, when I had finished. "What shaped your life?"

She looked at me and that lovely, charismatic smile stretched across her face, right up to her eyes. "You've been typing the story, haven't you?" she said. "You tell me. Whose life was it, anyway? Elizabeth Cochrane's or Nellie Bly's?"

I opened my mouth, I was ready with my answer, but she put a finger to her lips and got to her feet. "I'm just tired, now, Beatrice," she said. "So very tired. And you should go home. You'll be back again before you know it."

The next morning, Pauline arrived first and found Miss Bly still asleep in her bed. Her breathing was shallow. Pauline said she was drenched in sweat and running a fever. They took her to St Mark's in an ambulance, and there she stayed. I never had a moment with her alone again.

***

Her brother Harry, her lawyer John Warren Hill, her publisher Arthur Brisbane, and other family came and went. Not Albert, he would never be welcome, but Charles's children and Kate's all came to pay their respects. Bronchopneumonia and heart disease, they told her. She spent the days quietly, putting her affairs in order. John Warren Hill agreed to look after Brisbane. When he came and collected him from the hotel suite, I cried for an hour.

And what about Dorothy? She couldn't stay in that hotel suite all alone. Pauline and Mary had children of their own. Miss Bly's family lacked the space – and the inclination – to take her in. The obvious answer was for the Society to take her back under its protection and find Dorothy another place in an orphanage. I knew what that would do to Miss Bly. I told my mother it was only temporary. And then moved into Miss Bly's room in the McAlpin Hotel.

Nellie Bly died in the morning, less than three weeks later, on January 27th, 1922.

***

A maid at the McAlpin looked after Dorothy while we all attended Miss Bly's funeral at the Church of Ascension at Tenth and Fifth Avenue. The service was short and melancholy, as most funerals are. Afterwards, Ernest and I had a long talk about the little girl's future. It was the hardest decision I ever made.

***

Two days later, the three of us drove out of the city and met a man called Morris Bosworth. Dorothy wore a red velvet coat and a matching bonnet with a white fur trim, gifts from Miss Bly for Dorothy's "first proper Christmas" only a few weeks before. Ernest said he believed it was for the best, but until we saw Morris Bosworth, I wasn't sure I'd be able to let her go.

"They have been thoroughly vetted. This man's sister and her husband have been childless for fourteen years. They want her. They will love her."

"But to pass her to a stranger like a parcel," I'd said. He had shaken his head. Told me to wait and see.

And I did see, and he was right. Morris Bosworth looked like all his Christmases had come at once when he met Dorothy. He hunkered down before her so they could square up eye-to-eye, and even shook her dainty hand.

"Are you ready for an adventure and a new mother and father?" he asked her in the kindest of voices. "And to meet my own little girls who can't wait to have a cousin to love?"

Dorothy looked over at me and I nodded. There were tears in my eyes, but Ernest really was right. Here was a good family, ready to take her and love her. We didn't even have our own home as yet. Our time for family wasn't now, and for Dorothy it was long overdue.

I opened my arms and hugged her, one last time.

"You know Miss Bly told your mother you'd do well in the countryside," I said. "*Somewhere with fresh air and wholesome food.* Those were her exact words. What do you say? Was she right?"

"Wasn't she always?" said Dorothy.

Historical Afterword

Elizabeth Cochrane/Nellie Bly (May 8th, 1864 - January 27th, 1922)

Nellie Bly was an extraordinary woman: vigorous, brave, determined, kind, and quick-witted. She was also complicated, contradictory, outspoken, and unconventional.

All the details of her early family life in Pennsylvania revealed in *The Girl Puzzle* come from the biographical record. In January 1885, she wrote a letter to her local newspaper, *The Pittsburg Dispatch*, calling herself a "Lonely Orphan Girl". As a result, she got a job as a reporter. Two years later, aged 23, she left Pittsburgh and went to New York to try and forge a career in one of the big newspapers. Her first assignment was to enter the Blackwell's Island Insane Asylum and pose as a madwoman in order to report on conditions. Nellie's exposés in *The World* and the counter articles published by *The Sun*, described and quoted in this novel, can be found and read online.

After her great success, Nellie worked at *The World* for three years, including embarking on her famous 72-day round the world trip. Anyone wishing to read about that can do no better than to pick up Matthew Goodman's excellent account of it, *Eighty Days*. She also tried her hand at novel writing. Her book, *The Mystery of Central Park*, is available online and while it's not a terrible read, it wasn't a roaring success at the time and Nellie never wrote another. As I've hinted in the novel, success in the newspaper industry wasn't all Nellie hoped it would be. In 1890, she left *The World* and struggled with illness and depression while writing for *The New York Family Story Paper*. By 1893, she was back at *The World*, where she stayed until taking up a job at *The Chicago Herald* in early 1895.

Her time in Chicago, exposing prison conditions (although as a visitor, not an inmate), was short. By April 1895, as Beatrice tells Ernest, Nellie had married Robert Seaman – an industrialist and millionaire who, aged nearly seventy, was almost forty years her senior. It seems safe to assume that after years of looking after her family, both emotionally and materially, Nellie hoped to find some security. The marriage was not a success. In the only comprehensive biography of Nellie, *Nellie Bly, Daredevil, Reporter, Feminist*, Brooke Kroeger relates how Seaman regularly had her followed by a private detective. Worried that the marriage would not provide the financial security she craved, Nellie returned to work once again for *The World*. Despite this bad beginning, Seaman and Nellie stayed together until his death in 1904.

With Seaman gone, Nellie became a businesswoman. She ran the Iron Clad Manufacturing Company, and worked with her employee, Henry Wehrhahn, to patent the steel barrel. But poor choices and fraudulent employees led to litigation and bankruptcy. In debt and still in legal trouble, when war broke out in Europe in 1914, Nellie, then aged fifty, headed to Austria to report from the front lines. By 1919, she was back in New York, estranged from her mother and brother Albert over funds and the family business. Nellie returned to journalism to make a decent living, and took up a number of causes, including the adoption of some of the city's many orphans. She died in January, 1922.

Fact and Fiction in *The Girl Puzzle*

The 1887 story is heavily based on contemporary accounts about Nellie Bly's time in the asylum. All the characters imagined there are taken from Nellie's or *The Sun* newspaper's reports, with very few embellishments on my part. Anne Neville, for example, who Nellie believed was sane, was reported in the newspapers as suffering from religious delusions and had been in an asylum in Utica prior to meeting Nellie at Bellevue. Frank Ingram, as with all the doctors and nurses named, was a real person, and there were hints of some form of romance or relationship between him and Nellie – although if true, they came to nothing. Frank Ingram died in his early thirties in 1893. In a few minor instances, I have changed names of patients to make things easier for the reader. Mrs. Doyle, for example, is Miss Connor in *The Sun*'s account, but there were too many women with similar names in Hall 7, so in my story, I made a change.

When Nellie started working for *The New York Journal* in 1919, she lived in the McAlpin Hotel (now an apartment block called Herald Towers, just opposite Macy's) and ran an informal adoption agency. One of her secretaries was called Beatrice Alexander, and Nellie did have an at times uneasy working relationship with Ernest Coulter of the New York Society for the Prevention of Cruelty to Children. The relationship between Beatrice and Ernest in *The Girl Puzzle* is fictional, but the essentials of Dorothy's story are based in fact. The Coney Island trip really happened, as did the story of poor little Love of Mike.

The principal sources for this book are contemporary newspaper articles and Brooke Kroeger's wonderful biography. I'd encourage anyone interested in Bly to read both.

Nellie wrote about the asylum experience three times. The first time, she wrote two lengthy articles, *Behind Asylum Bars* and *Inside the Madhouse*, published by *The World* on October 9th and 16th, 1887, respectively. A few months later, they were re-published in book form with an additional chapter that includes the birth of a baby and mention of doctors dancing with patients, as well as her return visit with the Grand Jury. In January 1889, she wrote about it all again in *Godey's Lady Book* in an article called *Among the Mad*. Nearly five of the seven pages of *Among the Mad* are taken up with explaining how she got the asylum assignment, and describing her time in the Temporary Home and in Bellevue. Only the last two pages describe her ten long days in the asylum. Anne Neville, Tilly Mayard, Josephine Despreu, and others, are not named. The baby and the dancing are missing again, as is any claim to have helped acquire an additional million dollars in funding for the asylum. As a novelist, I wondered why that might be.

Any mistakes about Nellie's life and work included here are my own – apart from two! Mrs. Stanard of the Temporary Home for Women was in fact called Mrs. Stenard, but as Nellie was 'writing' Elizabeth's story in *The Girl Puzzle*, I kept to her spelling of the name. I've also quoted Nellie Bly several times in the book, but in one case – the one about how little sympathy there is in the world – I've corrected her grammar. It feels quite presumptuous to have done so but I hope she would not have minded. Nellie's longtime friend and colleague from Pittsburgh, Erasmus Wilson (also known as Q.O., the Quiet Observer) recalled their editor, George Madden, having this to say about her when she first started her career at the Dispatch and wrote *The Girl Puzzle*:

She isn't much for style, but what she has to say she says it right out regardless of paragraphs or punctuation. She knocks it off and it is just right too.

To find out more about *The Girl Puzzle*, Nellie Bly, and my other novels, please visit my website at **kate-braithwaite.com**, or find *The Girl Puzzle* on twitter @thegirlpuzzle1

Fantastic Books
Great Authors

darkstroke is
an imprint of
Crooked Cat Books

- Gripping Thrillers
- Cosy Mysteries
- Romantic Chick-Lit
- Fascinating Historicals
- Exciting Fantasy
- Young Adult and Children's Adventures

Discover us online
www.darkstroke.com

Find us on instagram:
www.instagram.com/darkstrokebooks

Made in the USA
Las Vegas, NV
02 February 2023